A WEST COAST HOCKEY ROMANCE
(BOOK TWO)

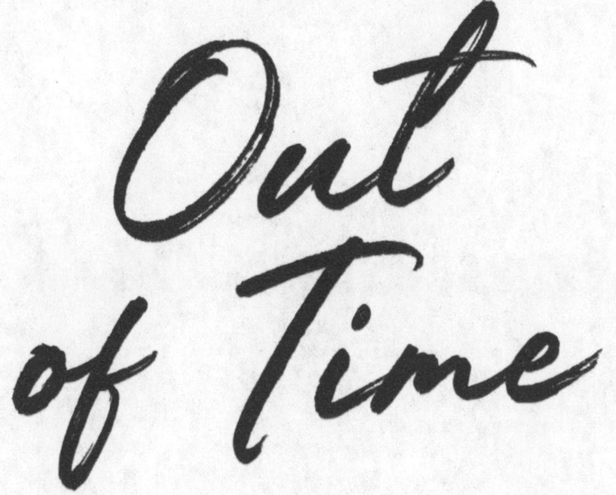

Out of Time

LUCILLE JAMES

Contents

Dedication

For Aaron and Kassie. Thank you for sharing your vision loss journey with me. Your vulnerability and willingness to tell your stories helped shape this book into something honest and true.

Dear Reader,

Don't be fooled by the sweet cover, Out of Time is a hockey romance that contains open door/explicit sexual situations; it is written for adult audiences only. Please keep in mind that while Out of Time is a love story it does contain mentions of alcohol use, mental illness, vision loss, loss of a family member (off page), and explicit sexual content; proceed with caution.

-Lucille James

Prologue

News Break:

"Another loss in the books for the Anaheim Condors tonight, Lacey."

"That's right, Mark. Another devastating loss indeed. What started out as a hopeful pre-season for this team has very quickly declined and left the entire NHL to ask the question: Does Max Miller still got it?"

"Max Miller, who is easily considered one of the best goalies the Anaheim Condors have seen in front of their net, has found himself struggling to make the save as we start this NHL season. Some of the goals getting past him are amateur mistakes that result in professional consequences."

"It just seems to me, Mark, that Max Miller might find it hard to sign his big contract at the end of this season if he doesn't sort out his place in front of the net—and fast."

"That's right, Lacey, with Anaheim having a fresh, strong backup goalie in the brick wall that is Jack Brown, Miller's days might be numbered as a starting goaltender for this Anaheim team."

Chapter One

Max Miller sat shirtless on the expensive Pottery Barn barstool. Every light in the house was on. The buzz of a tattoo gun echoed off of the long, pictureless, sterile white walls of his San Clemente, California home. His team, the Anaheim Condors, had lost—again. They had lost because their goaltender couldn't save a puck if it were the size of a frisbee.

He was their goaltender.

He was the reason they had lost their fourth game in a row, causing the team to have their worst start to a season on record.

He dipped the needle of the tattoo gun into a plastic cap of black ink, causing it to splatter on the fresh plastic wrap he put down to keep his expensive marble countertop clean. After adjusting the small mirror he had propped up against a bowl of fresh fruit, he lifted his left arm over his head and proceeded to draw a line on the skin of his rib cage.

Not a line—a tally mark.

One for each game he had lost since his first game in the NHL with the Anaheim Condors.

It was the fourth time this season he had to do it—to tattoo a tally mark on himself. The last one had completed a grouping of five, slashing through the previous four lines. Now, another tally mark sat on his flesh, a permanent reminder that he had let his team down—again—this season.

He sat the tattoo gun down and ran a paper towel over the small black line. Droplets of blood gathered on his skin there; he had gone too deep. The loss was permanent now.

Was Max Miller's time up?

Max knew, like any other goalie, that his time in the NHL was short, and the victories were sweet, but this was supposed to be his *big* year. The last of his bridge contract. He *had* proven himself, breaking every record set by the goalies that came before him in Anaheim. This was the year he was set to seal his big deal with the Condors and stake his claim in the hockey history books.

Only tonight, he couldn't be so sure.

It was a job that was hard on the body. His knees, his back, his ankles, his groin... his *vision*? It wasn't the easiest being the last line of defense, it was physically and mentally draining, and for every goalie approaching his thirties, there was a new young player ready to take the start in front of *his* net.

Packing up the tattoo equipment, he made sure everything was cleaned properly for the next loss, the next tally mark, the next time he went to make a save but *couldn't* for reasons he didn't understand.

He didn't know what was causing it—the floaters, the light sensitivity, and the inability to see sharp images in the dark. He was suddenly Alice in Wonderland, up was down, and down was up, and the green pill made you bigger and the red pill made you smaller, but where was the pill that helped you make the save? Where was the fountain of everlasting youth that kept you healthy and relevant? Where was the switch to turn off the mind-fuckery he was experiencing? He couldn't focus on anything moving half the time. Hell, he couldn't focus on anything still. The world around him was out of focus, blurred, and drunken; only he hadn't taken a single sip.

He stood from the bar stool, the intense kitchen lights causing his head to ache.

He would be fine.

This would be fine.

Tomorrow he would hydrate. Maybe take a walk outside, get some fresh air. He could go down to the beach before practice, enjoy the city he paid a lot of money to live in... he didn't do that enough.

He played hockey.

He ate.

He slept.

Repeat.

He clicked each light off as he made his way to the massive couch that filled the space of his living room. It was a couch intended for family, guests, game nights, Christmas movies, and lovers. But Max wasn't well versed in any of those things, so for him, it was where he slept. It wasn't because he didn't have a bed of his own. He had a perfectly fine king-size bed in his king-sized bedroom, another king-sized bed in his spare room, and another in another room. It was a lot of rooms for a man with no family. It was a lot of space for a man with nothing and no one to fill it with.

Max slipped off his pajama bottoms and fell back onto the couch wearing only his boxer briefs. He closed his eyes, willing away the dread that overcame him after he shut the lights off, the darkness engulfing him. The cool October ocean breeze came in through the open window, making it just chilly enough to need the throw blanket that was draped over the arm of the couch. He pulled the soft fabric up over his body, the sting of the new ink on his ribs barely present with the anxiety he faced in the dark.

Chapter Two

R emi Davis was a lot of things, but a morning person was not one of them. So, every Wednesday morning, when her alarm woke her up at 5 a.m. to clean the house of her one and only celebrity client, Max Miller, Anaheim goalie extraordinaire, she made sure to count her blessings that a guy like *him* continued to use *her* small but humble cleaning service, Busy Bee Cleaners.

It *was* San Clemente. No one cleaned their own homes there.

She pulled on a pair of black jeans and one of her "Busy Bee Cleaners" t-shirts and wondered if today would be *the* day she finally bumped into the infamous Max Miller.

She had been cleaning his house for four months now, and not once had she seen him, or any traces of him. His home was always spotless. The beds were unused, the floors were clean enough to eat from, and the bathrooms were pristine— not a single man-hair to be seen. Yet, she went through the motions. She mopped the already clean floors, scrubbed the already clean toilets, and washed the unused linens.

Max Miller was an enigma.

She pulled up to the famous hockey player's beachfront mini-mansion, as she had every Wednesday for the last four months, with a burnt gas station coffee in one hand, and her cleaning cart in the other; it was time to start her day.

His house was extremely beautiful. Spanish-style exterior, with a completely renovated interior. Yet, since she had started cleaning for him, he had not once added his own personal touches to the home.

It was, for lack of a better word, sterile.

The walls had no pictures on them, no traces of family, friends, or travel. The rooms were like something out of a catalog, they had no real pulse. They were rooms filled with furniture for the sake of being rooms filled with furniture. Remi found her client, Max, to be the most unknowable person on the planet, and that was hard to believe, considering he was a professional hockey player.

Several times over the last four months, she had let her mind wonder about him after a long day of work, trying to find anything she could on the goalie. His social media presence was generic, likely run by an intern for his team. His wiki page was stock images and responses. Google searches on the guy were lacking any kind of real intel. He was a celebrity goalie, and yet he left no traces of human life outside of hockey.

Maybe he was an alien. She could get behind that theory.

She punched her personal code into the front door and when she opened it an automated voice echoed throughout the smart home, "Busy Bee Cleaners. Entry time: 6:05 a.m."

She rolled her eyes at the overly feminine bot voice. "Yeah, yeah," she said to no one, "I know I'm five minutes late. Fire me."

Setting her coffee down on the white marble kitchen countertop, she headed to the master bedroom. She always stripped the beds first to get the wash started.

The palette of the home was mute colors. One room, a series of navy blues and beiges. She called this the GAP catalog room. Another room was a series of grays and whites, she called it the fancy prison cell room. The master bedroom was—well, it was sad. She couldn't be sure Max even slept in his own bed when he was home. The indentions on the massive luxury couch in the living room said otherwise, which seemed odd. *Max* seemed odd, but Remi wasn't surprised by this. She didn't *know* hockey, but she knew enough to have heard that goalies are a bit bizarre, leaving Max to fit the stereotype perfectly from what she could gather on him just by cleaning his house week after week.

She loaded the sheets into the industrial-sized washer and headed to the kitchen to get to work. "Alexa, play a punk mix," she said aloud to the smart home. The music started with a blast throughout the house, startling awake the massive body she had somehow failed to notice asleep on the couch.

"Oh, shit." She covered her mouth with her hands, only to immediately move them up to cover her eyes after realizing Max Miller was standing in front of her wearing only his underwear.

Were his black boxer briefs extremely small, or was his body extremely big?

She would have to reassess that query later when her high-profile client wasn't standing in front of her practically naked.

"Alexa, stop music," she shouted, and the punk music stopped on demand. "I'll turn around, so you can, you know, ummm..." she sputtered, turning quickly to face the refrigerator.

Max was fumbling about the living room behind her. She heard the AC kick on. She heard the freezer drop fresh ice, and then refill with water. She heard her heart hammering in her chest and her blood pumping through her veins. This was bad. This was awful. This was *not* how she expected it to go the first time she met this man.

After waiting what seemed like an eternity for him to give her a sign that the coast was clear to turn back around, she cleared her throat, and he gave her nothing in return. Slowly, she removed her hands from her eyes and turned back to face him. Only, he was gone—the throw blanket folded neatly on the couch.

No trace of Max Miller to be found.

"A fucking enigma," she said under her breath as she got back to cleaning the kitchen.

Chapter Three

Since when did the cleaning company come on Wednesdays? Max thought she came on Thursdays, but no, it couldn't be Thursdays, because he was here last Thursday, and she hadn't shown up then. Maybe she came whenever she wanted? She blasted her music like she owned the place. The craziest thing in all of this was that Max didn't even know his house *could* play music like that; he didn't even know the walls had a built-in sound system.

Somehow, he had fallen asleep, alone in his house, and woke up to a stranger treating it like *her* home. Did she not see him asleep on the couch? He was a massive, red-headed, grizzly bear of a man, surely she had seen him.

Max moved about the master bedroom fitfully, throwing on clothes. He slipped his feet into a pair of black Sk8-Hi Vans and bent to cuff his dark Levi's jeans. Standing quickly, he began a mad dash to the garage in an effort to avoid the housekeeper altogether—that was easier than talking to her. She *had* just seen him practically naked; he could bet on his life that she didn't want to talk to him after that. His heart hammered erratically as he felt panic come on strong.

Reaching for the bedroom doorknob, he tripped over something on the floor he hadn't seen. Before he could catch himself, he fell into the bedside table. The heavy clay lamp hit the floor and shattered, the sound of it echoing throughout the house.

"Fuck," he said, gripping onto the wall to try and center himself as he regained his balance. His eyes, glued to the shattered lamp, were still struggling to focus with the sudden loss of light in the room.

The bedroom door clicked open, and there she was, his house-keeper. Her face was panicked, her voice shaky with worry.

"Mr. Miller are you okay?" she asked, taking his hand in hers like a concerned old friend would do.

He blinked. And blinked. And blinked *again*. It didn't help.

She squeezed his hand. "Mr. Miller, should I call an ambulance? You don't look well. You're really pale, and..."

He could feel her tiny hands sure on his body as she guided him to take a seat on the bed. It was *his* bed, though he couldn't remember the last time he laid on the thing, let alone slept there.

"Mr. Miller," she began, but he cut her off, hating how formally she felt the need to address him.

"Max. Just Max," he corrected.

"Sorry. Just Max, okay," she revised, her voice frazzled. "Just stay here, I'll go get you some water," she said quickly and then she was off.

Max stood; much too abruptly considering what had just happened, and his eyes strained against the dull lighting. Sitting back down, he accepted that he might need to stay put while this—whatever *this* was that was happening with his eyes—passed.

Sometimes when these "episodes" happened, he found it helped to close his eyes, take a few deep breaths, and re-center his equilibrium.

With eyes closed and his hands on his knees, he began.

Breathe in...

Breathe out...

Breathe in...

Breathe out...

"Max?"

Her voice, soft and gentle, as if not to alarm him, still managed to catch him off guard. Slowly opening his eyes, he found the housekeeper crouched in front of him. Handing over the cup of water, she wore a worried look on her face. His finger trailed over hers as he took the cup and electric currents surged through his body at this slight dose of human interaction that wasn't hockey-related; his body heating with some kind of longing. A longing he hadn't felt in a long time.

He took a sip of the water while the woman watched, her head tilted to the side in wonderment, like he was some kind of science project.

"Hi there," she finally said, her worried expression lighting up just a bit, replaced with a simple, encouraging smile. "I'm the owner of Busy Bee Cleaners. I don't have any medical background, but I think, by the looks of it, your sugar might be low. I get like this too, when I forget to eat."

He waited for her to go on, but when she didn't say anything else, the silence grew just awkward enough to force him to speak. "I got dizzy," he lied.

And that was that.

Words often escaped Max when he was around people, hell, words escaped him when he was alone. His knee began to bounce with anxiety and his upper lip collected nervous sweat as he waited for the woman to respond.

"I can see that," she said, hinting at the shattered lamp. "Do you want me to get you some food?"

His eyes avoided hers, looking down at the mess of broken clay and glass from the lamp instead. It was easier to focus on *it* than the woman's piercing blue eyes. If he looked into them any longer, he might drown in the oceans of them.

"Protein bar," he managed, and she nodded at his response. Following it up with a single word, he added, "Pantry."

She stood quickly and left the room. Max looked up instantly to watch her leave, suddenly very self-conscious of himself, his home, and his cold, emotionless room. He looked around at the basic decor; everything about him, down to his bedroom was so uninviting.

She probably thought he was a creep.

When she returned, she had a protein bar in one hand and a broom and dustpan in the other. She handed him the bar and this time he made sure not to touch her—that felt dangerous—as she began to sweep up the mess the broken lamp had made.

Pulling down the wrapper on the protein bar, he began to eat, watching her anxiously as she cleaned up the mess he had created. He felt useless. He *was* useless. Just like he had been last night in front of the net, and the game before that.

Panic flooded him.

Would his career end with him on the bench?

His heart hammered in his chest. "You don't have to do that. I can sweep," he said.

"You're still looking a little pale. Finish that protein bar and then we'll talk about sweeping," she said, looking back up at him with a gentle beam. Max tried and failed to smile back. He kept eating instead.

Her smile was natural and light. Her teeth were big and bright behind her full lips. She had the kind of smile that seemed like it never ended. She was pretty, *very* pretty, and Max couldn't remember the last time he was in the company of a woman who made his body come alive this way. His face began to blush, his cheeks growing a deeper shade of pink, which was always an obvious thing on a redhead. Tapping his foot, he tried like hell to mask the weird rush of adrenaline he felt just looking at her.

"Besides," she added, with the final sweep, "it's *literally* my job to clean up after you. And this might honestly be one of the first legit messes I've cleaned up here. Why do you even have a housekeeper if you're never home and there's never any real messes?"

He thought about it and gave her the only answer he could come up with on the spot. "Dust?"

She stood up straight, pausing what she was doing to look directly at him before she began to laugh. And fuck, it was a good laugh. It made the depths of his empty stomach flutter with some kind of profound satisfaction. Her laugh was like hitting every green light on the Pacific Coast Highway. Her laugh was like eating dairy and not getting a stomach ache. Her laugh was an effortless save that won the game. Her laugh made his vision blur—or maybe it was just another episode coming on, he couldn't be sure—but his eyes struggled to focus on anything but her smile while she was standing in front of him.

"I don't think you need a cleaner once a week for dust, Max. But I'm not complaining either. Your house is the easiest part of my paycheck," she teased with a wink.

She went to leave, the dustpan full of lamp fragments, when it dawned on him that he didn't even know her name.

"Excuse me?" he called after her. She quickly turned back to face him. "I don't think I caught your name."

Leaning forward she stuck out a firm, yet tiny hand to shake. "I'm Remi."

Max instinctually wiped his palms on the denim of his pants before offering up his clammy, anxious hand to her. "I'm Max."

This made Remi laugh. "I know, *just* Max, right? You're kind of a big deal," she teased.

Shaking his head in disagreement, disappointment lined his face. "I've lost every game this season," he said as he eased his hand from hers, unable to handle her soft touch a second longer. He wiped his nervous, sweaty palms off on his pants again and hoped she didn't think he was trying to wipe away the reminder of her touch, but he just couldn't help it. He wasn't good at this sort of thing. It made him... nervous. Holding her hand made his skin crawl, and not in a bad way.

"*You've* lost every game this season?" she asked incredulously. "Aren't there like, seven other men on the ice that the puck has to get through before it gets to you?"

"You know hockey?" he asked.

"I know enough to know that you're not the only one in charge of making sure the other team doesn't score."

"Yeah, but I'm the goalie."

"Yeah, but it's a *team* sport. Don't beat yourself up over it. You're just going through a rough patch. It'll pass, you'll bounce back, and Max Miller will live to see another win."

Max looked down at the small remaining pieces of the broken lamp. It reminded him of how he felt; cracked, broken, obsolete—*done?*

It will pass.

It will pass.

It has to fucking pass, he was just getting started.

"So," she went on, "is it really *just* Max? Or is that short for something interesting like Maximus, or Maximillian?"

He noticed the way she was so effortlessly comfortable standing in front of him. Her hip popped out, her shoulders leaning back against the door frame as she waited for his answer, she was completely okay in his silence. It was oddly calming.

"Just Max, there's nothing interesting about me," he said, because words were hard on a good day, but words around Remi with her subtle beauty and effortless confidence were like picking pennies out of dried concrete—*impossible.*

"Your color is coming back," she said, hinting at his cheeks. "Probably from the protein bar. Must have been low sugar after all."

He wished he could be that optimistic.

It had to pass.

"Yeah, probably low sugar," he lied, then went on, "I'm sorry, I'm not great at... talking."

Especially around women like you, he thought.

It was the way she wore a t-shirt and tattered jeans like some women wore ball gowns. And the way her sun-bleached hair sat atop her head in the most perfectly imperfect bun. The way her skin looked like a walk on the beach when the sun was almost *too* hot, creating a warm inviting glow. And the way her cheeks had a faint hint of pink under her crystal blue eyes. She looked like the sun gods kissed her every morning when she woke.

He wondered if he got close enough to breathe in the scent of her, if she would smell like salt water and the cool ocean breeze.

Breaking his gaze, realizing how intently he was staring at her—*really* staring at her—he looked away. Remi shot him a sort of cocky, all-knowing smile before she left with the broom and broken lamp in tow.

"Finish that protein bar," she called over her shoulder playfully as she made her way down the hallway that led to the kitchen.

He wondered if she would come back to check on him. Would it be presumptuous of him to sit on his bed and wait for her to return? Or, were they done talking? How do conversations end between two strangers?

His leg bounced anxiously. Under his breath, he began to count, "One, two, three, four..." If she wasn't back by sixty, he would leave. He didn't know where he would go, but he would leave. She could get back to cleaning his house in peace, and they could pretend none of this happened: The nearly naked encounter, the tripping over his own feet, the caring for him, the way his entire body heated at the simple brush of her fingers against his... "Fifty-eight, fifty-nine, sixty."

Of course they were done talking. Of course she wasn't coming back. Max knew that talking to him was like talking to a tree stump. He stood slowly, pushed back his disappointment, and headed straight for the garage.

Chapter Four

Remi didn't usually watch hockey, but she hadn't been able to stop thinking about Max since the other day. She wouldn't say she was star-struck over him, but there was definitely a lingering element of wonder. And sure, she had googled him in the past, but meeting him made her curiosity towards him intensify. She couldn't shake the feeling that Max was sad, lonely, or going through something in secret. It was always a bad idea to go meddling in your client's dirty laundry, especially when their actual dirty laundry paid your bills, but she couldn't resist. She couldn't look away. She had seen too much, or maybe not enough, and if she was honest, what she did see in Max, aside from a man who looked very good in tight black undies, was a man who might be a little broken—like the shattered lamp.

Black briefs aside, Remi found herself wondering more seriously about Max. Her curiosity had turned into concern since she had met him. Who did he have in his life that cared for him, and if they cared, how come they never came to visit? Cleaning his house was proof enough that he never had any guests over. There was never any trash to be taken out, no signs of parties, or holidays being held there. She wondered if Max was the same with everyone else as he had been with her: awkward, shy, and a little withdrawn.

He said he was bad at talking; she agreed.

He said there was nothing interesting about him; she begged to differ.

Remi found Max to be a cabinet of curiosities just begging to be opened.

The hockey game started on her TV screen, and Remi found herself smiling as she watched number 31, Max Miller, get the start in front of the net, despite his awful stats this season so far. His helmet made her smile; matte black with a shiny cartoon Condor on the back, outlined in silver. The bird's eyes were silly, looking in opposite directions, with shiny black pucks coming at it from all directions. She thought it might be the best goalie mask she had ever seen.

The puck dropped and the game was off to an intense start. The Condors were playing their rivals, the Los Angeles Knights, and as usual things got chippy as soon as the puck hit the ice. Remi was born and raised in Anaheim, California, so she considered herself a Condors fan by default.

She opened her laptop to get some work done while the game played as background noise in her little beachfront house. It wasn't actually *her* house; it was a rental. She had always promised herself that one day when she was old enough to have a real job, she wouldn't live anywhere where she couldn't hear the waves from her porch and smell the ocean breeze through her open windows. Even if that meant living in an overpriced one-bedroom hut in Huntington Beach. She couldn't complain though, it was enough space for her and Bozo, her 4-year-old betta fish.

Remi had started her company, Busy Bee Cleaners, alone and had since hired three women to clean for her small and humble company. Her love of cleaning all started as a way to process her childhood trauma. Growing up with a hoarder for a mother wasn't always the cleanest or safest environment, so she started cleaning houses in high school for practically nothing. After she graduated, she took all the steps she needed to have an officially licensed business.

She found it therapeutic really, to see the before and after. Some days were harder than others as a cleaner. Some houses were dirtier than others, and some clients were pickier than others. But it wasn't just a job, it was *her* job, and her future, and she held a lot of value in knowing that she had done it entirely on her own. Busy Bee Cleaners was helping to break a generational curse that Remi knew had been handed down to her mother from her mother's mother, and so on.

And sure, Remi knew her mother loved her growing up, but love wasn't the issue. The issue was one bag of trash turning into a heap of filth. Love didn't keep the rodents out. Love didn't stop the mold from growing. Love didn't protect Remi from her mother's mental illness. A home should feel safe, and Remi rarely felt safe growing up. It was hard to feel safe at night when the roaches fell from the ceiling into her bed. It was hard to feel safe when mold lived on the very countertops she was supposed to eat from. It was hard to feel safe when the stuff, the trash, the debris, piled up to her waistline. It was hard to feel safe knowing the next eviction notice was coming because of her mother's hoarding.

She remembered praying every time the landlord brought the pink slip, telling them they had thirty days to go, that things would change. That her mom would get help, and talk to someone about her mental illness. She imagined each time that they would leave the junk behind and start over, a clean slate, a fresh surface.

But it never failed, each new apartment, rental, trailer, or condominium ended up destroyed by her mother's inability to throw anything away, to stop hoarding.

Remi ended up spending her childhood and adolescence feeling isolated, unable to make real life friends over the fear that they might find out her dirty little secret, no pun intended. She lived her childhood and adolescence terrified someone might see what her life looked like behind closed doors. So, she kept everyone at arm's length, with each move, each eviction notice, each change of schools, as she continuously reinvented herself as her mother stayed the same.

Was that why Max tried to live a secret life as well? Maybe he had a reason to keep people at a safe distance like she had at one point in her life. Maybe he was too afraid to let someone see into his world, and she couldn't blame him if he was. She could only imagine the anxieties that came with being a sort of celebrity, hell, she herself was guilty of googling him on several separate occasions.

Remi looked up from her laptop to watch as a Los Angeles player skated the puck up the ice. The commentators' voices were amped up on the TV, the game was finally picking up as they said aloud on a live broadcast what Remi was thinking, *"Can Max Miller make the save?"* She held her breath and watched as Max readied himself for the shot in front of Anaheim's net. The Los Angeles player took the shot and Remi let out a sigh of relief as Max made the glove save for the Condors.

Maybe he really had just gone through a rough patch for the team's first few games of the season. She sure hoped so; she didn't know the guy per se, but that didn't mean she wasn't rooting for him to succeed.

Chapter Five

The game was just getting started and Max held his breath as he watched the Condor's captain, Patrick Carter, battle for the puck against the L.A. Knights captain, Roman Graves, behind the Knights' net. Graves regained possession of the puck and Max tried like hell to follow it as he made a clean pass across the ice to Liam Harvey, Graves' right-hand-man.

Max blinked frantically. The corners of his vision blurred.

He blinked again.

Harvey skated right at him, giving Max nothing more than a split second to get into position, focus, and take a deep breath, readying himself for his first big save of the night.

Max watched as Harvey weaved through the Condor's defense. He was fast. Too fast. Where was the puck? Where was Harvey's stick? What was his body language giving away?

Max felt his heart race, as his vision strained.

"*No*," he said under his breath. Not now. Not now. Not *now*.

Harvey took the shot—top right corner of the net—and Max's gloved hand snapped up to make the save on instinct. He heard the roar of the crowd before he even looked down his nose to find the puck safe in his glove.

His heart rate slowed.

He took another deep breath and allowed himself a second to celebrate the save, then he let the moment pass, readying himself to keep his head in the game.

Save after save, Max felt hope for the future of his career creep back in. Save after save, even with his vision straining in the corners, struggling to make out the sharp lines of the goalposts, he felt optimistic. He considered the idea of playing like this, with his vision very obviously impaired. Maybe this would pass too. Maybe it wasn't so bad, or such a big deal. Maybe, just maybe, his brain was fucking with him, and tonight, after a big win, he would see his world come back into focus as the stress of losing his career faded.

The game went on, and Max, surprising himself, continued to get his job done—no tally marks tonight to document another loss, another permanent reminder of his failures. The clock ticked down slowly, second by second, and Max was grateful for the final minutes being spent with the Condors completely dominating the puck in front of the Los Angeles net.

Three-two-one.

The horn wailed.

The Condors had won, and his losing streak was finally over. He would take the win, no matter how he got it done.

By the time Max got home from the game it was late. As he made his way through his big beachfront house, he switched on all the lights and opened all the windows to allow the night's breeze in to cool his warm skin. The excitement from the win had left his body on fire, ablaze with hope.

Does Max Miller still got it?

Hell fucking yes, he did. And the score tonight should be enough proof to shut the naysayers up for a while.

He flopped down on his couch and kicked up his feet, the adrenaline from the win making him feel invincible, hopeful, and excited for this season *and* the potential of his big contract.

His mind raced, optimism flooding him, and oddly enough, his brain took him somewhere new. Not hockey, not the win, not the big contract. Instead, he thought of Remi.

Disappointment hit him as he looked around his living room, not finding anyone there as usual. There were no random cleaners in his kitchen, no Remi to be seen. No music blasting from the hidden speakers. Without overthinking it, he said aloud, "Alexa, play a punk mix."

The music boomed throughout the house. At first, it was a little unnerving, but Max let it play. He let it blast. With nothing on the walls, the sound reverberated all around him. Even his chest rattled with the thundering baseline and gritty lyrics being sung on the track that played.

He hadn't grown up listening to much music. There was no time for that sort of thing when you were at the rink all day. But he thought if he did, he might have liked whatever *this* was.

A text came through and it wasn't unusual for his teammates to shoot him a congratulatory message after a win. Usually, the messages made him feel half-human, like he meant something to someone. But he also found it hard to accept sincere acknowledgment for how hard he played in front of the net when the truth of it was, he hadn't done anything extraordinary, he had only done what he was paid to do.

Win.

Tonight, the messages felt different. They felt necessary because the win hadn't come easy. Tonight, it felt like so much more than just him doing his job, it felt like he had overcome some crazy obstacle. It left him wishing he had more to look forward to than a few "good job" texts from his teammates. For the first time in a long time, these texts left him craving more. He wanted to share this moment with someone, face to face. He found himself craving the way his body reacted when he was in *her* company—*Remi's* company.

He couldn't stop thinking about the first time he saw her, which still managed to make him blush each time he replayed it in his mind. The look on her face when she found him half-naked, startled by his presence, was something he could never unsee, and he wasn't sure he wanted to. He needed to see her again, apologize for scaring her, *and* thank her for taking care of him. She had managed to take up space in his life so effortlessly considering it was such a short encounter. She already felt significant to him, and he wondered if *he* could ever feel that significant to anyone else outside his hockey team. Maybe he was blowing it all out of proportion in his head, but she made him feel like he wanted more than a Stanley Cup for the first time in his life, which only managed to make him feel tiny in this big house. Meeting her in person that day made Max realize two things about himself: He was really bad at socializing, and that he might actually be lonely.

After responding to the whole damn team, Max put down his phone, shouted at the house to stop playing music, and switched on the TV to watch the highlights from tonight's game. His work in front of the net landed him the second star of the night. It had been a while since he had received a star. He pulled a pillow behind his head and settled in as he watched two of his big saves replay on the television. The sports announcers gave him praise, but not without mentioning his blunders from the past four games, causing sweat to form on his upper lip and panic to flutter in his chest at the memory of those losses. He ran his hand over his ribs—no tally mark tonight, but the skin there was still raw from the last four.

He clicked off the TV. His adrenaline from the win was finally crashing, leaving him struggling to keep his eyes open. Pulling his throw blanket off the back of the couch, he went to settle into his spot, only he didn't want to sleep on the couch tonight. He had a bed, and he was ready to start using it, ready to make himself at home. Something about meeting Remi had lit a fire in him, a longing for normalcy, a longing to settle in and make this space his, and one day, he could share it with someone else.

Heading to his room, he clicked off light after light. The blackness behind him grew more intense. The outline of his couch blurred, any real focus becoming nonexistent in the dark. His eyes strained in the sudden lack of light. The white marble countertops distorted in front of him; maybe he was just tired? This was normal, right? Night vision was an issue for lots of people, right?

"No." He growled in frustration. "No, no, no! Please just give me one more good year. Please..." he said and trailed off, rubbing the palms of his hands into his eyes, willing them to focus. His own words sounded foreign to him as they echoed through the empty house.

He was so alone.

There was no one there to guide him. No one there to clean up the mess if he made one. No one there to hold his hand, to reassure him that this, whatever *this* was, would go away.

He stumbled back to the couch, gripping at the walls he knew were there but couldn't see. Pulling the throw blanket up over his body in defeat, he settled on the massive couch, and even as he closed his eyes the room spun around him, his heart racing at the thought of what this could mean.

He would be fine.

He *would* be fine.

He would be fine. *Right?*

Chapter Six

Max sat anxiously awaiting Remi's arrival early the following Wednesday morning. Over the last week, he had gone back and forth, trying to figure out how he would handle their last encounter. He knew an apology was in order for scaring her with his half-naked surprise attack. And he knew he needed to thank her for helping him out after he had tripped and broken the lamp. But no matter how many times he played today out in his head, he knew he would never be ready to confront her. Because she was Remi, and he was, well, he was awkward.

He had showered, styled his hair, put on cologne, and hoped this cleaned-up version of himself would help diminish the memory of the last time she had shown up to his house and found him asleep on the couch.

The smart home announced her entry, and he stood to greet her, putting his nervous hands into the pockets of his dark blue Levi's. His heart hammered in his chest as she rounded the hallway corner and entered the open living space; travel coffee mug in hand as she dragged her rolling cleaning cart behind her. She noticed him immediately, the small smile on her face giving him instant relief over the situation.

He let himself enjoy the single-dimple smile she gave him before he took a step forward and cleared his throat. Words escaped him, and he had practiced what he would say to her late into the night for the last week. He had memorized the apology for the way she had found him, only now, the words were gone.

"Well, isn't *this* a pleasant surprise?" she said, eyeing him up and down. "Good morning. Clothes look good on you, Max Miller, you look handsome," she added with a playful wink, breaking the awkward silence he often lived in.

He frowned at her compliment, not expecting it.

"What?" she asked with a laugh. "You don't agree? You can always strip down to your undies if it'll make you more comfortable. I'm no stranger to that version of you."

He felt his face blush. She was teasing him, but she was also admitting she thought he was handsome, which shouldn't shock him, but it did. He knew he took pride in his appearance: He wore trendy t-shirts, clean Vans, and fresh dark jeans with a nice cuff, keeping his thick red hair and beard manicured. He knew he *tried* to look good, embracing the West Coast style, but being told he did by a woman like Remi, someone who *wasn't* a puck bunny; that was new. It caught him completely off guard.

"I actually wanted to apologize to you for what you walked in on last week. That's why I'm here," he offered.

Remi rolled her eyes, but her smile never faltered. "Is that the only reason you're here? Is it not because this is your house? Or because you knew I would be here today, and you think I'm awesome? Bummer. I thought you just really liked my company last week."

"I do... I did... I've just, I really wanted to properly apologize about it since then. It was unprofessional of me. I should have known you were coming and put on pajamas or slept in my own bed. But I didn't have a way to reach you, so I've just been ..." He paused.

"Let me guess, you've been beating yourself up over it ever since?"

"Yes. That," he agreed.

"Why am I not surprised?" she asked, walking over to set her coffee on the kitchen island.

"I don't know, why aren't you surprised?" he asked.

"Well, Max, if I'm being honest, and I have a bad habit of being extremely honest, sometimes to a fault, I would say that you come across a little... anxious."

His heart raced. Was it that obvious?

"I'm just quiet."

"Okay, call it what you will, but it didn't offend me at all. It was boxers, some men wear smaller bathing suits than that. Trust me, I've walked in on far worse things than hockey players in their undies in this profession," she said with a smirk before looking around slowly to take in his house in its pristine shape, as per usual.

"It won't happen again," he said, standing there awkwardly, unsure what came next.

"I wouldn't mind it if it did," she said teasingly, wiggling her eyebrows at him, then added, "We're both adults here, I think I can handle a little skin."

"Well, it won't happen again. I can assure you. I even bought pajama pants to make sure of it," he said.

"Please tell me they have like, Shrek on them, or baby Yoda or something."

This made Max blush instantly thinking back to his trip to Target. It felt like she was in his head because he *had* looked at the pajama bottoms with silly characters and wondered why any grown man would wear pajamas with cartoons on them, but maybe he was wrong to be so judgmental. Was this something women actually liked?

He corrected her, "It's Grogu."

She scrunched up her nose. "What is?" she asked.

"The baby Yoda. His name is Grogu."

Remi laughed. "Oh, yeah, Grogu. I knew it was something like that. He's so cute, I want one."

Max just nodded his head in agreement. He had also thought while watching *The Mandalorian*, that he wouldn't mind a little baby Yoda as a sidekick.

"So, tell me, Max, what do you have planned today?" she asked, leaning back against the island countertop. "You had a pretty big win last night, and now the day off. You hitting the beach? It's absolutely gorgeous outside."

He didn't know what he planned to do now that he had apologized, and Remi was ready to clean his *already* clean house. He would typically work out, have a nice meal, then watch a show or a movie.

"I haven't gotten that far," he admitted.

"Not a big planner?" she asked.

"I honestly couldn't think past this conversation."

"Rough stuff, Max. I promise you I'm fine. You can forgive yourself, there are far worse things in life than half-naked hockey players, I promise."

"Well, I am sorry, for what it's worth. I wish you had a better first impression of me."

"It was an amazing first impression, are you kidding me? Honestly, it was the boxer briefs for me. I'm a sucker for them," she said, then added, "And now... we never speak of it again."

He watched as *her* cheeks flushed, and for the first time he saw Remi act a little shy—her blue eyes managing to look like the ocean up against the blush of her cheeks. This made Max nervous, noticing eyes and blushing cheeks, and Remi; her presence alone made him feel weak in the knees.

"I should go," he said quickly.

Remi brought one foot to the other and kicked off her battered black and white checkered Vans. Her toenails were painted bright coral. "Pretty sure it's *your* house. You should stay. Keep me company."

Him? Company? Had she not suffered enough of his awkward pauses and clumsy eyes on her? Was she some kind of glutton for bad conversation?

"I'm not great company," he admitted, pulling his hands from his pockets to wipe them anxiously on his jeans.

"Oh, I think I'll be the judge of that."

"I don't think I can stand around and watch you clean," he said.

Remi looked around, raising her hands in question. "I don't think you'll have to. Your house is clean enough to eat off the floors, Max. I seriously don't understand why you keep me employed."

He didn't either, but if keeping her employed meant seeing her from time to time on Wednesdays, he would gladly write the check himself.

"I got fresh hummus from the farmers market this morning and a bag of pretzels," she said, pointing to a battered bag hanging off her cleaning cart, one of the straps hanging on by a thread.

He glanced over at it, then back at her, unsure what she wanted him to do with this information.

"I could share it with you," she offered.

"For breakfast?" he asked, unsure if he liked the idea of hummus this early, before coffee even.

"Or lunch."

"But lunch is hours away."

Remi looked at him incredulously, wrinkling her nose. "Do you want to have hummus with me or not? Because if I don't share it with someone, I'm likely to eat the whole tub of it alone. I have zero restraint when it comes to any kind of dip situation."

"You don't have anyone else to share it with?" he asked.

It wasn't what he meant to say. What he meant to say was, *why me*? He didn't understand why she would want to share anything with him, especially her time, let alone her hummus.

He was so bad at this.

This was why he played hockey and kept his head down.

He wanted the hummus, sure, but he wanted her company even more. But what was in it for her? Awkward conversation with a grown-ass man. A man who hadn't dated since college. A man that couldn't articulate that he wanted the damn hummus.

Remi rolled her eyes and shook her head at him. "I have plenty of people I could share it with, Max, but I offered to share it with *you*."

He watched as she got to work, moving on from the topic of hummus. Pulling cleaners from her cart, she sat them on the marble countertop before making her way to his room.

He called out to her, "I want to have hummus with you."

His entire body heated. Overheated even.

She turned back and gave him a double-dimple grin. "Good. How does noon sound?"

"It sounds good."

"What will you do until then?" she asked.

Max realized he didn't know. This *was* his house, but he felt like he needed to give Remi space to clean, or pretend to clean, or do whatever it was he paid her to do.

"Wait, I guess," he said, and Remi playfully shook her head at him, her smile never faltering.

Chapter Seven

She had just started making the bed in the master bedroom when she heard the garage door open, the smart home announcing his arrival. He had snuck off at some point when she was mopping, and she honestly wondered if he would return for their beach picnic.

"Hey," she called out, "I'm just finishing up your bed."

He crept in quietly, lingering in the doorway of his bedroom, watching her as she pulled the top sheet up into place.

"It's noon," he said, and Remi didn't miss the nervous undertones in his voice.

Turning to face him, she saw that he had a farmers market tote hanging from his massive arm.

"Whatcha got?" she said, hinting at the floral print tote she had seen for sale at one of the vendor booths this morning while she was picking up the hummus and pretzels.

"Oh, this?" he said, looking down at the bag. "I got the one with flowers. I thought you could use a new one," he said, hinting at her battered old tote hanging from the barstool in the other room.

Remi pulled her bottom lip between her teeth to keep herself from smiling too big. It *was* just a farmers market tote, but the gesture made her heart hammer in her chest. The thought of him choosing the floral tote for her and then proceeding to shop with it was an image she couldn't help but feel giddy over. Massive Max Miller, with his tight black Violent Gentlemen shirt stretching over his big chest, pulling on his biceps, walking through the Huntington Beach farmers market with his vibrant floral tote.

She wished she could have seen it in person.

"It's beautiful," she said, turning back to finish making his bed. "Thank you for thinking of me when you saw it."

Before she realized what was happening, Max was at the other end of the bed, helping her pull the comforter up.

"I don't sleep in here," he said.

She didn't stop what she was doing, she didn't want to make a big to-do over him admitting it. It was obvious that he didn't sleep in this bed, but she didn't push back. Max would tell her things in *his* time. She felt her role in this friendship was to just be safe. Safe enough that one day Max could share freely. Safe enough that one day Max might consider *her* a friend.

A new friend sounded nice.

"More of a couch guy?" she asked with a playful wink.

He took a moment before responding, placing the pillow she tossed him in its spot. "I think sleeping in a bed makes this all feel too official," he said shyly.

This made her pause.

"What do you mean by that?"

Max ran his hand along the pillowcase, smoothing it out. "If I sleep in this bed, I'm afraid I might realize how this isn't a proper home. It might make it more real how messed up it is that I have all *this*," he said, hinting at the house, the view, the beach, "and no one to share it with."

"And why is that?" she asked, in the most welcoming voice she could muster. She didn't want him to feel pressured to talk, but she also wanted him to know she was safe if he chose to.

"Why don't I have anyone to share it with?" he asked, his eyes on her, laced with so much emotion she thought her heart might actually break for him.

"Yes, Max. Why do you keep this all to yourself when anyone would be so lucky to be invited into your space, and *so* lucky to get to know you?"

"I already told you. I'm not good at this sort of thing."

"But what if you are? What if you just need the right person to show you that you are capable of friendship, and conversation, a house full of memories, pictures, and *love*?"

She watched as he shrunk into himself.

"And what? *You're* the person to show me that?" he asked, a hint of challenge in his voice.

"I'd like to be."

"Why?" he asked.

"Because, Max, I've got all this hummus and a free afternoon."

"I might disappoint you," he said shyly.

"You *might* disappoint me. That's always a possibility. But you also might surprise me, and you might just surprise yourself, too."

***

When he got down to the beach, he found Remi had already laid out a blanket for the two of them. She sat cross-legged, her feet bare and her hair pulled up in a messy blonde knot on the top of her head. When she turned to smile at him, he noticed she wore classic Ray Ban sunglasses, just the same as him, and everything about her vibe was welcoming.

Remi was a cool ocean breeze on a hot day. She was all of the best parts of the West Coast in human form: sunshine, carefree comfort, walking barefoot in the hot sand.

His stomach fluttered.

"Why do you still have your shoes on ya' big goon?" she teased, and he looked down at his Sk8-Hi Vans and wondered the same damn thing.

"I didn't think to take them off," he said, sitting next to her on the blanket.

"So, what's in the bag?" she asked.

"I didn't know what you like, so I got a little bit of everything," he said shyly, reaching into the farmers market tote to pull out a glass bottle of fresh lemonade. "This was made this morning," he said, "but it just dawned on me that we don't have any cups."

"That's okay, we can drink straight from the bottle. I won't back-wash, I promise."

His entire body stiffened.

"Or not?" she said reluctantly.

It wasn't that he didn't want to share a drink with her. He didn't care. He shared a locker room and showers with a bunch of men, so sharing a bottle of lemonade didn't scare him.

His body had stiffened at the thought of her lips and his lips sharing something. It was so far from being a kiss, and yet the most intimate thing he could imagine doing with her at this moment. Sharing a drink felt like something sacred when sitting next to Remi. He wondered what sharing himself would feel like. His life, his past, his mind... his heart?

"No, it's fine. I don't mind," he said.

"Okay, but if you don't want to, I can run up to your house and get some cups." She looked behind her at his house only feet away from where they sat in the sand, the ocean pushing and pulling, working masterfully in front of them.

He didn't do this enough—enjoy *this* enough.

"It's fine. Really." He continued to pull other things he had gotten from the farmers market out of the tote, fresh strawberries and blueberries, a bag of plantain chips, a jar of pickled veggies, and a bag of "California" trail mix that was essentially just normal trail mix with dried pineapples added.

"Well, looks like we have ourselves a proper picnic now, thanks to you," she said, reaching into her own worn tote and pulling out the infamous hummus and pretzels.

"I've never done this," Max said, looking at the spread of fresh goodies in front of him.

"Had a picnic at the beach?"

"Yeah. You would think I come down to the water often, considering I live here. But I'm on the road a lot with hockey, and I sometimes forget to enjoy the simple things in life."

"I *live* at the beach," Remi said, popping a handful of blueberries into her mouth.

"As in you live close by, or you come often?"

"Both. I live in Huntington, close to where the farmers market is. I have a little rental. It's tiny and out of date. I don't think you would even fit in the bathroom, it's *that* small. But I always promised myself I would live close enough to smell the water when I got older."

"And you kept your promise to yourself."

"I did."

"It's good to keep promises," he said as she opened the bottle of lemonade to take a drink.

He watched as her pink lips pushed against the glass, her neck elongating so elegantly as she pulled her head back to drink. She was beautiful.

There, he had let himself think it.

It wasn't as if he was on to something revolutionary. Any person within reason would look at Remi and see her beauty.

She handed the bottle back to him, and he hesitantly brought it to his lips to drink. It was more bitter than he expected but refreshing. When he finished, he decided against wiping away the sweetness that lingered on his mouth, because that sweet lemony reminder was all he might ever know of Remi's lips.

"So, tell me, Max. Where did you grow up?"

She came in with such a simple question, completely unaware of how difficult it would be for him to answer.

He wanted an out: to say pass, next question, please. His leg began to bounce, shifting the blanket below him.

Looking over at her, her face was inviting, even as she squinted with the sun in her eyes. No one had ever been this nice to him, not since his college year at the Mayberry house, and Allison...

"I grew up all over the place," he finally answered.

She shook her head in agreement. "Me too," she said, patting his knee before gripping it and holding it in place, slowing his anxious movements, "we already have something in common."

"What other states have you lived in?" he asked, wanting to keep the attention off himself.

"Only California, but I never stayed anywhere long. We bounced around a lot. My mom had issues, so we were constantly getting the boot."

"What kind of issues?" he asked, then immediately took it back. "Unless you don't want to talk about it."

Remi dipped a thick pretzel stick into the hummus and took a bite while she considered his question.

"My mom was a bit of a mess," she started.

"Oh," Max said, assuming that was all he was going to get—it was all he would have given if the tables were turned.

"I mean that literally and figuratively. She was an absolute mess."

"How so?" he pressed.

"She wasn't healthy—she had some mental stuff going on—so she drank a lot to mask her problems. She was a hoarder."

Max felt his facial expression falter with shock; Remi began to laugh.

"Didn't see that coming, did you?" she asked, busying herself by picking through the bag of trail mix to find all the chocolate candies hidden amongst the nuts, raisins, and pineapple chunks.

"I *didn't* see that coming. I think I always assume people have a perfect life because I..." He paused, struggling to admit what came next.

"You what?" she encouraged.

"I don't ever get to know anyone well enough to know these sorts of things actually exist. I thought hoarders only happened on reality TV."

"Nope. I'm the product of a hoarder childhood," she said, pressing out her shoulders in a bit of mock pride.

"Is that why you clean for a living now?" he asked.

Remi brought her finger to his nose and tapped it as she said, "Ding-ding-ding."

"Do you find it cathartic, cleaning up after others?" he asked.

"I do. I always wanted to clean up after her, but she was fragile, ya know? She hid under her trash, her pizza boxes, empty bottles, and filth. What a clean house does for my peace of mind, a mess did for hers. It's hard to explain if you didn't know her. She wasn't a bad person; she was just trapped in something I couldn't help her out of as a child. It was a vicious cycle. Move, drink, hoard, evict. Over and over."

"Where was your dad in all of this?" he asked.

"He would come and go. But usually, it was just to drink with her. They would go on a bender together, trash the place, and then he would be gone. Toxic love is a real thing, I saw it firsthand throughout my entire childhood."

Max wondered if that's what he had with his parents. Parents who on paper look like saints, but the older he got, he wasn't so sure they were all that great.

He looked out at the ocean. It was beautiful and terrifying, like this girl sitting next to him and the conversation they were having.

"You're burning. You need sunscreen, even in October," Remi said, running a gentle finger up the warm skin of his freckle-spattered forearm.

"Redhead problems," he offered, causing Remi to laugh.

"I like it," she said, bringing the same finger that was just on his arm, up to brush a stray hair off his sweaty forehead. "The red hair, the red beard, and now, after fifteen minutes in the sun, the red cheeks."

"I should have worn a hat."

"Next time," she said, bumping her shoulder into his.

Next time, he thought. Would there be a next time? Had he somehow convinced her to consider him for a *next* time?

"Hey, Max?" she asked.

He turned to face her, the dimple on her left cheek was present; his heart raced.

"You're not as bad at this as you think you are."

"I'm not?"

She smiled up at him, through squinted eyes. "Not at all. I think you just needed someone to give you a chance."

"A chance to what?" he asked.

"A chance to talk."

Max looked away. It felt like a lot of pressure. A lot of expectations to live up to. She had done the talking, he had only asked the questions, prying into the details of her past, one he wasn't even sure she wanted to share had he not been so nosy.

"Sorry for asking questions about your mom."

"Don't be. I think sometimes I only talk about her flaws, which makes her seem awful. How much she loved me often gets lost in all of that."

It was crazy to think that Remi's mom had managed to love her while struggling with mental illness, a toxic relationship with Remi's father, *and* a drinking problem, while all his mother managed to do was send him away. His mother was healthy, and wealthy, and never left a dirty dish in the sink a day of her life. It made Max consider how he perceived love. He guessed it looked different for everyone depending on where you were standing.

To most people, they would have seen him as an entitled boy with a mother and stepfather who loved him so much that they invested in his hockey career—sending him off to the finest training camps and billet homes. But to Max, he saw a lonely child who didn't want any of that, one who only wanted his mom back, and her affection and time. Time, she didn't have with a new husband and new kids. It was a life Max suddenly didn't fit into. He would have done anything for a father who hadn't run out on him. A father who told him "good game" and celebrated his wins.

"What about you? What was your family like growing up?" Remi asked as if reading his mind.

The sun suddenly felt much too hot, and his brain was starting to feel fuzzy as the sweat gathered on his forehead.

"To be continued?" he offered hesitantly, taking the uncomplicated way out. He wasn't ready for that conversation. Not yet anyway.

Remi leaned into his space, her body pressing against him, a calming reassurance that it was okay to take a pass this time. And for that he was grateful.

Remi began to pack up her hummus. "Deal. To be continued, Max Miller."

He also gathered his things, putting the cap back on the lemonade, and closing the bag of trail mix.

Standing at the same time, and without having to ask the other, they shook the sand from the blanket, with each of them holding an end in their hands as they walked together to fold it in a team effort. When they met in the middle, with only the blanket between them, Max thought he saw something new in Remi. The way she tilted her head to look at him, and the way she *didn't* smile this time—not even the single-dimple kind; he thought maybe she saw something in him too. But the moment passed before Max could act on it. They finished folding the blanket, and without saying another word, they made their way up the trail back to his house as he fought off the strobe-like flashes of light he was experiencing from being out in the bright sun.

Chapter Eight

The Condors were in Seattle, and despite Max being unpredictable in front of the net, Coach still gave him the start. It was their last game in October before he flew home for two days, and Max knew a win wasn't guaranteed with him in front of the net. Even with his coach's confidence in him, Max knew Jack Brown had become the team's safe choice.

There was talk in the locker room. He heard their hushed voices and felt their eyes on him. Not everyone on the team felt as confident in him as their coach did, and he didn't blame them. If he didn't trust himself in front of the net, how could he expect his team to?

He wasn't a dumb man; he knew something was definitely going on with him. Something was off, but that didn't make it easier to accept whatever it was that was happening with his vision and face it head-on.

It would pass. It had to pass. That was the only option.

"Hey," a gruff voice said before he felt the heaviness of a hand on his shoulder.

Looking up, Max saw Patrick Carter, the captain of the Condors, standing next to him.

"Mind if I take a seat?" he asked, and Max hinted to the left side of the locker room bench. Carter shook his head knowingly. Everyone knew that Max thought it was bad luck to have someone sit on the right side of him before a game.

"How are you feeling, Millsy?" Carter asked, using the team's nickname for him.

Max liked his captain. Carter was young, but he was talented and had a natural ability to lead. "I feel fine." Max lied, because in all honesty, he felt nervous. He could feel his chest growing tighter and tighter the closer they got to puck drop, because no matter how many times he blinked, or how many times he put drops in his eyes, or how many lights he kept on, Max couldn't seem to fix it. He didn't know what *it* was, but whatever *it* was, scared him because it was only getting worse.

"Okay. But how do you really feel, Millsy? Because if I were you, I wouldn't be okay."

"This season just started off on the wrong foot," Max said, knowing he wasn't fooling his observant captain.

"You getting the start tonight has the boys worried. And I'm not telling you this to discourage you, I'm telling you this to light a fire under your ass, Millsy. I know you're in your head over the losses, but I want you to remember you're the best goalie in Condors' franchise history. Remember *that* tonight. The start of the season is in the past, it was just a slow start for you, but you got this. We're going to play hard in front of you, Millsy, but I need to know that you'll be there if we let a puck through."

"I will. I'll be there," he said, but that didn't change the fact that he couldn't make out the shape of the team's logo under his feet on the locker room carpet.

Carter gave his shoulder one last squeeze. "We believe in you, but you've got to get back to believing in yourself."

If only *that* was the real problem.

Carter went back to his locker, and Max willed his eyes to stay unfocused. He didn't want to see the way the rest of the team was watching him get ready with their uncertain eyes and hushed voices. And while Max appreciated his captain's little pep talk, he knew it wasn't enough. Because while Max *was* in his head about his losses, he knew it was more than that. He needed help. He needed to go to the doctor to see what he could do to fix it, because if he didn't figure this out, he would throw away his final season, and he refused to retire from the bench.

***

Remi sat cross-legged on her living room floor as she glued sequins to the bodysuit of her Halloween costume. The Condor's game played on the TV in front of her. Max got the start, and it pained her how nervous that made her feel.

This Saturday was Halloween, and she had been invited to a party by one of the bartenders at Moe's. The party was, as to be expected, a costume party, and Remi was crafty if nothing else. So, balls deep in sequins, she sat gluing her costume as Max took his place in front of the net as the second period started. The Condors were winning, 2-1. Remi watched as Max had been able to make a few saves. And while Remi was no hockey expert, she couldn't help but notice that those saves didn't happen without struggle. He looked off tonight. His saves seemed messy, like he was frantic in front of the net.

She told herself watching him play didn't make her miss him.

Not at all.

Not even a bit.

She absolutely did not miss him.

She was an *awful* liar.

She hadn't seen him since their little beach picnic, and she *also* had not gone a day without thinking about it. Max was at the forefront of her mind for what seemed like every second of every day since she met him. She couldn't shake the feeling that he might need someone in his life, a friend or maybe even a lover? She tried not to think of him in a sexual way, but it was getting harder and harder to do the more she watched him play. She hadn't always been into a man in uniform, but she would be lying if she said the goalie gear didn't do something to her lower regions.

She was already breaking her rules of conduct for Busy Bee Cleaners by spending time with Max, breaking the fourth wall. He should be invisible to her when she was cleaning his house. But he was hard not to see, partly because he was massive, and partly because he was awkwardly there, but mostly because he was beautiful.

She wondered what Max would do for Halloween. He didn't have a game that night, so he might be in town. She couldn't be sure; with the way he was always flying from one city to the next. If he *was* in town, she knew one thing for certain, she wanted to see him.

Ripping a piece of paper from the spiral notepad on her coffee table, she wrote him a note inviting him to the party. It was a fifty-fifty chance Max would say yes, but so was everything else in life, so why would she let that stop her now? The glass was right in front of her, why not take a chance at making it half full?

Chapter Nine

It had come on faster than ever—the strobing lights, the little orbs falling from the sky—and within six minutes of the last period, Max had let in three goals, causing his team to lose against Seattle.

His career would be over if he didn't get help.

But what if it wasn't fixable?

What if yesterday's game was his last?

What if his final memory as an Anaheim Condor was him skating to the locker room after he lost them the game?

Max thought of Jack Brown and how he should have had the start. He knew it, the whole team knew it, but Max still made the choice to skate out onto that ice, with his vision straining, his heart racing, and uncertainty heavy in his chest.

He was thankful the Condors had Brown to count on in front of the net these days. It was one of the only things he found solace in lately when it came to hockey, but he'd be lying if he said he wasn't bitter. That was *his* net, and he was certain he was watching it slip away as it became someone else's spot in the starting lineup.

He grabbed his bag from the trunk of his Jeep, and the second he opened the door to his house the lemony-scented cleaner Remi often used when she mopped filled his nose, awakening his senses and causing the loss last night in Seattle to seem like a distant memory. His heart raced at the thought of her being here only hours ago. She had just been here walking barefoot on his floors. Her toes with little bits of sand between them from the beach, her hair a tangled mess of beachy waves, her petite frame that took up so much space with the confidence that surrounded her, and that damn dimple. The one on her left cheek that he saw more often than the one on her right.

Everything about her did him in.

Made him breathe a bit deeper. Made him smile a little wider, even if he was smiling alone. The thought of Remi, the smell of lemon cleaner, and the traces she left behind without even realizing it made him crave something deeper; a connection, a spark, a life shared, a messy bed, a fridge full of leftovers from late-night meals left unfinished. He wanted to fall asleep with sand between his toes, and wake to his sheets filled with the memories of long walks on the beach with someone who listened and cared. Someone who stuck around long enough for him to figure out how to get all the words that lived on the tip of his tongue to finally jump from his lips.

He thought of the glass bottle of lemonade they shared at the beach; her lips pressed against it. Running a finger over his own lips, he let himself wonder for a split second what it might be like to share a kiss with Remi.

Rolling his suitcase to the laundry room, he clicked on every light as he went, just as he did every night when he got home. Grabbing a bottle of water from the empty fridge, he sat down at the bar with his tattoo kit. Sitting next to the bowl of fruit was a handwritten note. Opening the folded piece of paper, his eyes darted to the bottom of the note where he saw her name, *Remi*. His heart began to hammer in his chest at the sight of her handwriting. Her delicate letters, the way she made the M in Max a little bigger than the rest of the letter...

> Max, Hi. I know you don't have a game on Halloween because it's public information. I promise I'm not creepy. I also noticed your team is playing at home November 1st. This leads me to assume that you are free on Halloween. I don't know how you feel about costumes, candy, and cheap beer, but I got invited to a party, and I was wondering if you wanted to come with me and enjoy some spooky festivities. No pressure. I promise I won't be offended if you say no. Think about it. But don't OVERTHINK about it!
>
> -Remi
>
> PS: If you do come, you have to bring a bottle.

A party.

A costume party.

With Remi.

No. Absolutely not.

He could hardly make eye contact in everyday clothes with this woman, he couldn't imagine trying to keep a conversation going in a scarecrow costume, or whatever it was people dressed up as these days.

He sat the note next to the bowl of fresh fruit and began to cover the marble countertop in plastic wrap. He was exhausted from the travel, the game, and the loss.

Filling the plastic cap with black ink, he looked over to read the note again before switching on the tattoo gun. No, absolutely not. No Halloween parties, no costumes.

The buzz of the needle felt louder than normal, and for a split second, he let himself consider not doing it. Not dipping the needle into the ink. Not pressing it against his bare flesh. He wondered what would happen if he didn't do it, if he didn't add another tally mark to his long list of losses. What if he just accepted it and moved on?

Superstition won. Bringing the tattoo gun to his side, he eternalized this loss on his ribs in one quick motion, tattooing a line next to the last like he had every other loss that came before it.

He looked down at the note again, he couldn't stop staring at it. Her dainty handwriting, so convincing.

Just go Max, just say yes. Take a chance, wear the costume, and accept that this beautiful woman wants you around, and wants you in her life.

He cleaned up the tattoo gun mess, packing the equipment away before making his way to his room where he slipped into his navy cotton pajama bottoms before heading back to the couch. He settled in, trying to ignore the invite on the island countertop.

Turning off the TV in defeat, he got up to get the note and entered her number into his phone just so he had it, just in case... for emergency purposes. Because there was no way he was going to a Halloween party. No way in hell.

Chapter Ten

Remi got ready for the Halloween party, The Strokes blasting and the windows open, the cool October breeze carrying the smell of rain into her small beachfront house.

Trying like hell, she failed to push back the disappointment that sat in the pit of her stomach. The disappointment associated with Max not accepting her invitation. And why would he? He was a professional athlete, and she was his housekeeper. He most likely dated models and celebrities. Shy or not, he probably had some big crazy party in a mansion he would be going to. Why would he want to come slumming it in Huntington Beach with her?

Her phone chimed, and despite not wanting to get her hopes up, she lunged for it, her heart sinking with disappointment when she read the name "Randy" on her phone's screen. Randy was the bartender who was throwing the party, and the text was a simple reminder to bring a bottle of alcohol.

She sat her phone down and willed herself to accept that she would be going to this party solo, and that was fine, right? She would know plenty of people there, it wasn't like she was going to be alone. If she drank enough, everyone would eventually feel like a friend or a date.

She pulled the pastel sequined bodysuit off its hanger and admired it for a second; she had knocked it out of the park this year, it turned out perfect. She stepped into the body suit, pulling it over her glittery white tights, it fit like a glove. She stood in front of the mirror, and realized she looked like Taylor Swift in her Lover era, but that wasn't where her costume ended.

She slipped her feet into a pair of pastel purple and white checkered Vans she had gotten to go with her costume, because give her Vans or give her death. Her phone chimed again with another text.

"I know, Randy, the party starts at seven," she said, opening her phone, shocked to find a text from none other than Max Miller, the mutha-fuckin'-enigma.

Max:

Invite still open?

Remi laughed, and with shaky fingers, responded.

Remi:

Depends.

She waited, and when he didn't respond, she remembered her audience and texted him again.

Remi:

I mean, it depends on if you have a costume or not.

She watched the three dots dance on her phone screen before they disappeared; no text came through.

"Come on, Max, don't overthink this. For once in your life just say yes," she said aloud to herself.

He responded.

Max:

> I don't have a costume.

She laughed. Of course he didn't have a costume. He didn't even have pictures hung in his house, he didn't sleep on his own bed, and he was, well, he was so very *Max*.

Remi:

> Don't worry about it, I'll figure something out. Meet me at my house, and we can walk to the party. It's only a block away.

***

Max found a parking spot a few streets away from Remi's address and paid to park there until 2 a.m.—optimistically. He had never gone to a Halloween party. Hell, he'd never even dressed up for Halloween, his mother couldn't be bothered by such nonsense.

As he walked up the small beach road, he noticed the tiny houses sitting closely together that lined the street. Each of them had tiny porches and small patio furniture sets. Some of the homes were nicer than others. Some of the homes, it was obvious, belonged to people who had lived there since the day the house was built and had never done any upkeep since; the moist ocean air stripping what seemed to have been vibrant colors of paint. Remi's house was the last on the street, the only thing separating it from the sand was a walkway, where a man on rollerblades flew past wearing a Minion onesie, blasting music from a small portable speaker.

Remi's house was, as she had warned him it was, *tiny*. The exterior was pale blue, the paint chipped and faded. Her porch had a small wicker patio set and an abundance of potted plants. He opened the small gate that surrounded the patio and made his way to the front door, which was open, the only thing keeping him from being inside was a battered screen door. He could hear music coming from deep in the house and a breeze pushed through, carrying with it the lemony scent he associated with her.

The old screen door rattled under his knuckles as he knocked. He waited until he heard her familiar voice call out. "Come in," she shouted from deep in the house.

Panic flooded him.

Instead of stepping inside, he stood there battling between entering her home like an old friend or waiting until she came to let him in like the stranger he was.

He saw her approach the door from the back of the house and his vision blurred, but it had nothing to do with his eyes and everything to do with Remi wearing some kind of glittery bathing suit, with her sparkly legs on display and her hair in two space buns on top of her head. He didn't know what she was dressed as, but he liked it.

She opened the screen door for him, a huge toothy grin on her face, and he noticed she had little pastel jewels surrounding her blue eyes. They were stormy tonight, and he wondered if they were predicting the weather that was upon them.

"I'm so happy you agreed to come. I was certain you would say no."

And to be fair, so was he.

"Welcome. It's not much, but it's home," she said, and something about that statement filled Max's heart with longing. A longing for a sense of what she had here—a sense of home.

"It's nice," he said.

"It's *just* okay. Nothing in comparison to your house," she teased, and she couldn't be more wrong.

Remi's house was everything. It was colors, pictures, and little sentiments tucked away on shelves. It was a life lived and being lived. There were memories etched in the chipped flooring; maybe a bottle falling during a drunken night. There was love and happiness in the mismatched furniture. There was a sense of family present, in the small fish tank, with a singular betta.

She was so wrong. His place had nothing on this.

"So, did you come up with a costume? Or do I have to force you to wear something from my box of Halloweens past?" she asked.

"I brought a jersey, figured I could be a hockey player," he said, feeling stupid.

"No. That won't do."

"I didn't have anything else," Max stated.

"Well, lucky for you I have just the thing," Remi said, bolting from the living room.

When she returned, she had a headband with cat ears on it.

"No," Max said instantly.

"You have to dress up, it's the rules."

"I can't be a cat."

"And why not?" she asked.

"Because I'm a massive redhead."

"Yeah, exactly, you can be a ginger cat, it's a whole fucking breed," she said, handing him the ears.

"But these are black," he argued.

"Max Miller, put the cat ears on or I'll find something else, and trust me, it'll only get worse."

Max put the bottle of alcohol he brought under his arm and took the headband cat ears. Hesitantly, he put them on as Remi bounced on her toes in front of him with excitement.

Once they were on, Max held out his hands in a "ta-da" gesture and Remi squealed with joy.

"Max Miller, you are the hottest black cat I've ever seen."

He felt his face blush. "I thought you said I was a ginger cat."

"Whatever kind of cat you are, you look purrrrrrrrrty good," she said with a wink, and Max laughed for the first time in what felt like forever. He genuinely laughed, and his reward was a double-dimple smile from this beautiful girl.

"Okay, let me grab my bottle and the rest of my costume and we can head out."

Remi turned to grab her things, and Max tried and failed to not watch her walk away. Her body was so readily available for him to look at, and while he knew he shouldn't, he feasted on the sight of her. The way the costume hugged her ass, and the way her legs were so long and fit. He felt a stir in the pit of his stomach; he ached for her. He ached for more of her than she was offering. It was an ache that would only be dulled by him slowly pushing the sequined straps of the bodysuit from her shoulders and pulling it down her body.

"Ready to go?" she said, appearing out of nowhere, snapping him from his inappropriate sex-fueled fantasy of her.

She invited him as a friend. She was his cleaning lady. He had to draw a line in the sand somewhere, right?

"Ready," he said, noticing they both had a bottle of Pink Whitney to bring to the party.

She tapped her bottle of pink vodka against his. "Twins," she said with a wink, before leading the way out, locking the door behind her, then handing him her house keys. "Can you hold these for me since you have pockets?"

He took the keys without hesitation. "Hope this isn't offensive, but what are you supposed to be?" he asked incredulously.

Remi took the umbrella she had in her hands, which Max assumed was for the storm that was headed their way and opened it. As soon as the umbrella opened colorful ribbons fell from it. Remi flipped a little switch on the handle and the umbrella lit up. She did a small twirl, making the dangling ribbons dance around her and finally, it all made sense.

"A jellyfish?" he asked with a raised eyebrow.

She leaned into him and tapped his nose, "Ding-ding-ding."

"It's..." he said quietly, "you're perfect."

Remi blushed at his compliment.

Max blushed at his compliment.

And then without another word, they made their way to the party.

Chapter Eleven

The party was... interesting. Max was completely blown away by the outrageous costumes some of these people had come up with. The amount of skin on display was surprising. He had seen a half-naked cop, a half-naked reindeer, a more than half-naked sexy nurse—who was also a man—and a T. rex with a tray of Jello shots. Remi grabbed two of the small plastic cups from the stumbling dinosaur and handed him one.

"On the count of three," she said.

Max took the plastic cup from her and squeezed it a bit, detaching the sludge from the sides to make it easier to shoot.

"One–two–three!"

They both sucked down the slippery Jello and Max was shocked at how easy it was. Not just the shot, but being at the party, with his cat ears on—that no one even batted an eye at—*and* being with Remi. She made it easy for him. The loud music made it easy. The *alcohol* definitely made it easy.

"Let's go out to the patio so we can talk. It's too loud and stuffy in here," she said, grabbing him by the hand as she led the way to the beach access patio. His entire body heated at the simple gesture, her confident grip on his hand, guiding him—he felt safe, even while completely out of his comfort zone.

"I can't believe it's going to rain tonight. The weather's been so unpredictable," she said.

"I like the rain," Max said, watching as Remi brought her bottle of vodka to her lips, taking a long swig before handing it to him. He lifted the bottle and did the same, the vodka warming his insides.

"Don't you have a game tomorrow night?" she asked.

"I do, but I'm not getting the start in front of the net. It's probably not the best decision I've made in my lifetime, drinking straight from the bottle the night before a game, but I think I can handle a little hangover from the bench."

Remi looked up at him, and her smile softened. "Yeah, the whole *bench* thing," she said, "we don't have to talk about it if you don't want to. About hockey and all that. We can save it for another night."

Maybe it was the liquor, maybe it was Remi, or maybe it was the cat ears causing him to feel so bold, but Max *did* want to talk about it. He wanted to get it off his chest, say it out loud to someone, *anyone*, because carrying it alone had become so heavy.

"I think there's something wrong with me, with my health," he admitted, not wanting to be too specific.

Remi's entire body tensed up at his confession.

"Like, I think I need to see a doctor or something, to be honest," he confessed, breaking her gaze to look down at his blurry feet. The party raged on, but suddenly the space around them seemed to go silent and still.

"Max..." she said, encouraging him to go on, to give her more, to say everything he was hiding.

"It'll be okay, I don't think it's something that's going to kill me. I plan to make an appointment soon," he said, pulling back from the conversation by offering her a simple solution, one he wasn't even sure he was ready to hold himself accountable to.

Remi nodded her head encouragingly, but he didn't miss the way her entire demeanor had changed at his confession.

"But hey," he said, offering a comforting smile, "I'm sorry I even said anything, I didn't mean to kill the mood. I guess I just needed to get it off my chest. I can't be honest about this stuff with my team."

"Don't apologize. I'm happy you told me. When you're ready, I'd like to know more about it, whatever *it* is."

"Yeah?"

"Yeah, Max. I worry about you," she said, giving his hand a comforting squeeze.

"Don't worry about me. It's nothing, really. I think I just needed to say it out loud, ya know? Admit to someone that something might be wrong, something bad enough to land me on the bench."

"Well, I'm happy you told me. Maybe saying it out loud was the push you needed to make the appointment to get some answers, set your mind at ease, and get you in front of the net more consistently," she said, kicking the toe of his shoe with hers.

A partygoer pushed by, bumping into Remi, causing her body to stumble closer to his. Her hands landed on his chest, keeping them from getting *too close*. They both played it safe and laughed it off before she took a step back, giving him his space. Only, he didn't want his space. He liked having her close.

The sky lit up around them as lightning struck in the distance. Everyone on the patio cheered and looked up towards the sky. Everyone except Max and Remi. He couldn't take his eyes off her, and she seemed to be on the same page because she didn't look away from him either.

"Are you scared?" she asked, another drunk partygoer pushing her towards him again, only this time she didn't move back. She stayed. A little too close, yet not close enough.

"Of lightning?" he asked, looking up at the storm rolling in.

"Of what a doctor might say. Jesus, Max, focus." She laughed.

Thunder rolled, chasing the crash of the lightning.

"I think I'm more afraid of *not* knowing what's wrong with me at this point," Max said.

He didn't see it happen, but Remi's hand found his. Their bodies pressed closer as the patio began to fill with people hoping to see more of the storm. Max thought he might kiss her, and when he looked into her eyes, he thought *she* might kiss *him*.

"Do you want to get out of here?" Remi offered calmly, as the partygoers around them rambunctiously pushed and shoved to get down to the water, which Max found to be stupid and unsafe, considering the lightning.

"Only if you do."

"I think it might rain on the walk back," she said looking up at the thick grey clouds above them.

"Well, it's a good thing you're a jellyfish then."

***

Remi popped open her jellyfish umbrella and hung it over her shoulder as she and Max walked up the beach trail that led back to her house. Max still had his cat ears on, and she wondered if he had forgotten, or if he was just invested at this point.

She looked around before taking a sip of the vodka she had brought along, scrunching up her nose as the aftertaste hit her. "You want?" she asked, holding it out to Max. "I don't usually drink like this, but something about this storm is making me feel reckless."

Max took the bottle and drank as well, something about Remi was making *him* feel reckless. She watched as he braved the taste of it, hardly making a face.

"Am I a bad influence?" she asked.

"No," he said shyly.

"How are you feeling?" She giggled.

"Buzzed. You?" His cheeks grew more flushed with each shot of vodka.

"Buzzed," she said, bumping her shoulder into him causing them both to stumble.

"Do you want to know something I've never told anyone?" he offered, and yes, fuck yes, she wanted to know all the secret things about Max Miller, the enigma.

"All the things, Max. I want to know them all," she said, looking up at him eagerly.

He smiled, one of his rare smiles, and then looked away. "I've never been trick-or-treating," he said.

Remi's jaw dropped.

"What?"

"Yup. Never wore a costume until tonight."

She stopped dead in her tracks and turned to face him. "Max, tell me you're joking."

"Not joking. My mom didn't like Halloween. She didn't allow us candy either. She was... *hard*."

"Max, we have to take you trick-or-treating. It's a childhood staple."

"I'm not a child though, I think that ship has sailed."

"Well, we have to do it anyway," she argued.

"When?"

She grabbed his hand and dragged him towards the row of beach houses.

"Now. I'm taking you trick-or-treating right now, Max Miller."

He pulled back, hesitating. "I'm too old."

"Not a thing. You're never too old to trick-or-treat."

"It's late, no one's going to answer," he said, trying and failing to convince her to stop.

Remi knew he was right. Of course he was too old. And yeah, maybe showing up as adults to a stranger's house slightly intoxicated asking for candy any other night of the year would be frowned upon and grounds for a phone call to the local police, but it was Halloween, someone had to have some candy left.

She stopped in front of a pink house with a white iron gate. "So, here's what you do, you just ring the doorbell, and when they answer you say, 'trick or treat' and smile."

"I'm not doing that," Max said, pulling his hand away and taking a step back.

"Max, this is a life event no one should be denied."

"Remi. I can't do this."

She looked up at him and pleaded, "Please. I'll even go with you."

"What if they don't answer?"

"Then we move on to the next house until someone answers and gives you candy."

She watched as Max considered it. He looked down at the bottle in her hand.

"Oh, yeah, *this*. We should probably ditch it before we go to the door," she said, but before she could throw it out, Max grabbed the bottle and took a long swig. Remi laughed as he winced at the taste of the vodka this time. "Liquid courage?" she asked.

"Something like that."

He handed the bottle back and she downed the last of it. Her head was definitely spinning, and her heart was racing. She was happy, and didn't realize it before, but she was a bit nervous too. "Okay, practice round. We walk up, knock, they answer, and you say?" she asked.

"Help, this crazy jellyfish dressed me up like a cat and is forcing me to beg for candy?" he said with a coy smile on his face that absolutely took her breath away.

She grabbed him by the hand and pulled him forward. "Close enough."

***

They both held their hands up to the door and at the same time, gave it a knock. Max's heart hammered in his chest as he waited for someone to open it. It might have been the longest minute of his life, and just as he was about to walk away, the door swung open.

An old man with a small Yorkie in his arms greeted them, a confused look on his face. Max looked over at Remi, who was holding her jellyfish umbrella in place. She smiled up at him, encouraging him to go on.

Max felt the alcohol surging through his body. He felt euphoric and alive, and at the same time nervous and very aware of the cat ears on his head.

"Tri... trick or treat?" he said, more as a question, and the second he finished saying it Remi jumped up into his arms, hugging him and laughing.

"You did it! You have officially trick-or-treated," she said, her voice booming with excitement.

Max tore his eyes away from her infectious joy and gave the older man a weak, apologetic smile.

"Son," the old man said, "are you telling me you've never done this before?"

Max shook his head. "No, sir. This is my first time."

The old man stroked the small dog's head and smiled at Max. "Well, I've seen better black cats tonight, but you might be the biggest, so I guess that counts for something."

"I'm actually a ginger cat," Max said, the drunkenness causing him to feel a little silly.

The old man burst out with laughter, scaring the tiny dog and sending it into fits of high-pitched barks. "Oh, stop that, Bella," he said, setting her on the ground. "Give me a second to go see what I have left."

Max looked at Remi and her smile was unreal, it nearly killed him.

"I'm proud of you." She beamed with pride, her eyes a little drunk and wild.

"For trick-or-treating?"

"Yeah, that. But also, for telling me what you told me earlier. Even if you didn't tell me what's going on in-depth, I'm happy you found me safe enough to share."

Max's smile faltered but Remi's confidence in him did not, and the comfort that seemed to radiate from her brought him back to the moment. "Thank you for being safe. Now I need to work up the courage to actually talk to a doctor."

The man reappeared, the small dog back in his arms. "I'm clean out of Halloween candy, but I like to keep these dinner mints on the kitchen table. I hope that works," he said, opening the door to hand them both three red and white spiraled dinner mints.

"It's perfect," Remi said cheerfully, peeling off the wrapper and popping one of the mints into her mouth immediately.

Max smiled and took his first-ever Halloween bounty. "Happy Halloween, sir."

The old man reached out and shook Max's hand. "Happy Halloween, son, and good luck tomorrow at the game. Go Condors," he said with a knowing wink.

They made their way back to Remi's house with mint candy in their mouths, smiles on their faces, alcohol in their veins, and a sense of something new brewing between them.

Their hands brushed together, her shoulder bumping against his arm as they walked on drunken feet, swaying and laughing as the ocean crashed violently close by. Every bump of their bodies, every graze of his knuckles against hers, only made him want more. And just when Max thought he couldn't get close enough to Remi without making it too obvious, the sky opened up and the rain began to pour.

Remi pulled him close, lifting her lit-up jellyfish umbrella above them. Now face to face, her breath heavy with drunken laughter, and something else. Max couldn't be sure, but he thought it might be anticipation. Anticipation for what? He didn't know, and he wasn't a brave enough man to find out. No amount of liquor could summon the courage he needed to act on his feelings for this beautiful, wild, jellyfish of a girl.

She looked up at him under the colorful lights of the umbrella and he noticed one of the pink jewels above her eye was about to fall off. With gentle fingers, he plucked it from her face and before he realized what he was doing, he put it into his pocket for safekeeping.

"What do we do *meow*?" she said jokingly as they stood in place while the rain beat down around them.

"Two options," he said, loving the way the string lights she had attached to the umbrella lit up her already infectious smile, "we stand here until the rain stops, and only get wet from the waist down, or we run."

Remi gave him a dubious grin, and before he saw it coming, she pulled the umbrella away, shut it, and took off in a sprint towards her house.

Chapter Twelve

Remi woke November first to a raging migraine, a desperation for water, and an ache in her stomach that could only be cured with a McDonald's breakfast sandwich. The only thing missing was Max. She didn't know when he got up to leave, but her clock showed that not only had she slept through the alarm she set last night as they sat on her carpet, drinking, and laughing, but she had also slept through the entire McDonald's breakfast window; it would be cheeseburgers or nothing to cure this hangover.

The blankets Max used on the couch were neatly folded up with a handwritten note on top.

Remi,

Thank you for the fun night, and for letting me crash on your couch.

-Max

She couldn't help but smile at his precise handwriting. Each letter was so perfectly written in all caps.

Max-fucking-Miller.

She smiled again to herself. She had spent the night with a professional athlete and yet he had somehow managed to be the most down-to-earth, if not a little odd, guy she had met. It was refreshing, and if she was being honest, it was hopeful.

After their mad dash to her house in the rain, Max switched out his wet black tee for the jersey he had in his car while wrapping his lower half in a blanket with a huge image of the Virgin Mary on it as his wet clothes went through a cycle in her small dryer.

Before she knew it, they had finished an old bottle of vodka she had in the freezer, and they were both too drunk to do anything but laugh and make cat jokes, as Max continued to wear the ears even as he settled in on her couch to sleep.

"Tonight was cat-tastic," he said.

"It was purr-fect," she agreed.

"Thanks for inviting me to the paw-ty," he said.

"Are you kitten me? I loved having you there."

"I think I might need to take a cat nap now." He yawned, pulling out his phone to set an alarm.

"I'll get you some blankets right meow," she said, with her final cat pun of the night.

She read his note again.

"Don't do it, girl," she said to herself. "Don't you dare fall for this man."

But Remi knew it was too late. She knew the second she saw him half naked on his couch that day that Max had instantly become an itch that she had to scratch. After last night, seeing him come alive, watching him smile, hearing him talk without overthinking his every word, she wanted more.

Pulling out her phone she typed up a text. She didn't know when he would be able to check his messages with it being a game day, but she wanted him to know she was thinking about him. What better time was there than the day after Halloween to throw all caution to the wind and allow herself to fall?

***

Max finished his pregame warmup and headed to the locker room to change. The lingering reminder of confessing his fears about his health to Remi last night sat in the pit of his stomach. It made it more real, having spoken it out loud, confessing it, owning it; something was wrong with him, and he needed to see a doctor.

He pulled out his phone to check the time, only to find a text from Remi.

His heart raced, and if he was nauseous before with last night's pink vodka threatening to make him lose his protein shake, he was even more so now at the sight of her name on his phone.

He stared at what she had texted him, so honest, so sweet—she always knew what to say. He tried to summon the courage from last night's version of Max. The version of him that was carefree, funny, and intoxicated. He wanted to be that version of himself around her sober, and he knew if anyone could help him accomplish that, it *was* Remi.

Max:

I would like to see you again.

I kept the cat ears. They're mine now.

She responded promptly.

Remi:

A memento from your first time trick-or-treating.

Max:

Thanks for that, by the way. I missed a lot of normal childhood experiences growing up in billet homes.

Remi:

BRB, going to google what a billet home is.

Max:

I have to go meow. Time to get ready for the game.

He smiled in approval at his cat-related text and hoped that Remi would get the reference to last night.

Her response did not disappoint.

Okay, let's "paws" this conversation. Text me later. Good luck tonight, Max Miller.

After the game, Max slowly made his way home, ten miles per hour under the speed limit the whole way. Driving at night had become harder over the last month, his ability to focus in the dark a serious struggle on the extensive list of vision-related issues.

The Condors had won. And of course they had won, Brown was in the net. Max forced down the mixed feelings that were creeping in. His gut told him to be angry; angry that he was watching his career come to an end from the bench, while his heart told him to do something about it, talk to someone, see the doctor... but that made it too real. Real was hard, denial was easy.

He made his way to the couch, and despite needing to pack for the upcoming road trip, he wanted to talk to Remi. He had been looking forward to it all day. The memory of last night with her was the only thing that kept him from breaking down completely as he watched Jack Brown make save after save with no signs of slowing down in front of *his* Condors net.

Just got home. We won.

He waited for her to respond, crossing his fingers, allowing superstition to creep in. When she finally did, he felt the weight of hockey shift, as well as the weight of his health, his career, and his future.

Why was everything always so heavy?

Remi:

I saw.

I was bummed you weren't in the net. I love watching you play.

Max:

It was for the best.

Remi:

Did you talk to your coach about seeing a doctor?

Max:

Pass.

Remi:

You're almost out of passes, Max Miller.

Max:

What happens when I run out?

Remi:

You have to actually start letting me into your world.

Max didn't want her to have to clean up his messy life, but he also knew there was no way he could keep her from seeing it. He had somehow convinced her to come into his space. After a half-naked introduction, a broken lamp, an impromptu beach picnic, and trick-or-treating, she *still* wanted more of him.

Another text came through.

He looked at his watch, it was 10:45 p.m. His flight left for the East Coast at 7 a.m. tomorrow, *and* he wasn't packed. Not to mention he might still be slightly hungover from last night.

He hit send before he could convince himself otherwise.

Remi:

Excuse me? Did you just respond quickly with a yes? Who is this and what have you done with Max Miller?

Max:

Max Miller is a carefree cat now.

Remi:

Having nine lives looks good on you.

Max:

Let me unload my stuff and then I'll be on my way.

Chapter Thirteen

Remi waited for Max at the corner of 14th Street and Pacific Coast Highway. She stood outside her favorite pasta place; the lingering scent of the night's dinner rush still surrounded the small restaurant, and she realized she hadn't eaten anything since her hangover cheeseburger around noon.

Max pulled up to the curb and the locks clicked open for her to get in. Climbing into his Jeep, she instantly felt flushed at the sight of him. Max was still wearing most of his game-day suit, and something about him dressed like this made the depths of her stomach flutter. His white button-up shirt was tight around his biceps, and somewhere between the game ending and now, he had lost his tie. Where the top buttons of his dress shirt were undone, Remi found a dusting of red chest hair that she thought was extremely sexy. She buckled up and immediately crossed her legs, trying to dull the ache between them. It was this man and his goalie thighs, massive hands, chest hair, and his perfectly groomed facial hair and...

"Should I put the address in the GPS?" he asked, pulling her from her spiral.

She laughed. "Sorry, yeah, that might be the easiest option."

He pushed the screen on his dash. "You can just type it here."

She punched in *Donut Palace* and hit enter.

Max pulled off onto PCH, making an illegal U-turn to get them heading in the right direction.

"Seal Beach?" he asked.

"Yeah," she affirmed and watched as his posture stiffened. "Is that okay?"

"For a donut?"

She leaned over and gave his massive thigh a playful pat. "For the *best* donut."

She could feel the muscles in his leg tense under her touch, and for a second, she wondered if she had gotten this wrong. This thing between her and Max. Sure, he was shy, sure he was weird, and sure he was kind of awful at conversations, but she was almost positive she had felt something *more* happening between them on Halloween. Maybe it was the alcohol and wishful thinking, but the way he looked at her with his drunken smile that night felt like the prelude to an epic romance.

But this *was* Max Miller.

And he *was* an enigma.

She pulled her hand away hesitantly.

"Hi, by the way," she said, causing him to look over for just a split second to give her one of his soul-crushing shy boy smiles. "Thanks for coming with me *and* for driving."

"No problem. But I have to warn you, I drive slow at night," he mentioned.

She noticed his tense hands on the wheel and smiled over at him, only he didn't smile back. He kept his eyes intent on the road with a white-knuckle grip on the steering wheel.

Was he still nervous to be around her? Had they not gotten past that part? Or was he just an anxious driver?

"Thanks for coming with me after a long day, you must be exhausted," she said.

"I'm fine. All I did was sit on a bench. Besides, you did say they were the best donuts."

"Do you even like donuts?" she asked.

"I haven't had one in a long time," he admitted.

"Diet restrictions?"

He put his blinker on, and changed lanes very slowly, very cautiously, then he seemed to relax a bit. Resting his arm on the armrest between them felt like an invite to hold his hand, but she remembered the feeling of his leg tensing at her touch only moments ago, so she couldn't be sure, and she was usually pretty damn sure about things. His hands were huge, with light freckles scattered across the tops of them. She desperately wanted to touch them, to run her fingers over each little dot just to say she had, just to know that she could.

"I never think to get donuts," he said. "We weren't allowed food like that as kids, then growing up as an athlete I was always training, and that called for me to eat a restricted diet. So, I just don't think to indulge often, it's not part of my routine."

"Do you *ever* indulge?"

"Sure. I'm doing it right now," he said, and she didn't miss the smile on his face as he kept his eyes fixed on the road.

"So, you fly out to New York tomorrow?" she asked, despite already knowing the answer.

"Yes. East Coast road trip, then back home before the holiday break."

"Any chance you'll get the start?"

"No," he said with certainty. His answer was short and clipped.

It honestly felt like a hint for her to shut the fuck up about hockey, but she wasn't done yet, and he was all out of passes. It was time to push, just a little. It was time to challenge Max, and ease him out of his comfort zone.

"With you not getting the start, do you think it will encourage you to go see a doctor sooner? You can get the help you need for whatever it is that's going and get back to being in the starting lineup."

He slowly hit the brakes as they rolled to a stop at a red light. Looking over at her, his eyes were pleading with her to understand. "Remi, if I go see a team doctor, it might be the end of the season for me."

"Would that be so bad? You could take the time off, figure out what's wrong, and come back stronger than ever," she offered, wishing she knew more about the situation, hoping that he might open up and tell her the details, so she could better understand how to help him.

He shook his head and looked away, bringing both hands up to grip the steering wheel tightly. "If I go out on a medical leave, there's a good chance I'll never be relevant again," he said as the light turned green, "especially with the Condors having an amazing young backup goalie."

"So, what are you going to do about it?" she pried.

"Eat donuts, of course," he said, looking back over at her, and she knew it was a cop-out answer, but it was also so much more. The smile he gave her in that moment told her she wasn't crazy. Max felt something for her, and maybe it was just a friendship, but that smile hinted at it being something better, something she desperately wanted. It might be the start of him opening up and letting her in. And with Max, that felt like a rite of passage.

***

Pulling up, the donut shop looked like your typical run-of-the-mill place. There wasn't anything special about it. It was an older building; the windows were grimy with old grease and beach film. In fact, the only thing remarkable about the place was that Remi was standing in front of it. She managed to somehow make everything more beautiful. Each time he saw her he noticed something new he liked about her. Like the way she had perfect ears, or the way her long fingers looked so elegant compared to his rough hands, or the way she always scrunched up her nose when she stopped laughing. But aside from the physical things, it was also the way she made him feel truly *seen* by someone and *liked* by someone enough for them to stay—for *him* to stay.

"What should I order?" he asked as they stepped up to the counter to be greeted by a tired-looking older woman who leaned forward and tapped the sign that read: *Cash only.*

Max began to panic; he didn't carry cash. Who even *used* cash anymore? He instinctually patted his pockets, the universal pantomime for, *oh shit, I don't have money on me.* He felt her soft hands on him, calming his frantic movements before she tangled her fingers in his, looking up at him with a calming, all-knowing smile.

He felt relieved.

He felt the panic roll away, like a wave that was there and then gone.

He felt her tiny thumb brush over the top of his.

She confidently began to order for both of them before moving her hand away to pull a folded twenty-dollar bill from her pocket to pay for the donuts.

This was new; being with someone who wanted to care for him, pay for him, comfort him. His head began to spin, overwhelmed with the idea of it all. His brain said *men take care of women*, but his heart said *who made up that stupid ideology to begin with anyway*, people should just care for one another no matter what.

He wanted to push her away and tell her no, stop, he was a mess, and she had enough messes in her life to clean up in her line of work. But he didn't. Instead, he took the box of donuts and followed Remi down to the beach, each step uncertain as the night's darkness engulfed him.

They sat in the sand, side by side, closer than he intended. As if there were a gravitational pull between them, they ended up hip to hip, leg to leg, shoulder to shoulder. Max shuddered, his body unfamiliar with this kind of physical connection, it had been so long for him.

"So, I have an idea," Remi said while kicking off her battered checkered Vans. He noticed this time her toenails were painted neon green before she dug them into the sand.

"Okay. What's your plan?" he asked.

"I got a half dozen. All different donuts. I say we take one bite of each, and then we have to guess which one was each other's favorite. And if we get it right, the other person has to run into the water."

"How will you know I'm not lying about my favorite to save myself from the plunge?" he asked, a skeptic if nothing else.

"Because I trust you," she said simply.

"And how will I know *you're* not lying to me?"

"Because I think you trust me too," she said, opening the pink donut box. She reached in and pulled out the powdered jelly-filled donut. Taking the first bite, she covered her mouth to laugh as a drop of jelly covered the corner of her lips.

He took the donut from her and took a massive bite. Raspberry jelly oozed out from the other end and he pulled his legs apart just in time for it to miss his suit pants. Instinctively, he buried the jam in the sand. He wished he could move as quickly and be as alert with the puck as he had been with the guts of the raspberry donut.

"Next up, a classic: glazed twist," Remi said, taking a bite before she handed it to him. He watched as she happily chewed, doing a little celebratory dance, and he wondered if she might have just given herself away. He would hang on to the memory of her little dance, and the way her lips curled up in a smile when it came time to guess her favorite donut.

"You pick the next one," she said, pushing the box at him.

"I feel like this is a trick."

"What kind of person do you think I am?" she asked with a dubious grin on her face.

"I think you probably don't want to end up in that water just as much as I don't. So, you might have me pick the next donut to get some kind of idea of what my favorite might be."

This made Remi laugh, her head falling back, the moonlight hitting her collarbone and causing the tiny sun charm that hung from the golden necklace she always wore to shine. He wanted to lean in and kiss it. Not her skin, not her neck, but the charm. He wanted to press his lips against the golden sun just to see if the warmth of her body heated it enough to burn his lips, because Remi was fire, yet everything about her cooled him to his core.

"Okay, calm down, Sherlock," she said, bumping her shoulder against his, "I just wanted you to get the first bite."

Max looked at the box. One had coconut, and he hated coconut. He grabbed it and took the first bite. Because Sherlock or not, he was going to try like hell to avoid getting into that water. He smiled a bit, chewing up what felt like dehydrated suntan lotion strips, pretending to like it.

"Ah, a bold move," she said, taking her bite. "Not a fan favorite, but I like your enthusiasm."

He just shook his head, trying to hide his smile.

"Go again," she encouraged.

This time he took the real donut he was excited about, the maple bar. He loved syrup and any kind of food you could add syrup to. He even loved the movie Elf because of Buddy's childlike love for syrup. He took a bite and before he even finished chewing, Remi grabbed his hand and pulled him to his feet.

"Get in the water, Mr. Miller," she demanded.

"What?"

She pointed to the ocean firmly. "Go."

"But we still have two more to try."

Remi looked down at his feet and kicked a bit of sand at the nice dress loafers he was still wearing from the game. "It doesn't matter, because I know, right now, in this moment, that you loved that maple bar more than maybe anything you've ever eaten."

She wasn't wrong.

Was he that obvious?

They say gingers give everything away with how easily they blush, so could people also see when they fell in love too? Because he *absolutely* loved this donut.

He dropped his head. She had won. No chocolate round or crumb donut would compare. "And what about you? Was it the twisty glazed one?" he asked.

"How'd you know?"

"The happy dance gave you away."

"It always does." She grinned, and before he was ready, Remi lifted the loose-fitting tank top over her head and pushed her jean shorts from her hips.

She wasn't wearing much less than her jellyfish costume, but the very idea of this being her underwear—her bra and panties—caused his body to betray him, as he felt all the blood in his head rush instantly to his lower regions.

Cold water he thought.

Cold water would put a stop to that. He removed his shirt, kicked off his loafers, and before he had a chance to remove his pants Remi bolted to the water. This left him an ounce of privacy as he pulled his slacks down and bound for the ocean wearing only what he wore the day he met her—black briefs.

Remi screamed as she dove into the waves, and he knew that was the scream of someone taking a cold plunge. The beaches were never that warm in California, not like Florida beaches. She watched him run towards the water, and then before he could talk himself out of it, Remi yelled, "Do it!" and he crashed into the next wave.

Coming up for air, he was greeted by the sight of her bobbing in the water next to him, her hair slicked down to her face and her smile one of regret. She still managed to look beautiful like this, wet, cold, and filled with bad choices in the name of donuts.

"This was an awful idea." She laughed.

"Your worst idea yet," he agreed, through chattering teeth. The vast ocean in the dark was nothing more than a blank space to him.

"It's kind of scary, huh?" she asked, looking out at the blackness that surrounded them as waves rolled into pillows of white foam closer to the shore.

"The ocean? It's terrifying," Max admitted.

"And yet here we are."

"Pretty stupid of us."

Remi swam closer, and Max thought this was it. She was going to kiss him.

"A bet is a bet," she said, her face close enough that he could make out droplets of water clinging to her long dark eyelashes.

"A bet *is* a bet," he agreed, his voice sounding heavier than usual.

"And besides," she said, her face a little more serious than it had been just a second earlier, "it's good to do things that scare us."

Remi was right. Maybe this was her trying to convince him to tell his team about his health issues, and maybe it was her hinting at him to see the doctor, but maybe it was her letting him know that it was okay to kiss her, because that was scary too.

He was going to do it.

He was going to do one more scary thing tonight.

When he closed his eyes, before he had time to process what was happening, Remi flung her body onto his, dunking him underwater playfully. He let her weight overpower his strength—strength that he could've very easily used to toss her like a wet puppy. But he didn't. He went along with her game, dunking her back and allowing her to wrap her arms around him from behind to dunk him again.

It wasn't a kiss.

It wasn't even close.

But in the moment, it might have been better.

They got back to Remi's house after another slow drive down PCH, sticky with salt water and wrapped up in two blankets Max had in an emergency kit in the back of his Jeep.

"Why are we always wet by the time we get back to my house?" she asked.

"I don't know, but at this rate, I might need to keep an extra set of clothes here," Max said, instantly going red.

Remi smiled as if she liked the idea of that. He wondered if nights like this could eventually lead to his things showing up in her laundry. His favorite drinks in her fridge. His personal toothbrush on her sink counter. The scent of him on her sheets... the scent of *her* on his skin.

"I'm sorry we got your car wet," she said, drying her hair with a towel she grabbed from the laundry room.

"It's fine. It's just a car."

Just a car? This made Remi roll her eyes sarcastically, causing Max to blush an even deeper shade of pink. He didn't do it often, but sometimes it was easy to forget not everyone had the same privileges in life he did being an NHL goalie.

"I have to go. I have an early morning, and I haven't even packed."

"Yeah, of course," she said, reluctance lining her every word.

"I could text you," he offered shyly, "while I'm on the road."

Remi beamed, and Max took that as a yes.

"Good luck on your road trip," she said, her words gentle and inviting, and he thought she might *really* kiss him this time. He thought of kissing her, yet again. He thought of how the last time he considered this he ended up with salt water up his nose.

Before he could work up the courage, Remi added, "Do scary things, Max... on your road trip." And there it was. *Do scary things*, like talk to your team, talk to your coach, talk to your doctor.

He had gotten it wrong. This wasn't an invitation to a kiss; it was a pep talk for a career-changing conversation.

Disappointment and resentment flooded through his body at the realization.

"I'll try," he said.

Chapter Fourteen

The east coast road trip was going how Max wanted it to go, as far as his team winning. *How* they were winning, not so much. Brown had gotten the start in all three games on the East Coast, after Max fumbled his way through practice, putting the Condors back in the rankings. His career's future looked bleak from the bench, and the way the boys were talking to him was torture. It reminded Max of how people spoke to a dying person.

He wasn't dying for fuck's sake; he just needed an eye exam and maybe some glasses or at least that's what he told himself to get through the day with the fear of it being something bigger sitting in the pit of his stomach.

They would fly out tomorrow for two games in Florida, then back to the West Coast for games against Arizona and L.A., before heading home for a game in Anaheim.

The whole time he was gone he hadn't texted Remi like he said he would. He couldn't. He felt defeated and was too scared to talk to her because he was reckless when he talked to her—open and honest. Saying it out loud would make it all too real, and he didn't want her to know that his night vision had been elevated to code red. Every time the lights went from dark to light, he was met with intense strobe-like flashing. This was bigger than he let on, and he didn't want Remi to know what he thought was happening to him. He didn't want to tell her because he was still trying to lie to himself. Hide it from himself. Denial was his only companion.

When he got back to his room after dinner, he was surprised to find his coach and Patrick Carter, his captain, sitting on one of the beds in the room. Normally Max roomed with a rookie, Nate Kinder, the other token weirdo of the team, but from the looks of it, Coach was shaking things up tonight.

"Hey?" Max said hesitantly, putting his things on the dresser.

"Have a seat, son," Coach said.

Max took a seat on the bed across from them.

"Max, what I'm about to tell you didn't come easy. It's something I've been considering with staff, and after talking with Carter, I think it's in everyone's best interest if we put you on leave for the rest of this trip and bring Brody up from the minors. We have to keep what's best for the team at heart here, and right now, Brown is on a winning streak, and Brody has been standing on his head in San Diego with the Waves. It doesn't make sense to keep you on the bench when we have a goalie in the minors who is better equipped to step in and give Brown a break. We all wanted to see you in front of the net in Florida tomorrow, but after your morning skate, we think you need to take some time off to reset. When we get back to Anaheim you can skate with the team and we can go from there."

Max saw this coming. To be honest, he thought they would have put him on leave sooner.

He stayed silent.

The words on the tip of his tongue stayed put. He heard Remi's voice in the back of his head, *do scary things.*

"You good man?" asked Carter.

"Yeah. I saw this coming."

"Do you have any idea why your game is off? Is there something we can help you with? Are you injured, or maybe it's something different, something you need to talk about?"

"I..." Max faltered. "I just have a lot to think about," he said.

"Max, if you get yourself healthy, you're in. If I see you out on the ice performing at Max Miller level, you're in, no questions asked. But I need you to figure out whatever it is you've got going on before I can do that. I've arranged an appointment with the team's physician when you get back to Anaheim tomorrow. I want you to go and talk with her. Tell her what's going on, and maybe we can get to the bottom of this."

"Do I have to?" Max asked, and he watched as his coach's face fell with disappointment.

"No, son, I can't make you. But when I say I want to see you trying, I mean on and off the ice. So, take that how you will. Carter is rooming with you tonight. Get some rest, and I'll see you back in Anaheim next week."

Max didn't watch as Coach left, he just sat there, paralyzed with anxiety. The dizziness crept in, the floor becoming Jello under his feet.

"You know," Carter said, "Coach means well. We're all worried about you. The whole team is worried, Max."

"I know."

"We want you back on the ice with us. We love Brown, don't get me wrong, but he's not you, he's not Max Miller. It doesn't feel right winning without you."

"I don't know what you want me to say," Max said, because words were hard, and right now, they felt impossible.

"Say you'll get help. Say you'll talk to someone and find out why one of the best goalies in the NHL suddenly can't skate to the net in a straight line, let alone save a puck most days."

"It's complicated," Max mumbled.

Carter leaned forward on his knees, getting closer to Max, begging him to look up, make eye contact, and be *real* with him. "What is? Losing? Not playing well? Talking? You give us nothing Max. You don't talk to us. We're your family, we want to know if you're okay, but no one knows how to ask."

"I know I don't make it easy on you," Max admitted.

"That's for damn sure."

"It's just hard for me."

"What is, Max? What's hard for you? You can tell me anything. I know it's scary sometimes, but we gotta do scary things."

Max's head sprung up at Carter's last words, the image of Remi telling him the same thing the last time he saw her playing over in his mind. Was this some kind of joke? Had she somehow contacted Carter? Was this a fucking intervention? "What the fuck did you just say?" Max asked more aggressively than Carter had ever seen from the gentle giant.

"I said I know it's scary to talk about stuff sometimes, especially as a professional athlete. I know we're expected to be tough all the time..."

"No. *What* did you say? Word for word, what did you say?"

"I don't know, I was just talking from my heart."

"You said, we have to do scary things," Max repeated.

"Yeah, absolutely we do. And I want you to know I'm here for you, no matter what you say, I'm here."

Max stood up, the lighting in the room making it hard for him to make out the contrast of the space around him. He took two steps towards the dresser to grab his water bottle and tripped over something he hadn't seen at his feet. Falling into the entertainment stand, Carter hurried over to grab the TV before it came crashing to the ground.

"Max," Carter asked, placing a hand on his back to steady him, "you okay, man?"

He just stood there, his body trembling from the fall.

"Just... stood up fast... just need a second and I'll be fine," he managed.

"Here," Carter said, handing him his bottle of water. "Drink."

Max took the water bottle from his captain just to do something, to deflect the attention from his stumbling.

"I'm fine," he lied.

"I don't think you are, man."

"Just stressed," he said. This was not a lie, but it was also not the full truth.

"Come on, let's get you sitting down."

Max, despite not wanting to show any more weakness in front of this man, accepted his help.

"I know something's not right," Carter said, his voice shaking with an underlying hint of anger. "I know you've got something going on that you're not telling us. Hell, you might not even be admitting it to yourself, but I know what I see, and I know that whatever it was that happened when you stood up just now is not normal. And for the sake of your career, the team, and honestly, for the peace of mind of all of us who love you, I hope you take this time off seriously and get the fucking help you need you stubborn asshole."

The last part made Max chuckle. He sat back down on the bed and allowed himself to laugh through the shit show he found himself in. What was he waiting for? Why hadn't he gotten help yet? What was he so afraid of? Whatever the results came back as, it couldn't be worse than this. It couldn't be worse than being sent home while some rookie came up from the minors to take his spot in front of the net.

That was *his* net, and he wanted it back.

Chapter Fifteen

R emi had just finished cleaning the Henderson house when she got the first text from Max since he left on his trip. She had been lying to herself for almost a week now, saying she wasn't hurt that he hadn't reached out yet like he said he would. But now, seeing his name on her phone affirmed that yes, she absolutely had been upset with him.

She told herself every day since the night at the beach that it wasn't fair to be mad, that he didn't owe her anything. She didn't want him to text her because he owed her his time, she wanted him to text her because he valued hers.

Catching feelings wasn't part of the plan; she didn't mix business with pleasure. But she fell, like a fucking idiot, and she didn't know what that looked like for her because Max was good at a lot of things, but showing emotions was not one of them.

After placing her cleaning supplies into her trunk, and before she left for her next house of the day, she opened the text.

Max:

I'm sorry. I know I said I would reach out to you sooner, but I wasn't in a good headspace.

Of course he was struggling, he was an NHL superstar goalie, warming the bench. Guilt flooded Remi for any ounce of anger she had towards him over his radio silence. She had watched the games, had seen him on the bench, his eyes hollow, vacant, and *sad*. She typed up her response.

Remi:

I understand.

He texted back immediately.

Max:

Thank you. I don't deserve you.

She had two options: give him some space or take up some space. Typing her response, she led with her heart, in typical Remi fashion.

Remi:

Honestly… I miss you. I don't know if I'm allowed to say that. I don't know if that's helpful for you right now, but I want you to know someone hundreds of miles away is missing your company, your face, and your terrible conversation skills.

When he didn't respond immediately, she wondered if she had said too much, pushing the narrative too soon. The puck was in his glove now, the next save was on him. She admitted her feelings, and now, Max had to find the words he so often struggled with to share his. If he couldn't, Remi knew she had to nip these feelings in the bud. She would clean and fix and organize a house for someone, but she knew from growing up with her mom that emotions were a different kind of mess, and Max had to sort out his feelings for her all on his own before she would allow herself to get tangled any further.

Putting her phone on silent, she got to work on her last house of the day. Max would be in Florida by now, most likely preparing to take a seat on the bench and watch as Jack Brown did *his* job in front of *his* net. Her heart ached for him. She couldn't fix him, but maybe, if he let her, she could at least prove to him he was worthy of being cared for.

*****

When Max finally got back to his house, he unloaded his bag and made his way down to the beach. The heaviness of the failed road trip with the Condors sat on his chest like a weighted blanket. Taking off his shoes, he dug his feet into the sand, the natural elements seemingly grounding him, clearing his brain long enough to process what the next week looked like for him. It would be the first time since he was a young boy that he didn't have hockey to fill his every waking moment.

The sound of the ocean calmed his racing heart, and he thought about the last time he saw Remi. Hesitantly, he pulled out his phone and stared at Remi's last text that he had left on read; guilt shot through him. He had two options: He could tell her he needed space while he got his shit together, or he could ask her to take up space while he got his shit together.

Either way, he knew this week was not going to be easy.

His fingers traced over the text. He finally had someone who wanted him around and saw his flaws as endearing. Someone who challenged his comfort zone and was not afraid of his hangups. She liked him, and she didn't leave him guessing. The uncertainty he felt at the beach had been cleared up with one text from Remi, revealing so much about her character, her boldness, her relationship with her own emotions, and how aware of them she was. He both envied and admired that in her. He should have kissed her. Maybe he wasn't good at using his mouth to speak how he felt, but he was certain if he could press his lips against hers, he could use his mouth to *show* her how he felt.

Max:

> I'm sorry I didn't respond sooner.

To his surprise, she didn't leave him on read, like he felt he deserved.

Remi:

> Why does it always feel like you're apologizing to me lately?

Max:

> Because I never get it right with you the first time.

Remi:

Well, I guess I should thank you then.

Max:

For what?

Remi:

For giving yourself a chance to get it right the second time.

And he would get it right eventually. Maybe he would have to apologize to her a million more times before that happened, but for Remi, he wanted to stick around long enough to not only figure out how to get it right the first time, but how to do it without trying.

Max:

I miss you too. I'm sorry I didn't say it sooner.

He took a deep breath and waited for her to show him this was okay—that he was allowed to say these things back this time, and that he was allowed to care for her and want her.

Remi:

There you go apologizing again.

Max:

Can I make it up to you?

Remi:

You don't have to make anything up to me. You're doing just fine, Max Miller.

Max:

Just say yes.

Remi:

To what?

Max:

To everything.

Remi:

I do love a good adventure.

Max:

Well, I don't come with a road map, and I can't say I'll be easy to navigate, but it could be interesting if nothing else.

Remi:

Then, I guess I say yes.

Max:

Yes, to what?

Remi:

Everything, of course.

She said yes. And to be fair, he wasn't even sure what he was asking of her in that simple word, but she agreed to it, and now, he had to try to say yes back. He had to bury the past, face the future, and own up to the present.

Max:

Now that that's settled, I guess it would be a good time to tell you I'm home.

Remi:

What do you mean you're home?

Max:

Why don't you come over and find out.

Chapter Sixteen

Max rushed to let Remi in. As he pulled open the door, he realized it was the first time he had let her into his home as a guest. He wondered if it was weird for her to have knocked on his door as a friend after months of punching in her code as a cleaner.

When he opened the door, he found Remi standing there, a single-dimple smile present, but not lacking a hint of pity for him, and for the first time in his life he didn't want to think about hockey. In fact, he wouldn't mind Remi acting as a distraction from it for a while.

"Thanks for coming over," he said, stepping to the side to let her in.

She reached down and removed her signature checkered Vans, and Max couldn't help but watch in anticipation to see what color her toenails were this time.

"Pink," he said under his breath and then looked up to find her smiling at him.

"Pink?" she asked.

"Oh, it's just, they're a different color every time I see you," Max said, hinting at her feet.

"Oh," she said, looking down, wiggling her toes. "Yeah, it relaxes me," she admitted.

"Painting them different colors?"

"Well, just painting them in general. But I hardly ever do the same color twice in a row. I like to keep things interesting."

It was working, because Max found everything about her to be interesting, nail polish included.

Remi made her way into his living room with ease and familiarity.

"I see you're a big lights kinda guy," she said, hinting at every light in the house being on. "I guess hockey players don't sweat the electric bill," she teased.

"They're on dimmers if it's too bright," he offered, and Remi didn't miss a beat. She lowered the lights in the living room and without fail, his vision strained against the sudden loss of light.

Making her way to the couch, she stood there a little awkwardly, waiting for him to join her; only he needed a minute. Just a minute and things would refocus, and he could make his way next to her without stumbling over his own feet.

"Do you want something to drink?" he offered, trying to make it less noticeable that he wasn't moving from where he was standing.

"I'm good," she said, and to his relief, his eyes adjusted, not fully, but enough to get him from point A to point B without tripping.

Remi sat down on the massive couch, her tiny body engulfed by its depth, and Max realized they would both fit, lying side by side, if they happened to fall asleep together one day.

He sat next to her, nervously wiping his sweaty palms on his sweat-pants.

"So, do you want to tell me why you're home early from the road trip or are we going to ignore that part?"

"Am I out of passes?" he asked.

Remi turned her body to face him, tucking her bare legs under her.

"I'll give you a pass tonight," she said empathetically.

"Are you sure?"

She reached out and steadied his leg that was bouncing anxiously.

"I'm sure, but you have to promise me that tomorrow you'll tell me what's going on. I don't want to pry, but I *do* want to be someone you can talk to. I want to be that person for you because you need me, but I also want to be that person for you, because *I* need you."

"Why? Why trouble yourself with my bullshit?"

"Because if I don't know what you're going through, I won't know how to care for you."

"What if I don't want you to treat me like there's something wrong with me? I couldn't handle your pity."

"I don't pity you, Max, I care about you. Those are two totally different things."

"For tonight, can we just pretend that me being home has nothing to do with hockey? Can we pretend it's just a random night, and I'm fine, and you're here because you want to be here..." He paused and then added, "And can we pretend that I'm a brave enough man to kiss you?"

"Why would we have to pretend any of those things when all of them are really happening right now."

"Except the part about me kissing you."

"Maybe we just haven't gotten to that part yet."

"I'm working on it," he said with a playful smile.

Remi laughed. "I can wait. I'm patient if nothing else," she said, taking his hand in hers as she pulled him to his feet. "I have an idea."

"Donuts?" he asked.

"No, better."

"Cat ears?" he teased.

She tugged on his hand. "A tour."

"A tour?"

"Yeah, show me your house, Max."

"But you've seen it, you've cleaned it a million times."

"Yeah, but I want to see it through your eyes."

"I don't even know if *I've* seen it through my eyes. So far, it's just been a crash pad."

Remi pulled him along, nearly causing him to trip over a throw pillow he hadn't noticed on the ground. "Then let's see it together. We can pretend we're looking into buying it."

"Like..." He paused. "Like role play?"

"Exactly." Remi paused to think, then went on, "I'm Marsha Bumbly, I run a butterfly conservatory. Incredibly famous for my advocacy for the monarchs."

Max wasn't good at normal conversation, and now he was being asked to look at imaginary houses for sale with none other than Marsha Bumbly, butterfly conservationist extraordinaire—it was all too much.

"Who will you be?" she asked excitedly.

"You tell me," he said.

"Oh no, you have to come up with your own character."

Max smiled at her excitement over this new, silly game they were about to play. But really, when he considered it, it was the perfect opportunity to be someone other than himself for a while, so why not choose someone bold, brave, and outgoing? The kind of man that would not only tour this home with Remi, or should he say Marsha, but the kind of man that would do it with her hand in his, and his body finding any way he could to press against hers.

"Walter," Max finally said.

"Walter who?" she prompted him.

"Walter *Shmalter*?" he asked, laughing at his own absurdity.

Remi quirked her eyebrows and then began to laugh too. "Shmalter? Really?" she asked.

"I'm not good at this," he defended.

"No, no, it's fine. Okay, so Walter..." She chuckled then added, "Shmalter. What do you do for a living?"

"I don't know, maybe a car salesman?"

She broke character. "Of all the jobs in the world and you choose a car salesman? Not happening. Pick something ridiculous."

A goalie? he thought.

That seemed ridiculous in his current state.

"Okay, I'm Walter..."

She cut him off and giggled. "Shmalter."

"Shush, you," he said, shaking his head at her, "I'm Walter, and I'm a professional party clown."

The smile he wore for her was effortless. Remi made the muscles in his face work on autopilot, it didn't feel forced when he was with her, it felt the way smiling should feel. It felt like home.

"So, are we married and shopping for a vacation spot, or maybe engaged, looking for our forever home?" Remi asked.

The plot thickens, Max thought.

"Maybe we're dating, and we just really like to tour homes for a unique date experience?" Max offered, surprising even himself.

Remi pressed up on her tiptoes and brought her finger to his nose to boop it three times. "Ding-ding-ding! That's it. We are Marsha and Walter, and this is our favorite kind of date night."

Mine too, Max thought, because this felt like a date, an unconventional one, but a date, nonetheless.

"Shall we?" Remi asked, offering him her arm.

"We shall," he agreed, taking her arm and letting her lead him to the front door.

Remi looked up at him, and her smile was wild and silly, clearing her throat as she spoke with a posh accent. "Well, Walter," she said and giggled, breaking character for a split second, "I'm sorry, I still can't believe you went with Shmalter."

Max started laughing too, then cleared his throat and decided to take the lead. "Funny you should laugh at my last name, Martha, darling, considering Shmalter will be your last name soon since we're engaged to be married."

Remi pulled herself back into character, popped out her chest, and said, "And what makes you think I'll take your last name, Walter, darling?"

Max fought back a laugh. "How silly of me to assume."

"Silly indeed… but would you look at this entryway, darling. It's so…" She paused.

Blah?

Boring?

Lifeless?

Sterile?

"Stunning," she finally said. Max would have called it a million different things, but she was right, this entryway was rather stunning with her standing there. Because Remi made any room she stood in come to life.

"Indeed," he agreed, as she led him to the kitchen.

"This could use a pop of color, what do you think?" she asked, and Max wasn't sure if she was still speaking as her character Marsha, or as Remi, but yes, he absolutely thought the kitchen could use a pop of color. He had just never found the time to actually add any.

"Maybe a plant?" he offered, thinking of all the potted plants on her small front porch.

"Oh, yes, a plant would be lovely. Greenery always brings a house to life, Walter."

"I couldn't agree more, Marsha."

Remi looked up at him, and Max watched as Marsha's smug demeanor washed away, only to be replaced with Remi's soft smile. The blush of her cheeks returned, and then, with her voice a bit lower, a bit less campy, she asked, "Should we check out the bedroom..." She cleared her throat and added, "Walter, I know you'd love to see the master."

Max felt his face burn hot and damned his red hair and pale skin for giving him away every time because something about the mention of his bedroom with Remi made his entire body heat.

"Not as much as you'd love to see the walk-in closet," he added, no sign of Walter in his tone.

Somewhere in the last few words they'd exchanged, they had both ditched their characters, aside from the silly names, and they were speaking entirely on their own behalf. They were both saying the things they wanted to say under the guise of characters, in the name of roleplay.

"The bedroom is this way," she said, and of course she had seen his room before, only this time was not like the rest. This time she was here because he invited her, and because she wanted to be. There would be no paycheck at the end, no clocking in or out, no entry codes that were specifically created for the housekeeper.

Max's arm dropped, and her hand slid from his forearm down to his hand where she intertwined their fingers and tugged him towards his room.

"It's a bit disappointing," Max offered as they walked into the massive space.

"It just needs some personal touches," Remi said.

"I'm not good at that sort of thing," he said.

Remi turned to face him, stepping into his space, her fingers still gripping his tightly. "You keep saying that."

"I'm sorry," Max offered.

She smiled. "*And* that."

Rubbing his thumbs over her knuckles, he wanted to be brave, and for this to be the part where he kissed her. The part she said she was patient enough to wait for.

Each day as he woke up and tried to blink away the uncertainty of his career crumbling beneath him, he was learning that he had been waiting his whole life to see things clearly. And now, while his vision grew tired and unreliable, he realized Remi was the clearest thing he had ever seen in his life. He wanted to spend forever memorizing every fleck of the ocean in her blue eyes, every sun-induced freckle that spattered across the fine lines of her collar bones, and each beach day sunburn on her sand-covered toes.

He was done waiting.

Because time was always running out, and the clock slowed for no one.

The time was now, Remi was here, and he was somehow still breathing despite how close their bodies had become, pressed against each other.

"Indulge me, Walter," she said, her voice low, "show me the closet."

"If that's what you want, darling," he said, his tone matching hers. "I do love a good walk-in closet."

Max took the lead for the first time tonight, tugging Remi towards his pristine, organized closet. It wasn't exactly where he thought they would end up, considering he had a bed, but if she wanted to see the closet, he would show her the fucking closet, be it Remi, Marsha, or any other alter ego, roleplay character she chose to be. Hell, he would show her anything she wanted. He wanted her, and he had known it since that day on the couch, with the punk music, his black boxer briefs, and the lamp crashing to the ground.

He wanted her.

He wanted to take his time with her.

He wanted to rush every second.

He wanted the world to stop spinning just long enough that he could catch his footing.

They entered the closet and Remi looked around the space with an appraising eye.

"It's big enough to be listed as a bedroom," she teased.

"It's a good size," he agreed.

Remi pulled him all the way into the space. "Shut the door," she said in a whisper.

Max did not hesitate to do as told, pulling the door closed behind him. The closet he often found to be obnoxiously big suddenly felt so small with the two of them taking up the space there.

"We're in your closet," she said, taking a step towards him.

"It's definitely not something that was on my bucket list of things to do with you, but I like the way you surprise me, Remi. I've never been good at surprises."

"And yet you continue to surprise me too, Max Miller."

"How so?" he asked.

"Everything you say you're not good at, you end up being amazing at."

"Conversation?" he asked.

"Top tier." She smiled.

"Decorating a house?"

"Well, you mentioned getting a plant, which is a good start."

"And being brave?" he asked, pressing his body against her, leaving no space between them for uncertainty, no room left to guess what came next.

"I saw you wear cat ears; I think that's pretty brave."

Max brought his hand to the back of her neck and gently let his fingers push through the wild tangles of her blond hair. "And the kissing you part?" he asked softly.

"I was waiting to find out, but I'm almost certain you will excel there too."

Reaching for the light switch, he pulled down the dimmer, keeping his eyes intent on her face, trying like hell not to lose her in the lack of light.

"How's that?" he asked.

"Purrrrfect," she said in a low purr, a play on cat puns making a reprise.

"I'm going to kiss you meow," he warned, a faint boyish smile on his lips.

"Hurry," she said, closing her eyes. "I feel like I've been holding my breath for this moment since I met you."

And who was he? Who was Max to deny this woman the very air in her lungs?

He pressed his hand against her lower back, drawing her body up against his as he leaned down. His eyes closed tight as he let his lips finally meet hers.

It was a million glass bottles of freshly squeezed lemonade.

It was soft lips pressed against the sweet brim.

It was the lingering sugar coating his tongue with the faint reminder that hers must taste the same.

Max kissed her like he had a million things to say but didn't know how to articulate them.

He encouraged her mouth to open for him and with gentle strokes against hers, he showed her all the things that had been stuck at the very tip of his tongue in the way he kissed her.

He kissed her as though he was making up for a million words lost in translation.

She responded, her lips a perfect fit against his as his beard tickled the corners of her mouth. Deepening the kiss, she wrapped her arms around his neck, holding him close.

She wanted him in her space.

She wanted *him*.

In his closet.

In his house.

In all his awkward splendor.

He was glad she wanted to keep him close because Max wasn't sure how long he would be able to see the details of her face when she was far away.

Slowly, and with every trained muscle of his body, Max lowered Remi to the plush carpet of his closet, an unlikely place to share their first kisses, but what a story it would be. Max realized he had been craving this very thing. An uncommon kiss, a memorable date, a connection that lasted longer than three periods being counted down by a clock on a jumbotron, and Remi was all those things.

He let the darkness steal his vision as he counted on his other senses to enjoy this moment; the soft hum of her moans against his lips, the heat between their bodies, her fingers gripping his shoulders as she wrapped her legs around his hips allowing all their most intimate parts to align as he pressed against her fully clothed body.

He found optimism with his eyes closed so tight as he trailed his nose down along her neck and was able to make out the very shape of her body this way.

Because even in this moment of pure bliss, Max could not drown out the deafening reminder of what this pitch-black kiss held.

He allowed himself to breathe in the scent of her.

He allowed himself to listen to the sounds she made as he gently nipped at the lobe of her ear.

He allowed himself to taste the salt water that lingered on her skin.

He allowed himself to feel the way his body ached for more of her.

Max allowed himself to accept all of these things with his eyes closed tight, because he knew the day would come when he wouldn't have to close his eyes to avoid the lingering dimmed lights, because, for the first time in his life, Max admitted to himself that he was going blind.

Chapter Seventeen

Max had blue balls. That was a complete sentence, full stop. It wasn't for lack of releasing said balls after Remi had left last night, no, he had absolutely done that. But these were perma-blue. Wanting Remi and not having her after dry humping like teenagers on the carpet of his closet was like craving your favorite burger joint at 1 a.m. knowing damn well they closed at midnight. It was like needing water when all there was to drink was milk. She had given him a taste of the appetizer, and now he wanted the whole damn feast.

He pushed the thought of devouring her away, desperately not wanting to have to hide a boner from the doctor. He tried to focus on the bigger problem at hand—the fact that he was finally waiting to see a doctor, or an optometrist, if he was being exact.

He had woken up on the couch with an ache in both his groin and the pit of his stomach. One of those things was because he was obviously still horny, the other was because he had been sent home early from the road trip and he still didn't even know what was wrong with him.

While Max had every intention of finding out what was going on, he had decided he would only do it on his terms. He knew damn well if the team doctor found something wrong with him, he could end up benched for the remainder of the season, or worse. But after staying up way past his bedtime with a mild panic attack as he let the thought of hockey sneak back in, he decided to get help under the radar and go from there. He wanted his career to end on his terms, and he hoped like hell that it wouldn't happen anytime soon.

The optometrist knocked before entering the exam room, and Max's anxiety instantly skyrocketed.

"What are we seeing you for today, Max?" the doctor asked, obviously clueless as to who he was in the hockey world, and for that he was grateful. He needed this appointment to go undetected by the NHL.

"Eye exam," Max said.

The doctor typed something into the computer, then looked back over at Max. "The notes say you've seen some dramatic changes in your vision?"

"Yes," Max agreed.

"Well, let's get you looked at, and go from there."

"Okay."

The doctor pushed his wire-framed glasses up on his nose. "How old are you, Max?"

"Twenty-six, sir," Max said.

"It's not uncommon for a man of your age to start seeing a decline in his vision. Often times it's something that can easily be fixed with a prescription for some glasses or contacts." He pulled up the photos the tech had taken of his eyes earlier in the exam, then turned to face Max. "Have you ever been prescribed glasses?"

"No, sir."

"And it says here that your mother does not need or wear any corrective lenses."

"That is correct, sir."

"And you said no answer for your father, do you have any knowledge of his medical history pertaining to vision?"

"No, sir. My father was never in my life."

"And how was your vision growing up? Did you ever struggle to see the whiteboard at school? Or have you ever needed to pull a book closer when you read?"

"Night vision has been an issue for as long as I can remember. But other than that, I've never had any other issues with my vision until..." Max trailed off. Being diagnosed was one thing, but saying the symptoms out loud was something else. It was terrifying. Max felt like a dog with his tail between his legs.

"Until?" the doctor prompted.

"Until this summer, when I started to struggle adjusting to the change in lighting. It's like I can't refocus when it changes dramatically."

The doctor's face fell just a bit as he looked closer at the photos of Max's eyes, a newfound hint of worry lining his brow.

"I see. Any other challenges? Or is it just trouble adjusting?" the doctor asked.

"No, that's it," Max lied, and his leg began to bounce. The doctor took notice of this, and Max stilled.

"Well, there is only one way to find out what you've got going on here, son," the doctor said. "We'll start with testing your visual acuity." The doctor rolled over to the light switch and flicked it off. Max squinted at the sudden lack of light, trying to blink away the darkness that engulfed him as his eyes struggled to adjust.

"Ok, son. Go ahead and read me the first line."

Max took a second, then another second, and then one more, allowing time for his vision to adjust before he began to read.

As the exam went on, the doctor's demeanor changed, the easy inviting smile he introduced himself with grew weary, and then, Max watched as all notes for a positive evaluation faded. The doctor looked into his eyes after dilating them, letting out a discouraged sigh.

"Max, have you by chance looked into the symptoms you're experiencing at all?"

Of course he had. He had googled his symptoms. He had searched Web MD just like most idiots, realizing that the best-case scenario was that he needed glasses, and the worst-case scenario... cancer, because everything on WebMD had the possibility of being cancer. But it wasn't either of those things that scared him the most. The best or the worst he could live or die with. It was the in-between diagnosis that terrified him.

"I have," Max said.

"So, as you know, I am just an optometrist. I deal with your more common health and vision issues like myopia, hyperopia, astigmatism, eye infection, and inflammation, to name a few. But what I'm seeing when I use this guy," he said, holding up the ophthalmoscope, "is something I don't specialize in."

"What did you see?" Max asked.

"I'm seeing something we call pigment clumping, located in your retina, which is a characteristic of something called retinitis pigmentosa."

"And what does that mean?" Max asked.

"It can mean a number of things, Max, some of which could be more severe than others."

More severe than others.

He felt his entire body overheat.

Sweat gathered on his brow, and he felt all color fall from his face as panic flooded him.

He tried to swallow, but his throat was dry.

"So, before you panic," the doctor said, but it was too late, Max was already panicking. "I want you to make an appointment with an ophthalmologist. They have better tools and tests they can run to narrow down what's going on and get you more concrete answers."

"I thought you were an *optometrist*. Isn't that an eye doctor?" Max asked, suddenly feeling angry at the lack of help he felt he was getting. He didn't want another appointment, he wanted treatment, and to hear what he needed to do to be okay. To make the save. To get the start. To win the game.

"You're right, I am an *optometrist*, son. You need to see the guy above me I'm afraid. I can give you a referral to a good friend of mine if you'd—"

Max cut him off. "No, it's fine. I'll just..." Max stood to leave, but his head was fuzzy. He felt like he might pass out, or scream, or break something. Fuck, he felt like he might cry.

"Son," the doctor called out, causing Max to pause, "can I make a suggestion?"

No.

No suggestions.

Just answers.

He wanted answers.

"Yes," Max said.

"Talk to your mom. Try and find out if your dad has any history with his vision. You might get answers that way."

Max gave the doctor a nod and left without saying another word.

Chapter Eighteen

Max sat parked at the beach, his Jeep facing the ocean, the setting sun casting a mirror of orange and pink ripples across the water. He ran his finger over the screen of his phone, the name under his lightweight touch, a name he hadn't called in over a year. A name familiar to him, but one he never felt right calling out for, not even as a child, not as a teen, and certainly not now as an adult. But he needed answers, and she was the only one who might have them.

He hit call and waited nervously for the unfamiliar voice of his estranged mother to answer. If she didn't pick up, he wouldn't be surprised. If she *did* pick up, he wouldn't know how to address her, how to act, or how to ask what he needed to know.

"Hello? Max?" she said with hesitation after picking up on what he could only imagine was one of the last rings offered before the inevitable fake voicemail greeting she had recorded would play. In the background of it was the sound of her new family happily laughing and living a life that he didn't exist in.

"Hi," he said, because words often failed him, but with his mother, they felt like poison in his mouth, a bitter taste, a souring acid in the depths of his gut.

"We were just on our way to Justine's gymnastics competition. Can I call you back tomorrow?" she asked with ease, as if it hadn't been a year, a fucking year since they last spoke. A year since she last promised to call him back.

He felt his body shrink into himself like he often did as a young boy. Making himself small. Making himself unseeable, unknowable... non-existent in a world where he wasn't wanted.

"Mom," he said, the name on his lips felt foreign and forced.

"Max, what is it? Can we rush this along, I have to get to—"

He cut her off. "Justine's gymnastics competition, yeah I heard you the first time."

"Don't be rude, Max. Her competition might not be an NHL game, but that doesn't make her accomplishments any less worthy of my time and praise," she spat, her every word lined with disdain for her redheaded stranger of a son.

Max's heart raced in his chest. His need and want to fight back, to finally have the courage to call her out on her familiar bullshit, rose in his chest. He wanted to tell her his accomplishments had never been praised by her, her new husband, or his new siblings. His accomplishments had only served as a way to keep him far from her happy existence.

But he wasn't good with words, and with his mom, they were like a million daggers to the heart—but from behind.

"I just have one question and then you can go."

"Well?" she asked.

"My dad—"

She immediately cut him off. "Nope. Not going there, Max. And out of respect for the man who actually *did* raise you"—*sent you off to billet home after billet home*— "I suggest you drop it."

"I need to know if he had any…" He didn't know how to ask, didn't know how to speak. He felt like a helpless child at her mercy.

"If he had any what?" she asked, and he knew it had nothing to do with her wanting to help him. It had everything to do with her wanting the conversation to be over so she could go back to pretending he didn't exist.

"Did he have any medical issues," he finally got out.

"I don't know. He left, Max. He left me and *you*."

Taking a deep breath, he mustered all the courage a man terrified of his own mother needed to ask a question he knew would be met with resistance and hate.

"Mom, I need you to tell me who he is."

He heard her sigh on the other end, one he was not unfamiliar with. It was her signature sigh that said, *I don't have time for this, Max.*

"Mom. I *need* to know who he is," he pleaded.

"Your father is Nick," she said cruelly, offering up the name of his stepfather.

"Mom." He paused, his breathing erratic. "I need to *fu-cking* know who my *fu-cking* father is," he said, breaking up his words to add emphasis to his demands.

"Max Miller," she snapped.

"Mom," he pleaded, like he had his whole life, begging for her to give him anything without a fight since he was a young boy.

Mom, can I have a piece of candy?

Mom, can I go on the field trip?

Mom, can I come home for the summer?

Mom, can I have a hug?

"Max?" she held out.

"Please. I need to know if he's... sick," he said, not sure how else to try and get her to cave, to care, to let him have something he needed. It was a cry for her to just this once, show him she cared about him more than her pride, more than her ego.

"I can't do this right now, Max."

He felt anger rise up from the calm composure he often kept, and before he could settle the rage growing in his chest, he punched the steering wheel of his jeep, his knuckles busting on impact. "Tell me who my father is, or I'll drive to your house right now and rip every picture from the walls until you answer me. Just answer me. Just once in this lifetime, give me what I want, and not what you think I need. You have never protected me, you have only ever protected your new life without me, and if you think keeping him from me is helping me, it's the most delusional, selfish shit you have ever pulled as my mother, and you've been pretty fucking awful. So, I'll ask one more time, Mom," he calmed his voice, "tell me who my father is, please."

"Are you threatening—" she started.

Max screamed as loud as physically possible, his own eardrums rattling at the roar of his voice, "*Tell me his name, I swear to fucking god woman.*"

"Jim," she said, cutting him off. "Jim Alan Miller. Last I heard he was in Arcadia," she said in her fake, calm voice. "I hope you're happy with yourself, Max, you just acted exactly like him. A perfect example of why I want nothing to do with you or him ever again."

"No, Mom. You pushed me to act like this. And honestly, I'm starting to think that his leaving had nothing to do with his character and everything to do with your lack of any."

"I have to go, Max, Justine has—"

"Yeah, I know, you have family shit to do."

"Max, one last thing," she said, her voice low, calm, and unwavering from the emotionless tone she had always managed to use with him.

"What, Mom?" he asked, his voice cracking, raw emotion taking over.

"I never want to speak to you again."

A solitary drop of blood rolled from his battered knuckle onto the fabric of his jeans at the same time that a single tear rolled down his cheek.

"I can't say I'm surprised," he managed.

"I have to go," she said firmly.

"Yeah, you said that already."

The line went dead, and his vision blurred.

This time it had nothing to do with his eyes and everything to do with his heart.

Chapter Nineteen

Remi waited patiently, but the passing of time led her to impatience and finally anger. It was then that she let herself worry, just a bit. Her racing mind spiraled into worst-case scenarios and filled her with a fear so deep in the pit of her stomach she thought she might actually puke up the burrito she had just eaten.

Every text left on *send*.

Every call met with an automated voicemail.

Every breath she took felt like a punch to the gut.

She had been ghosted; by men, by employees, by friends, by her own fucking mother, but something about Max doing it, after he had made her silent promises, and kissed her with his eyes closed so tight, hurt differently. It felt personal.

She hit call one last time.

It rang and rang, and on the third ring, it went to voicemail.

"Max, I don't know what's going on, and maybe it's nothing. Maybe it's just you pushing me away, and if that's the case I can handle it, I'm a big girl. You don't owe me anything. But I'd be lying if I said it didn't sting. I *do* deserve to know you're okay. I *do* deserve to know that you're safe. So, can you, just for my peace of mind, tell me you're okay and that I don't have to show up at your house for a welfare check. Because I will. I'll fucking drive over there unannounced to make sure you're not hurt. So, yeah, shoot me a text. I'll even settle for a thumbs-up emoji at this point, and I hate those. Anyway... okay..."

She hung up, pulled on her checkered Vans, and headed to the only place she knew how to be alone, the beach.

***

Max declined her call, again, hating the notification for her voicemail. The temptation to listen was too much. The temptation to call her back, to drive to her and fall into her arms, to let her comfort him, it was all too much.

He searched for the name: Jim Alan Miller.

Jim Alan Miller, Arcadia.

His father's name was, oddly enough, a fairly popular name.

He hit call, he asked, was denied, and then scratched a line through the number.

He called the next number on the list, he asked, was denied *again*, and he scratched a line through the number.

Repeat.

Only forty-six more Jim Alan Millers to go.

When he saw the number of missed messages lit up on his phone, he opened the text thread with Remi. She was worried, and she had every right to be. He couldn't respond, because he knew if he did, she would ask the tough questions, and he was all out of passes. He was low on words, and it would take a fuck ton of them to explain everything; what the doctor had said, the conversation with his mother, and the phone call he was trying so desperately to have with his estranged father. On top of all of that, he was struggling with the idea that, in two days, he was going to report back to the locker room with no answers for his coach or team, and possibly even for himself. And he was scared.

He was so fucking scared.

His house felt so big with him being there alone, but he didn't know how to ask her to come. So, he denied her calls and avoided her texts and didn't listen to her voicemail.

Each deep breath he took before he called the next Jim in the phone book echoed in the sterile space around him.

He hit call.

He hit call.

He hit call.

"Hello?"

Max took a deep breath. "Hi, ummm, my name's Max Miller, and I'm looking for my father."

The phone went silent, and for a second Max thought the person had hung up. It wouldn't be the first time that had happened today, but then he heard the man clear his throat.

"I was wondering when I'd get this call," the man said.

"You were?" Max asked, completely shocked.

"I was. I knew she would never tell you about me, but I still followed your career, been watching you since you got drafted to Anaheim. And I just knew that one day you would call poking around, looking for answers."

"Why didn't you…" Max paused, unsure what he was going to ask.

"Why didn't I reach out?" his father responded.

"Exactly," Max said.

"Do you *know* your mother?"

This made Max laugh because he *did* know her. "Yeah, she can be..." Max trailed off again, words escaping him.

"A bitch?" his father asked.

"I was going to say hard, but that works too," Max agreed, allowing himself this one time to speak poorly of her.

"Well, go on then, son, ask me what you called to ask, and I'll try my best to help you understand it all."

"I just need to know if..." Max paused, took a deep breath, and then said the words he dreaded ever leaving his lips, "I need to know if you're blind."

Chapter Twenty

Remi let herself into the beachfront house of Max Miller to clean as she had so many times before. Only now, when she entered, she felt like an intruder. Having the code to his front door felt like a conflict of interest.

Now that he wanted nothing to do with her; his simple thumbs-up emoji— even though she said she would settle for it—followed by his silence led her to accept that whatever they had shared between them romantically, had ended as quickly as it had started. What hurt the most about his silence was that he asked her to say yes to everything, only to take away her opportunity to do it before she could.

Motherfucker.

She called out to announce herself after letting herself in, giving him any chance he might need to run and hide like the coward he was.

"It's Remi, your *house cleaner*," she said, making sure to emphasize her position.

The window coverings were drawn closed, and the typical inviting smell of clean linen and fresh ocean breeze was replaced with something stuffy and thick, like old air and sweat. The hairs on the back of her neck stood up. This was wrong, all wrong. Panic flooded her.

She should have reached out again.

She should have called again.

She should have shown up.

She reached for the light switch; the normally bright house was uncharacteristically dark, causing bile to rise in her throat as her stomach turned with uncertainty.

"Max, are you home?" she called out, this time her voice less informative, and more worried.

No response came. Flicking on the kitchen lights, she was shocked to find the house completely trashed, which wasn't an uncommon thing for a house cleaner to walk into, unless it was *this* particular house. Max Miller's house, which up until today, had always been pristine upon her arrival.

She opened the windows in the living room to get fresh air circulating, damn near tripping over dirty clothes strewn across the living room floor. Pushing open the slider that led to the beach, she allowed the bright sun to light up the living room around her. Following the sun's path over the trail of filth, like breadcrumbs from Hansel and Gretel, it led her to the massive, unmoving body of Max Miller laid out on the couch.

"Oh, fuck," she cried, falling to the couch beside him. "Max," she shouted, shaking his body, only to find him unresponsive. "Max, are you okay?" she asked, her voice filled with panic. Reaching into her back pocket she pulled out her phone. "Please don't be dead," she said. Her hands shook, her fingers struggling to dial 9-1-1.

Right as she managed to hit the call button, Max reached out and slapped the phone from her hand, sending it flying across the room.

"I'm not dead," he shouted. The voice of the operator boomed from Remi's phone that had landed in a pile of dirty clothes, "9-1-1, what's your emergency?"

She crawled over to retrieve her phone, and in a panic, ended the call, hanging up on the operator. She looked over at Max, who was now sitting up on the couch, his red hair sticking up on one side where he had slept, his beard flattened against his right cheek while deep red indentations from the couch's throw pillow lined his face.

Her phone began to ring; it was the emergency number. She looked back up at Max searching for help.

"Answer it so they don't send the cops," he said, calmly. His voice was extremely even-toned and steady considering the series of events he had just woken up to.

"Hi," she answered, "I'm sorry. It was a false alarm." She looked over at Max who was now holding his head in his hands, his body hunched over, accentuating how massive his shoulders were.

The operator responded, "I thought I heard someone say something about being dead."

Remi looked back over at Max who was currently massaging his temples. Out of the corner of her eye, she saw the empty bottle of Jack Daniel's on the coffee table and her stomach lurched at the very thought of smelling it.

"I'm sorry for the confusion. He wasn't dead. Just... really fucking drunk."

The operator went on to ask if they needed an ambulance and Remi reassured her it was just a misunderstanding before hanging up.

She sat back on her heels, her heart still pounding in her chest with adrenaline, fear, anxiety, and all the things one might feel when they think they just found a loved one dead on the couch.

Loved one? How had he so quickly become someone that meant *so* much to her?

A small sigh escaped her. Maybe it was relief that he was alive, but this caused Max to finally look up at her. She noticed he had dark circles that hung low on his cheeks, the whites of his eyes bloodshot.

"I'm mad at you," she said after a moment, her voice cracking. And she knew it didn't matter. His silence over the past few days had made it clear they weren't *a thing* anymore. He didn't owe her an explanation, but she was still mad, and her anger with him was valid. He needed to know that.

Max shook his head and looked down at his feet. "Not as mad as I am at myself."

"You scared me," she said weakly.

"I'm sorry."

"I thought you were—" she started, only to be cut off.

"Dead. Yeah, I know."

"I know you're allowed to get shit-faced on your couch. I know that. I really have no right to be mad at you. It's just, your house..." she stammered, unsure what her defense was. "Your house is never like *this*," she said, signaling to the mess all around her; empty bottles, take-out boxes, dirty clothes, black briefs, a porn magazine...

Her eyes instantly darted away from the magazine, just knowing he had been looking at it felt gross and intrusive. Her eyes locked back on him, on the top of his head because he was clearly too cowardly to face her.

"You can't just change it up on me like that, Max. It's not fair. You can't be so fucking consistent and then *bam*, have me walking into a fucking crime scene."

Her heart hammered in her chest; she couldn't catch her breath. The smell of the pizza boxes, musty laundry, and the putrid stink of whiskey; she thought she might puke as her past flooded her. This was too much to walk into unprepared. She always knew what she was going to get with Max, even despite their recent circumstances. His house was safe. Max's house had always been a sure bet walking in, unlike the home from her childhood.

Until now.

Finding him this way.

He could have been dead, under his filth, with sour whiskey-stained lips.

It was too much.

It was too familiar.

It was *exactly* how she had found her mother.

The need for fresh air consumed her. She needed to get the fuck out of his house until her brain remembered how to make her heart work again.

Heading out the back door slider, she didn't stop until she had made it across his patio and through the small gate that led to the beach. She didn't stop until she hit the shoreline. Only then did she let herself break completely.

***

By the time Max heard Remi return from the beach he had the living room cleaned up and had started working on the kitchen.

He should have gone down to the beach and comforted her. He had hurt her, upset her, scared her, and triggered something deep inside her, but he didn't go to her. Considering what he had recently put her through, he wasn't even sure he was allowed to try and comfort her.

So, he cleaned instead.

Shoes in one hand and her phone in the other, Remi let herself in through the back slider. Max turned off the sink water that had been running, in case she wanted to talk, but she said nothing. She sat her shoes down by the door, and he noticed her toenails were painted black this time, her feet so tiny, and tan. In fact, everything about Remi was tiny. But right now, in this moment, standing before him with a tear-streaked face, puffy eyes, and weak posture, she looked pocket-sized. Max considered going to her and bringing her into his massive arms. He could cover her body completely, hold her, and make her feel safe.

Only he didn't, because he was certain he wasn't allowed, not anymore.

Instead, he got back to loading the dishwasher in silence.

He tried not to look up and stare, but he couldn't help but watch as she took in the clean living room in surprise.

"You didn't have to do that," she said.

He put a plate covered in crusty pizza sauce in the dishwasher. "No, I did. I made a real mess of this place all on my own."

"It's my job to clean up after you," she said coldly as she crossed the room towards him.

Maybe she would scold him. He knew he deserved it if she did, though he hoped she wouldn't; he didn't think he could handle being told how awful he was. Not after finding out what he had from his father. Not after being put on personal leave from hockey. Not from her. Not from *Remi*. She was the last person he wanted to let down, and yet he had done just that the second his life became too heavy.

"This is a different situation, I think," he said timidly.

"How so? You make a mess. I clean it up. It's Wednesday. It's a mess. I clean it up. How is this time any different?" she asked, her voice elevating with each word.

"It just is."

"Because I freaked out? Or maybe it's because you fucking asked me to say yes to everything and then the second I asked for *anything*, for a simple response, you sent me a thumbs up. A thumbs up, Max. And then you let me walk into *this*?"

He loaded an old oatmeal-covered bowl into the dishwasher, shifting his eyes from her stone-cold gaze. "You told me to give you a thumbs up."

"Yeah, but that didn't mean I wanted one, Max. Read the fucking room. I wanted more. I thought you did too. I guess I was wrong."

"You weren't wrong to want more, you deserved better than a stupid thumbs up." He looked back up at her, afraid of what he might see in her eyes.

She held his gaze for what seemed like an eternity and then looked over at the dishwasher and then back to him. Her shoulders fell. The tense line between her eyebrows relaxed, her pursed lips fell into a lifeless frown as if surrendering to this mess—she was giving up. It broke his fucking heart that he had caused her to look this way.

"You're doing that wrong," she said weakly.

Max looked down at the jumble of dishes he had stacked awkwardly. When he looked back up, she was standing beside him.

Leaning across him to turn on the faucet, he watched as she stuck her hand under the water until steam rose up from the spray.

"That's your first problem, you need to use hot water. It helps break down the dried-up food."

Max made room for her between the dishwasher and the sink; she was so close he could smell the ocean on her skin. His heart broke for her, and he hated what he had already managed to put her through.

Wishing she wasn't so calm, he thought he actually might prefer her yelling at him over this. But she didn't yell, or scold him, instead, she reached down to grab the oatmeal bowl he had just loaded and began to rinse it under the hot spray. The oatmeal was old, and stubborn, and wouldn't budge with just the water. Embarrassment flooded him, watching her clean up after him. He didn't like it, but he let her do it anyway because it took words to tell her to stop, words he did not have at the moment.

She reached into the cupboard below the sink, pulled out a scrub pad, and began to work on the dishes he had already loaded, scraping away pizza sauce and curdled milk before reloading them into the dishwasher with precision.

"You have to basically wash the dishes before the dishwasher can *wash* the dishes," she said, offering him a weak smile. He noticed her small dimple appear on her left cheek and his heart ached to brush his fingertips across it.

She pulled a cleaning pod from a clear jar below the sink, held it up to show him, then placed it into the small compartment on the dishwasher door, making eye contact with him before closing it. Max knew she wasn't trying to make him feel stupid for not knowing how to load a dishwasher properly. She was simply showing him how to do something normal, something common, something kids who lived normal childhoods did daily.

Max hadn't had a normal childhood, but neither had she.

"All done," she said, stepping back, away from the sink, the dishwasher, and *him*.

As if gravity had shifted, he felt the loss of her in his space.

He looked at the dishwasher, then back up to her. "Seems silly," he said, because it did. What was the point of the dishwasher if you had to wash the dishes beforehand?

Her smile lifted a bit more, and there it was, above her lips on her right cheek, the other dimple. His heart hammered as his feelings warred inside of him; he longed for her, and he hated himself.

"It does, doesn't it? Seem silly?" she said, pondering the thought. It wasn't a profound conversation, but Max found a sliver of hope that she still wanted to converse with him at all.

Remi, without missing a beat, got back to cleaning the kitchen, leaving Max to feel like a speed bump in the middle of a busy road.

"Ummm, stupid question," he started.

"There are no stupid questions, only stupid answers, Max," she said, sarcasm lining her every word, causing him to squirm a bit under the pressure of this whole situation.

"Well?"

"Where would I find a broom?" he asked, ashamed he didn't know this for himself.

He was almost certain she was going to tell him to fuck off. Tell him it was her job to clean his house because technically it was her job, but something about today felt different, this mess felt different. It felt destructive, and somehow his self-destruction over the past few days had managed to trigger something in Remi too.

She didn't tell him to fuck off, she simply pointed to the hallway. "There's a broom closet next to the laundry room, that's also where your mop is."

Max found the broom exactly where Remi told him it would be, and when he returned to the kitchen, he found her peeling up ink-covered plastic wrap from the marble countertop from his last tally mark. He hadn't lost a game. He hadn't even played a game. But he felt the phone call with his father warranted a fresh line, this one for the biggest loss of his life. This one is for the loss of it all.

"What's this about?" she asked, picking up the small cap of black ink.

He played dumb, shrugging his shoulders as if he was just as confused as she was.

She didn't pry, and for that he was grateful.

He finished sweeping and was shocked when Remi met him with a bucket of mop solution that smelled like lemons. He wasn't sure what he was supposed to do with the high-tech mop bucket or the foot pedal thingy, and as if reading his mind, Remi took the mop from him. She dipped it into the water solution, then moved it to the strainer and began to press the pedal with her foot—he noticed her toes still had a little sand between them from earlier—the spinning made his vision blur. The majority of the solution had spun out before she handed it back to him.

"And now, you mop," she said simply.

Clever, Max thought.

Remi gave him a knowing nod, so he gave her one back, letting her know he understood the assignment.

He began to mop.

She began to vacuum.

It was like a dance. A silent dance, as no more words were spoken. Only, they had never danced together before, so they had to be cautious not to step on each other's toes while learning the next move as they went.

When the house was clean, and the dance was over, Remi picked up her checkered Vans that were still sitting by the back slider.

"I should go," she said softly, gathering her things as she made her way to the front door, pulling her cleaning cart behind her. Max followed at a safe distance.

"And Max," she said, turning to face him. "You should probably shower, you reek of whiskey," she said quietly.

His face flushed, he was embarrassed and ashamed. He didn't know if he wanted to beg her to stay, so he could apologize and make it right, or if he just wanted her to go. It would be easier for both of them if she just left.

He was a mess, and while she cleaned for a living, this wasn't the kind of mess she signed up for.

"I'm sorry about today," he offered.

"Me too," she said, her voice barely above a whisper. "I'm sorry for freaking out."

Max took a step towards her. What did he plan to do? Shake her hand? Hug her? She didn't want a sloppy hug from him now, not while he smelled of stale booze. Not after he had kissed her with everything in him nights ago, only to leave her without an explanation as to why he had cut her out of his life the very next day.

"Do you..." He paused, not being good at this sort of thing, but his question had to be asked. "Do you want to talk about it?"

She looked at him, *really* looked at him, and asked, "Do *you* want to talk about it, Max?"

He just stood there. It was a real deer-in-headlights moment for him. His fast reactions in front of the net meant nothing in the real world. No one ever asked him if he wanted to talk. No one stuck around long enough to notice he might need to. No one asked the right questions to see that maybe he wasn't quiet by choice, he was quiet by default.

And he did want to talk about it.

About what she walked in on.

The mess.

Hockey.

The phone call to his mother.

And the one with his dad.

The way he wanted to kiss her in the dark and still be able to see her face.

"Pass?" he asked quietly.

It was easier this way. Less messy. Less complicated.

Remi shook her head, her disappointment in him was obvious. "Yeah, I had a feeling you might say that. But Max, just a heads up, pass only works when you don't do it every time."

Hanging his head in shame, he knew she was right.

She placed her checkered Vans on the welcome mat, slipped her tiny feet into them, and without another word, she left.

Chapter Twenty-One

Remi pulled up to the run-down apartment complex after a long day of work and a fucked-up night with no sleep. She was lacking the energy she needed to finish her last job of the day. Walking in on Max like she had yesterday did a number on her. Seeing him like that reignited a fear in her that she thought she had moved on from. She thought she had let that part of her past go, laid it to rest, and healed.

But surprise, surprise, she still feared finding her loved one's dead.

Weird, right?

She rolled her eyes at her brain's sick sense of humor. It had been four years since she found her mother unresponsive, in the same way she found Max last night. It was so oddly similar that it made her stomach churn. The smell of the old take-out boxes, the heavy musk of his drunken body, the lingering scent of whiskey in the thick stagnant air... it made her skin crawl.

She was so mad at him.

She was also so sad for him.

She was *so* fucking confused.

Pulling her cleaning cart behind her, she knocked on Mrs. Keller's door and waited for the old woman to slowly make her way to let her in. She had been cleaning Mrs. Keller's house for almost a year now as a part of her Free Clean charity program. Remi had started Free Clean with Busy Bee to help people who were in the same situations she and her mother had been in when she was a child. Remi would clean the old woman's apartment, and even make sure Mrs. Keller's meds were in the small daily container to help her remember to take them.

The state failed people like Mrs. Keller time and time again, and Remi knew it wasn't her job to step in. It wasn't her job to do what she did for free, but it felt like the right thing. Each time she threw away the trash that lined the floor of the small one-bedroom apartment, scrubbed the toilet, and wiped down the countertops, she saw her mom in the back of her head, smiling and proud, telling her she was doing the right thing.

No one had ever intervened for her mother. No one had even thought to intervene for Remi. No one saw the mess and tried to help clean it up. All anyone ever did was sweep it under the rug, one eviction notice after another. Where were the people that were supposed to step in and offer to help? Where were the heroes that saved the kid and helped the mom recover? They never showed up. And because of that, Remi showed up—even on the hardest days. Even today.

The first time Remi cleaned for Mrs. Keller it was supposed to be a one-time thing after the elderly woman was served an eviction notice for her hoarding. A friend of a friend who knew about Remi's non-profit, Free Clean, contacted her and told her about Mrs. Keller's situation. A situation that ultimately would have rendered the older woman homeless. Remi showed up for Mrs. Keller, no questions asked, and then she showed up the next week, just to check in on the older woman, only to realize the house was trashed again. So, she showed up the week after that too, knowing this woman was stuck in the cycle of hoarding, and at her age, with no one to support her or get her the help she needed, she would never stop. It was a vicious cycle, one Remi was well-versed in, so she kept showing up and never stopped.

"It got bad this week," Mrs. Keller warned upon opening the door, a rank odor hitting Remi's nose the instant she stepped in.

"Mrs. Keller, what are you holding on to that stinks?" Remi asked.

"Probably that Costco chicken you brought me. I kept looking at it. I knew it needed to be taken out days ago. But I just..." she said, her voice lowering to a whisper as she trailed off.

"It's okay. We'll get it sorted out today," Remi assured.

"I wanted to throw it away before the maggots came..." she murmured, trailing off again, and Remi's heart broke for the old woman.

"It's fine Mrs. Keller. I'm no stranger to the little pests. I'll get them cleaned up in no time."

She *would* clean them up, but truth be told, the sight of the maggots brought on fierce memories of her childhood; the way they would pop under her small bare feet in the middle of the night as a child. She remembered getting up to use the restroom as a young girl, feeling the crunch of the maggots under the weight of her steps as she made her way past the rotting bags of food, and KFC chicken carcasses her mother refused to get rid of. Sadly, the little white bugs were a core memory from Remi's childhood.

Room by room Remi fixed the woman's house, and while she watched the small apartment transform back into a clean space, her brain on the other hand, remained a mess.

Remi realized that while she was good at cleaning up other people's messes, she sucked at facing her own. Especially the mess that was Max Miller. What she walked in on yesterday, and the fact that she knew he was hurting, killed her. While she wanted to fix him, she couldn't; that was his burden to carry and that scared her because while she was still angry at him, she was also worried about him, his career, his health, and fuck, the list went on and on.

The part that hurt the most about all of this shit with Max was that it was none of her damn business, he had made that very clear.

Chapter Twenty-Two

The cool air of the arena hit Max's face sending a chill down his spine. The smell of the building was so familiar, so refreshing, and so comforting—it was good to be back. His time off was up, it was time to face his coach and see where they went from here.

The words of his father felt like an anchor in his chest, securing his fate from drifting. This generational curse wasn't going anywhere, it was his to keep, his to share. It was his to carry, be it alone or with the ones who loved him.

He was going blind, that he was certain, and he didn't know what he was going to do with that information just yet.

He wasn't ready. He *wasn't* fucking ready.

This was supposed to be his big year.

"Have a seat, son," Coach offered, as Max entered the office. "How was your time off?" he asked. A dozen memories, good and bad, flooded Max's brain. Remi and closets, phone calls and doctor's visits, and the sound of his father's voice that resembled his own.

"It was hard to be away from the team," Max said.

"And do you feel like you sorted your shit out? Got some rest, got laid, whatever it was you needed to do to get back on your A-game?"

"I did." Max lied.

"How are you feeling about hitting the ice today?"

"I feel ready." He lied again.

Lies were becoming his entire identity.

"Good. Brody is out with an injury. That leaves Brown healthy, and you, well, I don't know, *are* you healthy?"

"I'm very healthy," Max said, and it *wasn't* a lie. His vitals were good, and his body was in amazing shape. There wasn't anything wrong with his *health* per se. So, unless Coach asked for specifics, on paper Max was pretty damn healthy. He wasn't going to drop dead on the ice or start bleeding from his ears anytime soon.

"I want to see you at practice. Suit up. If you don't perform, you're going to see the team doctor. And if you refuse this time, you can kiss your career goodbye. I've had enough of the runaround. I want you healthy, or I want you getting treated, but I won't settle for the unknown bullshit, Miller. You hear me?"

"Yes, sir," Max agreed, and the clock was officially ticking down to the end.

Max was greeted by his teammates with warm embraces and words of affirmation. They had missed him. He had been so wrapped up in his own shit that he didn't even realize he missed them too. They had been his only family since he was drafted. They were the first group of people that stuck around and showed up for him. He hugged them back and fought back the tears that wanted to make an emotional ass out of him.

While putting on his gear, Max could feel Brown staring at him from across the locker room. They were teammates, but they were also both goalies, so they spent a lot of time together in training camps and conditioning. Max realized that somewhere in all of this he had let resentment towards Brown seep in, causing him to distance himself from the young man. A man who at one time or another had called Max his hero and mentor.

Max met his gaze, and Brown's eyes dropped to the floor. Max wasn't good at this sort of thing, he was just as awkward as the next goalie, but he knew he needed to talk to the young player, tell him he was proud of him, and thank him for showing up for the team. *Their* team.

He made his way around the benches slowly. The commotion of pre-practice skate went quiet as Max broke his superstitious ways to go talk to Brown. Because what was superstition going to do for Max now? He was past the point of that. He needed more than good luck and a strong set of routines now. He needed a miracle, and he was pretty damn sure walking across the locker room wasn't going to change his destiny at this point.

"Mind if I have a seat?" he asked his fellow goalie, who immediately made room for him on the bench. Max scrunched up his face at Brown, realizing he was still a *little* superstitious. "Can I be on the other side?" Max asked, hinting to the left of Brown, "It's a goalie thing."

Brown quickly scooted the other way knowing all too well about goalie superstitions, and Max took a seat.

"I want you to know that I'm grateful for you," Max managed.

Brown tensed at his words.

"It's hard letting your team down." Max went on, "But I think it would be a lot harder if I didn't have you to take my place. If I can't help the team win, I'm happy you can."

"I don't want to take your place, Max, not yet," Brown admitted sincerely. "You're still the number one goalie for this team, Millsy. I know my place."

"It's *our* place. There is no number one. Not anymore. It's me and you, and one day, it's going to be you and Brody. And I need you to know that when that day comes, I'm good with it," Max said, his voice cracking despite how strong he was trying to be.

"Yeah, but you're just getting started, Millsy. You're going to sign your big contract this year, and I'm going to wait my turn."

Max lowered his head and ran his fingers through his thick red hair.

"Brown, I won't get the big contract this year," he said under his breath.

The young goalie just sat there, unable to speak, unable to process what Max had just said.

"I won't get the big contract, but I'm also not ready to say good-bye," he admitted.

"What are you saying?" Brown asked.

"I'm just saying what you're all thinking."

"We all just want you to be okay. That's all anyone wants."

Max reached out and patted the young goalie on the shoulder. "Buckle up, man. Your time is coming sooner than you expected," Max said, standing to leave.

"But what does that even mean?" Brown asked, his face lined with worry.

Max just gave him a knowing smile, brought his finger up to his lips. and gestured for him to keep quiet, because what he had just said was their little goalie secret—for now.

Chapter Twenty-Three

Remi turned on the shower, making the water as hot as possible. Mrs. Keller's house had been the worst she had seen in months. On top of the maggot infestation, she found the bathroom in a horrific state, as Mrs. Keller had stopped flushing her toilet well over three days ago—that was new, she had never done that in the past.

Some people had nothing to hold on to, so they held on to anything they could.

Remi thought of Max. *He* felt like something worth holding on to. He felt like something she didn't want to walk away from or turn a blind eye to. And while she knew she was a stubborn person, she also knew she was filled with compassion and grace.

As the small bathroom began to fill with warm steam from the shower, Remi pulled out her phone and typed out a text to Max. She wasn't ready to give up on him, and in her heart of hearts, she knew he didn't want to give up on her either. She wouldn't let him hide from her or let him ask her for everything and then take it away. She was in too deep, too invested, and she cared too much.

She was an idiot.

But at least she was an idiot with good intentions.

Setting her phone on the small shelf that hung above the toilet, she stripped off her clothes and tossed them into the laundry basket when what she really wanted to do was burn them. Stepping into the scalding water, she allowed it to wash away the lingering ick from the day, other people's filth, and the reminder of her childhood trauma. Maybe if it was hot enough it could also wash away the feeling in the pit of her stomach that was Max Miller.

The water nearly burned her skin, and she willed it so. She lathered her soap and scrubbed her legs, her feet, her arms, her neck. She could almost feel the maggots dripping down her skin, crawling in her hair. Using her fingernails on her scalp, she dug into her flesh. She would never feel clean enough in this moment, and she knew it.

The water ran down the drain full of soap suds, carrying away her day's hard work. It felt symbolic. It always did.

Her shower.

Her sanctuary.

It was where she washed away her sins and the sins of the others she carried every time she punched in their door code or knocked on their battered screen.

Closing her eyes, she let her head fall back, willing the hot spray of the water to relax her. Her body began to soften, the tight muscles around her shoulders eased, and the throbbing in her knees dulled.

She would be okay.

She took a deep breath and pressed her head against the cool tile when she heard a loud knock at her door, startling her. Turning off the water, she got out of the shower and quickly dried off before slipping on her robe.

The knock came again, this time louder.

"I'm coming," she called out, rushing to the door, hoping she was right in guessing who it was, but also preparing herself to find an Amazon package to avoid any more disappointment.

She pulled the door open, and there he was, hair wet from a recent shower, wearing his Anaheim Condor's sweat suit. It dawned on her that today was the day he went back to practice.

"Well?" she asked, her tone sharper and crueler than she had known herself to be.

His eyes darted up to meet hers. "I'm ready to talk," he said, his voice low and defeated.

"No more passes?" she asked.

"No more passes, Remi."

***

He followed her into her small space, the overwhelming calm he felt just being in her presence seemed unreal. How could just being around someone lift the weight from his shoulders with such ease, when only hours ago, in front of a net, *his* net, his team, and his coach, he had felt such immense pressure and an overwhelming sense of dread? He would never push her away again; his heart couldn't take it, and her heart didn't deserve it.

"I just got out of the shower," she said, hinting at her wet, blonde hair.

"Me too," he said, hinting at his.

"Did you just come from..." She paused.

"Practice, yeah," he said, finishing her sentence.

"How'd it go?" she asked.

"I was able to fake it," he said.

She offered him a weak smile. "Fake it 'til ya make it," she said, her attempt at a joke.

"Or fake it until they find out the truth," he said.

She took a step towards him, then hesitated, not getting *too* close. He didn't blame her, not after what he had put her through, not after the last few days, not after his silence.

"And what's the truth, Max?"

"The truth?" he asked, buying time.

"The truth."

"No passes," he affirmed.

"The *truth*, Max."

"The truth is that I'm going blind, Rem."

He watched her knees buckle at his admission. He watched her face, ever confident, ever strong, ever inviting, falter into something broken, confused, and sad.

He hated to see her like this.

"Remi?" he asked quietly, taking a step towards her, taking her hands in his.

"Are you sure?" she asked.

"Pretty sure," he said.

"How sure, Max?" she asked, her voice shaken with a hint of denial in her tone.

"Remi, maybe we should sit down," he offered, hinting at her couch. She did as he suggested, sitting down next to him, her body tense as they faced each other, panic on her face, worry on his.

"I went to see an eye doctor," he offered.

"Okay. And?" she asked.

"And he saw something."

"Something bad?" she asked.

"Yeah, Rem. Something bad," he said.

"Like, like... cancer or..." she stammered.

"No, not cancer. He saw something in my retina. I had like, clumps or something," he offered, not wanting to use the proper terms he knew by name after Google search upon Google search. Not ready to speak them into existence.

"And how do they fix it? When can you get treated for it?" she asked frantically.

"Remi," he said softly, gently taking her hand in his.

"Max, stop," she pleaded.

"Stop what?" he asked.

"Stop being so calm. It's freaking me out."

"Remi..."

"Just fucking tell me what we can do. I can drive you to your appointments. I can help."

"Remi, I... it's not treatable. It's hereditary. My dad ..." He tried to find the words to explain.

"You spoke to your dad?"

"I found him, yeah."

"And what did *he* say?"

"That he'd been waiting for me to call him. That he's watched my hockey career, and he knew…" Max bit back his emotions, he wouldn't cry, not now. "He said he knew I would find him when I started to see the signs."

"How? Why? What signs, Max? You never gave me any details. I don't even know what any of this fucking means. Make it make sense, Max."

"Remi, he's completely blind. He has—"

"What? What does he have?"

"He has an eye disease. It's called—" Max had not spoken it out loud, not yet, not since his father had put a name to it, making it real.

"What's it called, Max? Maybe I can help you."

"It's called retinitis pigmentosa, my father has it, and from what the doctor saw, and lots of research, I'm certain I have it too. And the only thing you can do to help me at this point is to let me back into your life. I know I've fucked up, more than once. But please, let me look at you long enough to memorize the details of your face, because I won't be able to see them one day, and I never want to forget."

She fell into his arms, and he welcomed her. He let his own stiff body relax into the weight of her.

"I don't know what to say, Max," she said, her voice no more than a faint whisper.

"Just say yes one more time."

She looked up at him, her eyes bloodshot, tears streaming down her face. "I did that once before, Max, and you pulled away."

"I won't this time. I promise."

"What am I saying yes to, Max? Tell me this time. I need more."

"To everything."

"What does that even look like?"

"I don't know. I can hardly see my feet, you can't expect me to see the future," he said, offering her a small, half smile.

Remi let out a soft chuckle amongst her small sobs. "Not a vision joke already?" she said, swatting his shoulders.

"If I don't laugh about it, I'm afraid it might kill me."

"Then I say yes. Fuck it. Yes, to everything. Part two. But don't make me regret it this time."

"I won't. I want to be with you, Remi. I want to take care of you for as long as I can. I want to spend what time I have left with my vision seeing how beautiful life can be with you."

"And hockey?" she asked, her voice breaking as she said it.

"Remi," he pleaded.

"Pass?" she asked.

"No. Not a pass. No more passes, I promised," he affirmed, bringing his hand to her leg, running it up her thigh. "Not a pass, just an, I'll get back to you on that."

"Okay, I can handle that," she agreed.

"Remi," he said, a hint of a smile on his face. "I need you to stop crying right *meow*, and I need you to show me to your room while I still have the courage to do what comes next."

Remi wiped away her tears with a small smile before standing.

"And what comes next, Max Miller?" she asked, as he stood before her, his body massive next to hers, engulfing her space.

"I kiss you, of course," he said.

"My closet isn't big enough, in case you were wondering."

"No, I think this time I might like to do this on a bed."

"But you always sleep on the couch," she argued, and he was glad to have this version of her back, feisty and fun, and so damn confident and beautiful.

"I wouldn't mind changing that. Sleeping in a bed sounds more appealing with the idea of you there with me," he said, leaning down to press his lips against her neck.

She tugged on his hand, pulling him towards her bedroom.

"I just realized I've never seen your room," he said before entering.

She smiled up at him before pushing the door open, color spilling into his senses; pictures and books, the smell of fresh linen and lemon cleaner, her curtains blowing about, the ocean in the distance a reminder of how small they were in this big, terrifying world.

"I'm scared, Remi," he said quietly standing across from her, unable to push away this fear buried deep in his chest, one he hadn't vocalized until now.

"I know, Max. I know," she said, running her hands comfortingly along his arms.

"I'm scared to lose my vision. That's a given emotion, that's to be expected. But the craziest part is that it's not what scares me the most."

"Tell me. Tell me what your biggest fear is so I can try and understand it. I want to know how to help you through this. And I want to do it with as much understanding and compassion as I can, while never having walked a day in your shoes."

"I'm scared that I'm nothing without hockey. It's been my entire identity my whole life. It's all I know. It's my only home and my only personality trait. I'm Max Miller, the goalie. I don't know what I am if I'm not that guy. I'm terrified I'll never be anything of importance once my career is gone."

Remi closed the space between them, wrapping her arms around his body in a tight embrace. Her face pressed into the fabric of his shirt, her warm breath heating him there as she held him close.

"You are so much more than hockey and being a goalie. You are so much more, Max. Maybe you can't see that in yourself yet, but I can, I have since the first day I met you. You're a beautiful walking contradiction, and you have no idea how perfect you are. I want to walk beside you and hold your hand as you discover yourself, Max. I want to be there when you finally see your worth outside the arena, off the ice, without the pads and pucks. Because when you do, you're going to absolutely shine in your self-discovery, I just know it. Your life has just begun, Max Miller, and I can't believe I get to be a part of it."

He pulled her face up to his and kissed her words into his existence. She was right, he was so much more, and this wasn't the end of the line for him. If *she* was lucky to have him, what did that make him for having *her*?

He couldn't articulate his feelings, there were no words, but he could show her. He could make her feel good.

"Can I take off your robe?" he asked, and she nodded as she took a step back, allowing him space to pull the fabric away from her naked body.

"You're the most beautiful thing I've ever seen," he said, stopping just a beat to appreciate her form.

"Now you," she said, hinting at his fully clothed body.

He pushed away his shoes and then his socks before looking up at her. "I'm very red," he said as he blushed.

"Carpet matches the drapes?" she teased.

"Oh yeah," he said pulling his shirt over his head to reveal the red hair that covered his chest.

Remi stepped forward, and at first, he thought she might run her fingers over the chest hair, but her smile faded and her hand gently traced across the tally marks that covered his ribs.

"Oh," he said, "about those."

"Max," she asked, a concerned line on her brow, "what does this mean?"

"It's every game I've lost in front of the net with the NHL," he said, and he didn't know why, but shame flooded him admitting that.

"Why?" she asked.

"That's a good question," he said. "A question I think I used to be confident answering, but now with you looking at every loss I've ever had eternalized on my skin in ink, I'm not so sure it was the healthiest way to go about losing."

"Okay, but *why* tattoo your losses?" she asked again. "Help me to understand this."

"I think I've always been so obsessed with losing that I never wanted to forget. I thought it held me accountable, and then, it became a bit of a superstition."

"And did tattooing your losses on your skin ever stop you from losing the next time?" she asked, gently sweeping a finger across the raised lines of ink.

"No, but it always made me want to fight harder for the win," he said, suddenly feeling self-conscious of his stupid tradition, his weird superstition.

Fucking goalie nonsense was what it was.

As if reading his mind, Remi leaned in and kissed the ink-covered skin. Her lips trailed across each tally mark, each bundle of five losses, each black line until she had run out of losses to kiss. His skin warmed with her mouth on him, her understanding and reassurance in each kiss.

"Tonight, we focus on wins," she said, pressing her fingers under the elastic band of his joggers before pushing them down along with his briefs. His need for her was evident in the way his hard cock sprung free the second his clothing was gone. Her eyes locked on to his erection, then moved back up to meet his with a wild grin on her face.

"And this," she paused to hint at his cock, "is absolutely a win," she said, looking back down at the size of him with satisfaction.

This made him laugh just a bit—she approved of his dick, which was always a win.

"I just have one request," he said.

"Anything," she agreed, wrapping her arms around his neck, pulling their bodies together for their first taste of skin-to-skin friction.

"Can we leave the lights on? I just really want to see you like this." *Before I can't,* he thought.

"Absolutely. I want to see you like this too," she said and blushed a rosy pink to his red.

"I'm not too red and hairy for you?" he teased, a minor insecurity he had growing up.

"Your body," she said reaching down between them to give him a firm stroke, "is incredible, Max. I want to memorize every freckle on your shoulders." Leaning in to kiss him there, she said, "I want to watch your face blush as you enter me for the first time."

He knew he wouldn't disappoint her there, because if his face was blushing now, it was nothing in comparison to how red he would become once she was underneath him.

She lowered herself to the bed and he wasted no time finding his place between her legs. Their skin was electric in every place it touched, their breathing heavy, their hearts racing.

"I can't believe you're here," she whispered.

"Hey, that's my line," he said, drawing his hand up her side gently, her skin reacting with goosebumps under his fingertips.

"I can't believe you're not an alien," she teased.

His lips moved down to graze the firm deep pink of her nipple, the tickle of his beard causing her to giggle. "Who said I'm not?" he asked.

"An enigma for sure." She moaned as his mouth sucked and pulled on her sensitive bud, causing her entire body to pulse and throb in the best way possible. "Max Miller, the motherfucking enigma," she said.

His mouth pulled away from her breast, and the way the cool air replaced his warm lips was a beautiful sensation. Slowly dragging his mouth along the sensitive skin of her stomach, he let his lips, tongue, and beard stimulate her as he moved lower on the bed. Pressing kisses across her sharp hipbones, he loved the way Remi hummed sweet sounds as his hands pushed her legs apart to make room for him there.

"Can I kiss you?" he asked, and ran a finger up her entrance before pointing to her most intimate part, "*here*?"

Reaching down, she gripped his full head of beautiful red hair and encouraged him to do just that. He wasted no time. No gentle kisses, no moments leading up to it; there was only before his mouth was on her and after. He expertly pressed the flat of his tongue against her clit, applying pressure before latching onto her, causing her hips to buck against his face as he began to expertly suck, lick, and flick his tongue with unwavering rhythm before bringing his hand between her legs to help.

Remi's head pushed back against the pillow as he slid a finger deep inside her. Gripping his hair tighter she forced his face against her wet entrance, and his dick wept against her comforter. She tasted so good; he couldn't get enough of her. He pulled his finger away only to fill her with his tongue, her orgasm building as he used his thumb to rub her clit while he buried his face between her legs.

"This is so good," she moaned, and he couldn't agree more.

He was grateful his mouth was busy because he wouldn't have known what to say if it wasn't. He felt her legs begin to tremble as her thighs started to clench against him, holding him in place as he relentlessly fucked her with his mouth, his thumb never missing a beat against her clit.

"Max," she called out, and this only made him work harder for her release. He wanted to come up for air with his beard covered in her arousal.

And then he felt it, the moment it all came to a head. The moment her body began to shake against her will, the way her entire sex pulsated against his mouth. She moaned a deep, beautiful moan. Her hands released his hair and she brought them to cover her mouth as she cried out his name over and over. "Max, Max, *Max...*"

The movement of his hands slowed, and he moved his fingers away from her sensitive clit as she came, but he didn't move his face, not yet. He let her orgasm roll through her, loving the way he felt her body tremble against his face as he licked and kissed her through the best part.

Slowly, he pulled his face away as her body settled on the mattress below them. Climbing up to find his way beside her, he watched as she took a moment to recover.

"That was so good," she said, looking over at his pleased face.

"I think I might have enjoyed it as much as you."

She looked down at his erection and laughed. "I thought you meant you came on my sheets."

"No, but I honestly could have," he said.

She reached over and wiped his beard with her hand, unable to push back a girlish giggle. "Beards are new for me," she said.

"Doesn't help that I'm a messy eater," he teased, and they both began to laugh.

It was the most comfortable Max had ever felt during intimacy.

"Do you have a condom?" she asked.

"Would you find it presumptuous of me if I said I did?" he asked.

"No. Would *you* find it presumptuous of *me* if I said I bought some a week ago just in case?"

Max laughed and looked over at her bedside table. "In there?"

"Yeah, you can grab one."

He opened the small drawer and pulled out the new box of condoms, but not without noticing the packet of birth control beside it.

Safe was good.

He tore off a condom and began to open it when Remi took it from him.

"Can *I* do it?" she asked.

"You want to put the condom on me?" he said, a little taken aback—this was new.

She brought her finger to his nose, "Ding-ding-ding," she said, then asked, "Is it weird that I want to?"

"Not weird. It's hard to be weird in comparison to a goalie. Trust me. If I'm being honest, I think it's sexy," he admitted.

She took the condom and sat up in front of him, his face growing two shades darker as she slowly began to roll it down his length, his dick twitching at her touch.

"This might be the hottest thing I've ever experienced," he said watching as her tan fingers pushed the slippery rubber down his cock.

"You have a really nice one," she said with a smile.

"Thank you?" he said more as a question.

"You're welcome," she said, laying back down, pulling him with her.

"I'm not going to last long. I already know it," he admitted.

"That's ok. I'm just happy we're sharing this moment."

He lined himself up at her entrance and while he knew he was rather well endowed, Remi felt so small beneath him.

She pulled him down to kiss her, spreading her legs wider to make room for his body as he slowly pushed inside. Her walls tightened around him as he sunk in as deep as he could go. Remi's eyes were set on him, watching him, loving him?

"I'm just going to take a second," he said, pausing to enjoy the feel of her body stretching to fit him. He might come just from being inside her.

"Take all the time you need," she said, kissing his neck.

Giving himself one more second, he gained his composure and then began to move, slowly at first. Their bodies adjusted quickly to this new way of connection, this intimate exchange; sweat-slicked skin, her hands on his back, and his lips gently kissing her neck.

"You fit so perfectly," Remi whispered, and he couldn't agree more.

He wanted to take it this slow, to memorize the way it felt the first time he was here, with his woman, all emotions laid bare, but his body craved more of her. His need to move overcame his desire for this slow, deep connection, so he let go of the matters of the heart and began to move with the rhythm of his need.

Pushing deep inside her, his thrusts became harder than they had been mere seconds ago causing Remi to grip his shoulders as a moan escaped her. His body moved with certainty and a need for her he had been wanting to act on since the day Remi's finger first brushed across his. Pulling her legs up, Remi made more room for him to move without restriction and his rhythm quickened. It came easily and naturally, being with her like this. It felt like he had done this a million times with this woman, it was the best first time he had experienced.

His body was on fire, his orgasm closing in on him as everything tensed and ached for his release. He felt Remi's body doing the same, her fingers now gripping at his back, her eyes intent on him, intent on their release.

"Max," she cried out. "There, there, there," she moaned, and he knew he was hitting all the right places, his momentum unwavering as his body pushed into hers again and again. With the sound of their skin smacking together, their quickened breaths, and their inaudible words mixed with the distant roll of the ocean, he knew he was done for.

Remi's body suddenly tensed under his weight, her legs wrapping around him and her eyes slamming shut as she cried out. He knew she was there, and he wanted to join her. Thrusting into her one last time with all he had, he held her body tight against him as he came.

Before pulling away, Max leaned down and kissed the small smile on her face, and then her left dimple.

"I remember the first time I saw that dimple," he said, lying on his back next to her as they both caught their breath.

"That dimple is for strangers," she said, looking over at him in the bright lights of her bedroom.

"So, what did it mean when you showed me both?" he asked.

"The second dimple, that one is for friends, family, or lovers."

"And what am I?" he asked.

Remi rolled over to face him, both dimples present. "You are all of the above, Max Miller."

He leaned over and kissed her properly. They were in her bed, naked, and they were safe. He was safe. This was absolutely what home felt like.

Chapter Twenty-Four

Max skated out to the net. The crowd went wild as he took the ice, and he allowed himself to look up into the stands of the arena as the national anthem was sung by a local Condors fan. It was a blur. With the lights down low, the starting line standing in unison, the fans on their feet with hats removed, a sense of home, belonging, and family flooded Max.

He was going to miss this.

He closed his eyes and took a deep breath, steadying his shaking body that trembled with nerves, anticipation, and guilt.

Was it wrong of him to take the start knowing there were no guarantees with him? Would his eyes work well enough to make the save? Was it wrong of him to just want one more game, until the clock ran out, until time ran out, and he was forced, prematurely, to hang up his pads and hand over his spot in front of the net to Brown?

One more season was all he needed. He needed to see as much, save as much, and celebrate as much as he could before the small lingering haze in the corners of his vision engulfed him entirely.

The lights came up.

The clock showed fifteen minutes.

Max blinked.

And blinked.

He thought of Remi at home, watching the game, watching him play, and despite the blurred lines on the ice, he managed to smile. Even if hockey seemed like a losing game for him, he found solace in the idea of her. Until now, he never had anything outside these arena lights, cool ice, and face masks designed just for him. Now he had Remi, and she said yes. Yes to everything, and to him that ultimately meant yes to letting him love her, because he was pretty fucking sure she was it for him. She gave him something to work towards, a new goal, a new forever outside the NHL, the Condors, and the Cup. For the first time in his life, his endgame had someone else in it.

The puck dropped, and it was up to the hockey gods now. One save at a time.

He blinked.

And blinked again.

His vision centered, and he watched, with only his periphery blurred, as his captain won the puck and skated towards the San Jose net. The rumble of the crowd's cheers echoed around him, and he wondered if it always sounded this loud. He wondered if it always shook the ice beneath his skates. If he could always feel the intensity of the game but just never noticed because he only ever relied on one of his senses. Now, his body, as if knowing his vision was slipping, was reminding him that there was so much more to depend on.

San Jose regained the puck after a scramble behind their net. Jonathan Pierce, last season's rookie of the year, skated up the ice with Stanos, a Condors defenseman, on his heels. Max readied himself. He could see enough to make the save; he could see what was in front of him and could read the body language enough to know that he needed to drop to his knees. Pierce was known for his "between the legs" goals, and Max wasn't going to let him pull his signature move on him tonight, not when it was a save he knew he was capable of.

He pulled his leg pads together, leaving no space for the puck to enter. The mad dash of players piled into his space and Max dropped his body to cover the puck.

The score remained zero-zero.

The clock still had twelve minutes on it.

It was just the first period.

There was a lot of fucking hockey left to be played.

***

Watching Max play hockey *before* Remi knew what he was up against was nerve-wracking. Watching Max play hockey knowing *everything* he was up against was going to give her a fucking heart attack. She couldn't imagine the pressure he felt to win, to prove himself, and to be able to play one more game.

Nothing was guaranteed for him anymore, and nothing hurt worse than uncertainty.

The puck dropped at the start of the third period, and Remi couldn't take her eyes off Max, no matter where the puck was. She couldn't look away, and she couldn't deny the warmth she felt in the pit of her stomach at the reminder of last night. The weight of his body on top of hers, and the way he took his time with her—her gentle giant, her sweet quiet man, she wanted him to win so he might let her celebrate him tonight.

She would celebrate his wins in front of the net until she had to celebrate him in other ways. The clock ticked down, and she watched as he made save after save, despite his circumstances. He was a fighter. He was brave and good, and he was hers.

A million times, yes.

The game cut to a commercial and Remi opened up her laptop. She used the break in the game to start researching. She pulled up a list of resources for people with loved ones who are going blind. Not another minute of her time would be wasted being uninformed. If she couldn't save his vision, she would prepare for its loss. They would navigate this together, as effortlessly as they could, one day at a time.

Chapter Twenty-Five

The energy in the locker room after the Condor's big win was electric. The start of the season's losses with Max in front of the net meant nothing with the winning streak Brown, Brody, and now Max had continued, putting the Condors in a great place playoff-wise. Max accepted the congratulations of his teammates and tried to avoid the knowing glare Brown was giving him from across the locker room. Brown didn't know exactly what Max was going through, but he knew enough to have his suspicions and worry. Max tried to catch him staring so he could give the young goalie some kind of reassuring smile, but Brown wouldn't have it, he looked away every time.

Maybe Max shouldn't have said anything to his fellow goalie, or maybe, just maybe, he should have said more. Said it all. Come clean. Entrusted his fate to one of his teammates before he dropped the bomb on the whole team. Maybe it would soften the blow?

The time would come for that, but it wasn't tonight, he wasn't ready. Not after a big win. Not when Max had miraculously defied the odds and won the game tonight.

He showered and got dressed to leave. Some of the boys were going out to celebrate, and Max rarely joined them, so it came as no surprise when Max declined their invitation to come along. This time Max had something to look forward to when he got home. He had someone waiting for him, and he couldn't get back to her soon enough.

Pulling out of the parking garage, the contrast from the fluorescent lights to the dark night sky made him strain to make out anything clearly past the hood of his Jeep. His night vision was getting worse with every sundown, just like his dad said it would. He hated that the man who never tried to find him or warn him this was coming had already been so right about all of this.

He took PCH at grandpa speed, staying in the slow lane, allowing any impatient drivers to go around him. It was the new way he had to do things—slowly and cautiously, until he couldn't drive at all anymore.

The streetlights blurred as he drove past, counting them down one by one, just like he had done with the seconds on the clock at tonight's game until he was pulling past the Subaru Outback, he knew to be Remi's that was parked in front of his house.

Entering the house, he was hit with a wave of a newfound familiarity he had only ever dreamed of—the scent of lemon, the sound of music, the rustle of his curtains blowing about, and his back door opened to allow the night breeze to freely enter his home.

Making his way into the living space, his heart raced at the sight of a new pop of color. Sitting on the kitchen island, next to the bowl of fruit, was a plant in a teal clay pot, with a note sitting next to it.

Come down to the water.
I'm waiting.

-Remi

Max slipped off his dress shoes and suit jacket, laying it over the back of the couch. Unbuttoning the top few buttons of his shirt. He made his way down to the beach. The night air was cool with California experiencing more rain than Max could ever recall. Something about the weather felt moody; it only fueled the burning need and desire he had for Remi, and it amplified the lingering adrenaline from the win. It made him feel alive.

He made his way past his back patio and through the small gate that led down to the beach access. He could hardly make out the shape of Remi until he was right there next to her, where she stood to greet him. Snaking her arms around his waist, she welcomed him home in a warm embrace. Instinctually, his arms came up to wrap around her shoulders, pulling her body close to his. Their hearts raced against each other, speaking a language only lovers understood, a pitter-patter of hello, I missed you, and I want you.

Max loved the way she melted into him. There was no stiffness left in her embrace, just her body against his body, and the comfort they both found in that. How could something so new and foreign to him feel so familiar?

He leaned down to kiss the top of her head. "Thank you for the plant. It really livened up the kitchen."

"It's a *congratulations on the big win* plant," she said looking up at him, her smile a closed-mouth one, but the dimple on her left cheek still made an appearance.

"You watched?" he asked.

"Of course."

"It was the longest game of my life," he admitted, guilt teasing the depths of his stomach.

"I imagine they all might feel like that from here on out," she said, her hands soothingly rubbing his lower back.

"I'm struggling with the guilt of it. Of taking the start knowing I don't have the team's best interest at heart."

"Sometimes you have to be selfish, Max. Just for a little bit. Just before it becomes your entire identity."

"And then what?"

"And then you let it go until you have another valid reason to be selfish again."

Max ran a gentle thumb across Remi's jaw, causing her to close her eyes at the simple touch, her smile fading into something heady.

"I want to be selfish with you tonight," he said quietly.

"You don't have to be selfish with me, I'll freely give you anything you want, Max Miller."

"I want to make you feel good," he said, bringing his lips down to meet the delicate skin of her neck, his soft facial hair causing her to giggle as it traced below her jaw.

"I want to make *you* feel good. You deserve the celebration. You played a hard game tonight."

He brought her mouth to his, kissing her for the first time this evening, the taste of her lips sweet and minty against his. Pressing up on tiptoe she deepened the kiss; the friction between them made every part of his body come alive.

Pulling her down to the blanket she had on the sand, he brought her to sit between his legs, both of them facing the ocean. Max was grateful he was still able to make out the white crash of the waves. He never wanted to forget how the moon illuminated the ocean at night, making it seem as if it were glowing in the dark.

Remi settled herself against him, and the heat of her body pressed against his groin made him harden with need for her. He ran a heavy hand over her breasts and then lowered it firmly down her stomach until he was gripping her sex. Remi instinctually let her legs fall apart, making room for him there.

"Is this okay?" he nearly growled into her ear.

"Yes," she hummed.

He firmly pressed his fingers against the cotton fabric of her shorts, grateful she had chosen to wear something simple that allowed him such easy access to her tender parts. Remi allowed her head to fall back against his chest, her eyes closed, and her breaths growing rapidly.

He looked down at her body, loving the advantage he had being so big in comparison to her. He loved his ability to have her in his arms this way, to watch as she bit down on her bottom lip while he slowly brought his hand to the elastic band of her shorts. Her hands gripped his thighs as he pushed below the thin fabric. Looking up, she gave him a smirk when he realized she had no panties on.

"Fuck, Remi, you're so soft. So smooth," he whispered as his fingers grazed her most intimate parts. Teasing her as he trailed a finger along her entrance, he pressed in just enough to feel how wet she was for him, but not giving her what she wanted—not yet, not while he was enjoying watching her come apart in his arms.

"Max," she hummed, and it wasn't a question or a statement. It was just his name on her lips, a whimper, *a plea*.

"You're so beautiful like this," he said, pushing his finger between her soft lips just enough to stroke her clit. Her ass rolled against his erection, making him suck in a deep breath. The ocean was loud in the distance, and he wondered if it would be loud enough to mask the sounds she would make when he made her come.

He ran his hand down her slit again, this time stopping to press a finger deep inside her. The warmth of her made his dick weep to be free, engulfed by the walls of her sex. When she pressed her body up against his hand, he curled his finger firmly inside her, his palm heavy on her clit, creating friction against her most sensitive parts with the strong palm of his hand.

His grip on her was rough and controlled, and he used that strength to make her body tremble. Shifting his hand, he brought his thumb up to massage her clit, pressing in deep circles. The walls of her sex started to grip around his finger, the pulse of her heart seemingly pounding against his palm. She began to cry out in little hums and moans. Her voice was deeper than normal, and her body pressed against his chest as he kept his rhythm, never missing a beat, never switching it up once he found the spot, the pace, and the pressure that made her come undone.

Without warning her knees clasped together tightly, trapping his hand between her legs as she came. Her toes dug into the sand; orgasm footprints would mark this place when they pulled the blanket up to go home.

Max smiled out at the ocean.

Tonight was a good night.

He couldn't understand how he had just found out he was going blind and that his career as a professional athlete was essentially over, and yet somehow, he was managing to feel the most alive and complete he had ever felt in his lifetime.

Sometimes, he thought, *it took losing something to see what you had right in front of you the whole time.*

"I don't think I'll be able to walk back to the house after that, *sir*," Remi teased, her eyes still closed and her hands still gripping his thighs.

"I'll carry you," Max offered, causing Remi to smile one of her effortless smiles—even in the dark, it felt like sunshine when she looked at him that way.

"I can't believe we just did that on the beach." She laughed.

"No one ever comes out here. It's pretty sad really. We all pay for these beachfront homes and these views, and none of us appreciate it. I know I sure as hell didn't appreciate it until recently."

"Hummus always helps people see the beauty of things."

"You call it hummus, I call it good company," he said.

Remi sat up and turned to face him. Her legs wrapped around him as she leaned in to kiss him, the smile on his face causing his end of the kiss to feel a little stiff, but for good reason.

"You know, I think you're getting pretty good at this talking stuff," she said.

"Thank god, because I'm trying really fucking hard," he admitted.

"I don't think you were ever bad at it, not with me anyway."

"I guess I just needed someone to feel safe with," he said, leaning down to place a kiss on the top of her head.

Remi leaned back and looked around, taking in the vastness of the ocean and the infinite stretch of sand.

"What do you see? Tell me," Max said, because truth be told, he couldn't make out anything past the blanket, his night vision loss seemingly the worst part about retinitis pigmentosa so far.

"Nothing worth looking at besides you," she said, leaning in to kiss his lips gently. "Close your eyes," she said sweetly.

"Why, I can hardly see as it is," he teased, causing Remi to laugh while shaking her head in disbelief. "What? Too soon?" he asked.

"Listen, *I'm* definitely not ready to make vision jokes, but knock yourself out, big guy. Whatever helps."

Max smiled and scrunched up his nose before doing as she asked by closing his eyes.

He felt her breath on his lips first, and then the gentle graze of her tongue along his bottom lip, his body shivering at the simple sensation.

Then, the tip of her nose gently ran along his jawline, pressing against his beard, causing his body to cover in goosebumps.

Her fingers gently rose into his hairline, starting with a delicate touch before quickly turning into a firm grip, pulling his head back.

His body was overwhelmed with sensation, and then it dawned on him, he could feel all of these wonderful things with his eyes closed.

He was going to be okay.

This was going to be okay.

His eyes shot open, finding Remi's deep blues intent on him, her eyes just as wild as his. "I want you," he said.

"Here?" she asked, slight panic lining her face as she scanned the beach again.

"Here," he said.

"Are you sure no one comes out at night?" she asked.

"I mean there's always a possibility," he said, because he couldn't lie.

"Your career would be over," she said.

Reaching down, he pulled her cotton shorts to the side exposing her. "It already is. I might as well enjoy the boat ride if the ship is going to sink anyway."

Remi scanned the beach again for good measure, then grabbed his hand and placed it on her chest "Feel that? My heart is pounding."

And it was.

Max took her hand and placed it on his dick. "Feel that? So is my need for you."

Remi's face lit up with a wild smile. Her hands frantically undid his belt and his zipper, tugging his suit pants down as much as she could with the weight of his body holding them in place. Max, seeing her struggle to undress him, pushed his body up with her still sitting on his lap, and with one hand managed to maneuver his pants and briefs just low enough to free his cock.

"I can't believe we're about to fuck on the beach," Remi laughed.

"Not long ago, I was nervous to share a bottle of lemonade with you in this same exact spot, now look at us. Look how far we've come," he teased.

Remi lifted herself to straddle him, her knees pressing into the blanket on the sand, her hips hovering above him as Max took his hard length in one hand and held it ready for her. Remi wiggled her hips, teasing against his tip before slowly easing all the way down, taking him deep with the weight of her body.

"Fuck," he said, biting his lip.

"I know," she agreed, her head falling back, "your dick is my favorite thing ever."

"No, I meant, *fuck*, fuck. No protection," he said, realizing in their idiotic lust-filled moment that they had forgotten how important that particular step was.

"Oh. Fuck," she said, agreeing.

"I hate how good this feels, Rem," he said, looking down at their bodies locked together.

"I don't. I know I should, but I don't. Yes, to everything, Max. And right now, yes to me fucking you on the beach. We'll sort out the bad choices later. Right now, we're already this far in, let's enjoy it."

Max didn't waste another second with worry. He gripped her waist and raised her off his dick to the tip before letting her slide back down.

The stretch of her around his girth was enough to cause his heart to miss a beat.

He lifted her again, this time meeting her as she came down with a quick thrust of his own. Remi winced as he hit her deep inside, but that didn't stop her from taking him again and again. She wrapped her arms around his shoulders, using him as leverage as she began to move her body, taking him to the hilt, then sliding up. Rolling her hips with each thrust, his strong hands helped to guide her, lift her, pressing her hard against him.

"This feels way too good," Max said through gritted teeth, his hands both gripping her ass while also keeping her cotton shorts pulled to the side as Remi took over completely. She worked her body expertly; thrusting, rolling, and those sounds she made—he wouldn't last much longer.

Heavy, steady moans escaped her as her rhythmic movements halted, and her body stiffened. She clenched onto his shoulders; her sex pulsing around him.

"I'm sorry," she apologized in a whimper, her face buried in his neck. "I can't move, I'm coming so hard."

The way her body tensed around him, trembling with release as she held onto him with all her strength, he lost it completely. If she couldn't move, he would have to take over. He lifted her off his dick, then pressed her down into his lap forcefully as his hips pushed up against hers. Lifting her body one last time, he thrusted up into her, holding her tight against him as he came harder than he had ever experienced before.

Remi's head crashed into his shoulder, their breathing erratic from the sex, the thrill, and the wild abandon they had both just displayed. Not smart by any means, but so fucking worth it. Max had never felt so wild and alive.

He pulled the sides of the blanket up to wrap around his naked ass, and to cover Remi as she lifted herself from his lap, his come deep inside her. A situation he had never put himself in before, possibly problematic, and yet it made his heart race with a weird sense of pride, to be in her that way. Raw. Real. His. She was his, and he wanted her this way for the rest of his life.

"Maybe we should head back to the house," he said, trailing kisses along her shoulder.

"Yeah, maybe we shouldn't stay out here and push our luck," she agreed, looking around with a dubious smile on her face. The fear of being caught was over. They had done it, they had sex on the beach, and neither of them was headed to jail for indecent exposure—another win for the books tonight.

Remi stood, her shorts stretched out around her thighs. His dick stirred at the sight of her like this and thoughts of his orgasm dripping from her as she walked across the beach made him crazy with lust. As if knowing his very thoughts, she sarcastically rolled her eyes at him.

"I'll need a shower," she said, leaning down to pick up the blanket.

"Me too, I think I might have some sand in my ass," he joked. "I'll start one for you when we get home."

Home. It fell from his lips with ease. He didn't know if she planned to stay, but he would have her if she would.

Max gripped the other end of the blanket, taking it in his hands like he had that first day on the beach after their picnic. As if on cue, they both walked together, bringing the ends of the sandy blanket to meet up, chest to chest. Max thought of how he wanted to kiss her the first time they did this, and how he wasn't sure if she wanted to be kissed by a man like him.

Without hesitation, he leaned in, and her lips met him there with no uncertainty, no unknowns, no what-ifs.

He kissed her with confidence backing it, because he could, and because she wanted him to. It was nice to be so certain of one thing when the rest of his life was spiraling into the great unknown.

Chapter Twenty-Six

"**O**kay, boys. Listen up. As we head into the holidays, we have advantages and disadvantages. The holiday break in December means we get to see our families, have a few days to relax, fuck your girls, fuck your wives, hell, fuck yourself," Carter said with a smug grin to his team after a quick practice in Colorado. The boys were amped up at the mention of getting their dicks wet, and Max found himself unable to deny the strain he felt in his cup at the mention of it as well. Seeing Remi and spending different holidays with her made him excited, it was uncharted water for him.

This road trip had been especially hard on the entire team with the Condors losing Levi Holland, the team's top goal scorer this season, to an upper-body injury from a bad cross-check by Sergey Petrov, an asshole defenseman who played for Seattle.

The captain went on after they all settled down. "We have a lot of hockey left to play before Christmas, so we need to keep our heads in the game. Next week is Thanksgiving and we all know what they say, if you're not sitting in a playoff spot by Thanksgiving, your chances are not as high. Right now, I think we're sitting pretty if we can keep playing our game and not get distracted." His eyes roamed over the team, landing on a few players who were known to party a little too hard. "If we keep taking chances," he said as his eyes fell on Marks, a rookie who had a four-game point streak, "and, if we stay healthy." His eyes then fell on Max, and Max's gaze fell to the ground; all the while, he could feel Brown glaring at him from across the locker room.

"Our advantage is that we're playing good fucking hockey lately, boys. Our disadvantage is that so is everyone else. We're all pushing to clinch a playoff spot. We're also all ready for the Holiday break, but we don't take a break until we win that fucking Cup, you hear me?" he said, his voice growing louder, more intense as the team began to bang their lockers with sturdy fists as they agreed with their well-respected captain.

"Get some sleep tonight. Colorado may be on fire, but *we're* taking the two points tomorrow," he said, ending his little speech by patting Brown, who was sitting on the bench next to him, on the shoulder.

Max looked over at Brown, waiting for him to make eye contact. Things had been weird since their little talk. Brown avoided looking at Max as he began to strip down from his pads, and Max knew the only way he was going to get the chance to have a much-needed talk with his fellow goalie was to get him alone. Lucky for Max, with Brody being sent back down to the minors, it left them rooming together tonight in Colorado.

When Max got back to the hotel after the team's practice skate, he stopped by the small convenience store to grab two tall cans of beer, way too many random bags of candy, and a bag of classic Doritos. It was a peace offering of junk food and a hope that Brown would hear him out and agree to keep his secret until Max was ready to tell the team.

In hopes that Brown would *carry* his secret while Max still had time left.

Normality left.

Vision left.

Hockey left in him.

Max knocked on the door before entering, waiting for Brown to give him the all-clear to come in. It wasn't a rule on the road, but it was common courtesy. After weeks of being away from loved ones, girlfriends, wives, and secret lovers, it wasn't unheard of for the guys to make a quick phone call or FaceTime or to even have a visitor over to the hotel room to help "relieve" some road stress.

"Come in," Brown shouted, giving Max the okay to enter. When he did, he found Brown facing the opposite direction, talking on the phone under his breath. "Yeah, I know," he said, "but if I get picked, I have to play babe. It's the all-star game, you don't get a choice."

Max ran a hand along the wall as he made his way to his bed, his eyes struggling to adjust to the dim lighting of the hotel room.

"Okay, babe. Yeah," Brown went on, "I'll let you know how it goes. I love you too. Bye."

Max took a seat on his bed and waited for Brown to acknowledge him.

He wasn't good at this sort of thing, at talking, at starting conversations, and yet, here he was, in the same room as his friend and teammate, trying. While he knew what he needed to say, old habits die hard, and the words didn't come, as they often didn't for Max.

He cracked open a beer and took a long drink, causing Brown to turn and face him.

"You bring me one?" he asked, his face uncertain, but Max was grateful the young player was the one to break the ice.

"I did." Max reached into the bag and pulled out the other tall can.

"Busch?" Brown asked.

"Listen, it wasn't a beer garden down there."

Brown smiled, this made Max relax just enough to hold out the bag of junk food. "I brought snacks."

"Why?" Brown asked, but not without reaching for the bag and sifting through the obnoxious amount of candy.

"Because I thought it might help me say what I have to say."

Brown shook his head. "Do I even want to know?"

"No. You probably won't like it, and I'll be asking you to keep it a secret from our team, so there's that."

"Then don't say it, Miller. That last talk we had got in my head, and it fucked with me. I feel like I'm keeping this big secret already, only, I don't know what the secret is. It's fucked up, man. It's fucked because I know something isn't right. I know you; I know your game. I know the way you play, skate, and make saves, and something isn't *right*, Max."

Max took the bag of snacks from Brown after he settled on a bag of sour candy.

"Your thoughts are valid," Max offered.

"Then what is it? Why do I feel like you're about to tell me you're leaving the Condors? Did you get a better offer for your bridge contract? Is it Coach? Was it the start of the season? Everyone has a few off games," the young goalie argued.

"It wasn't just a bad start to the season, Jack, and you know it. I'm pushing dirt around out there, and I know *you* see it because you just said so yourself."

"Yeah, but you're still making the save."

"*Some* saves, Jack."

"You can't expect to save them all," his fellow goalie argued.

"But it's getting harder and harder. Every game feels like my last," Max said, his voice trailing off.

"But you're making saves, *some* saves. We're winning. We're on track for the playoffs," Brown argued.

"This is all true, but it's not *if* I'm making the saves, it's *how* I'm making them. *And* for how long? I don't know, man. It's not good."

Brown brought his hands anxiously through his hair, his face distressed. "The candy, it's not making this any easier by the way."

"I know," Max agreed. "It was a stupid idea."

"So, rip the Band-Aid off, Miller. Spill the beans."

Max ran nervous hands over his sweatpants and his knee began to bounce. Words were what he always thought would end him, and now, he knew they might be all he had left one day.

"I went to a doctor," he said, then specified, "an eye doctor, outside of the NHL."

"Why?" Brown asked, and it was a question laced with so many different variations of that simple word. Why? Why an eye doctor? Why not the team doctor? Why are you telling me this? *Why.*

"Over the summer, I started to notice some drastic changes in my vision. At night, mostly, and now, looking back, it's been my whole life really. I was just living in denial—"

Brown cut him off. "Yeah, because you're getting old. You can get Lasik, you're a fucking millionaire."

"That's what I thought too, but it started to progressively get worse, and then it was time for the pre-season, and I was panicking. It was getting to a point where seeing the puck was hard. I didn't want to see a doctor out of fear that he might tell me my worst-case scenario, but *not* knowing what was wrong was messing me up in front of the net almost as much as not being able to see."

"But you were just in your head. Anxiety can make your vision blurry, man. I know. I've had that happen to me before in college."

"I wish I could say it was that, that it's just my vision getting worse with age. That a quick surgery, a pill, or some glasses would solve all my problems."

"But?" Brown asked.

"But that's not the case... *my* case anyway. The eye doctor saw something bad; he wants me to see a specialist to confirm his suspicions."

"So, you're not sure then, right? You still need to see the specialist to confirm what he said? He could be wrong, Max."

"No. He's not wrong. I talked to my dad on the phone," Max said.

"No way. How'd that go?"

Max cleared his throat, then went on. "As good as it could have gone considering he told me he's blind and that I will most likely be too one day."

Brown cracked open his beer and took a long swig, and Max did the same. They both took a second to process. It would have been an awkward silence, but this was two goalies; things were bound to be weird from time to time, it was in their DNA after all.

Max took another drink.

Brown spun the silver tab on the can over and over.

"So, what does that mean? What does him being blind have to do with you? What makes *your* situation so different from anyone else with vision loss? Why can't you just get contacts or something?"

"Because," Max said, "I seem to have inherited a disease from him, one that will inevitably make me go blind."

"And you're sure there's nothing you can do to stop this from happening? I mean, modern medicine is wild. There have to be other options."

"The only thing I can do is prepare for it. That's why I'm telling you," Max said.

"And then what? What happens next?" Brown asked.

"I have to tell the team that this is my last year."

Brown stopped fidgeting with the beer can.

Max placed his hand on his knee to steady it.

"When do you plan to do this?" Brown asked.

Max bit at his bottom lip, his red beard longer than normal and in desperate need of a trim.

"When I *stop* making the saves," Max said, his voice shaky, his words cracked and laced with a sad underlying certainty that this day would come, and it would be sooner than later.

"And what am I supposed to do with this information?" Jack asked. Max thought he sounded hurt, or confused, and Max could handle those things, he could handle anything as long as it wasn't pity.

"Be ready," Max said.

"Be ready for what?" he asked.

"Be ready to take my place when I can't stop the puck anymore."

Chapter Twenty-Seven

It had already been a long day, with three houses cleaned, two call-offs, and her phone reminding her it was time to check in on Mrs. Keller. Not to mention Max had been out on the road, and every time he took the ice and got the start over the Condor's backup goalie, Remi felt her stomach drop with nerves for him. She knew he could still play, and still win at this point, but that didn't stop her from holding her breath each time the other team skated the puck up the ice and took the shot.

He had lost a few games and won a few.

He had even warmed the bench a few times as well.

Knowing what she knew now, about his vision, she couldn't seem to watch him play without thinking about his future with the NHL. Worst-case scenarios of what that would look like for him emotionally, mentally, and physically constantly played on a loop in her head. Max had a long road ahead of him, and Remi was ready to put all the miles on her body walking that road beside him, hand in hand, no matter what happened.

"You're here early," Mrs. Keller said, opening the door for Remi to enter with her cleaning cart. The smell of something putrid hit Remi's nose the second she crossed the threshold into the small, stuffy apartment, and while she had cleaned the apartment many times before, something about being there today brought on an overwhelming feeling of dread.

She was probably just tired. On top of everything, she missed Max, and knowing he got back into town today only made this job seem harder. She couldn't wait to be home and showered, but most of all, she couldn't wait for the beautiful crash that came when she fell into Max's arms to sleep.

"I don't think so, Mrs. Keller. In fact, I'm late," she said with a forced smile as she took in the state of the apartment. It had only been two weeks since she last cleaned, and it was absolutely trashed.

"No, no. You're early. It's seven. You never come this early. You're lucky I'm awake," Mrs. Keller argued, and at first, Remi thought she was referring to going to bed for the night, but then, Remi really looked at Mrs. Keller, and it was obvious the woman was not okay.

"Mrs. Keller, its *7 p.m.* It's evening," she said slowly and kindly, as if talking to a fragile child.

Mrs. Keller paced the small square of carpet that wasn't covered with trash, laundry, and debris. Remi pushed boxes aside with her foot and very gently placed a hand on Mrs. Keller's arm, still managing to startle the old woman. "Mrs. Keller, are you feeling okay?"

"Oh, I was just going to watch my program on the TV, but you're more than welcome to stay and watch it with me," the old woman said through glazed eyes. Her lips looked parched and cracked in the corners.

"Mrs. Keller, it's Remi, your housekeeper."

The older woman ignored her, looking right through her as she sat down on the only livable space left on the small sofa. "Just set it on the table and go," the confused old woman said, making no sense.

Remi felt panic flood her. Something was wrong. She looked around the small apartment for anything amiss, aside from the normal chaos. It was a mess, but it was always a mess. It wasn't any worse than Remi had seen it in the past.

Her phone buzzed in her pocket, and she pulled it out to see Max calling.

"Hey," she said in a panic, answering the phone quickly.

"Hey, is everything okay?" he asked, taking notice of the worry in her tone.

"No, it's Susan—Mrs. Keller," she corrected, she never called her by her first name.

"What's wrong? Do you need me to come there?" he asked.

"Yes… no… I don't know. Max, she's like, *gone*," Remi whispered, instantly regretting her word choice.

"Oh shit, she's dead?" Max asked.

"No, she's like," Remi said as she stepped into the kitchen, never taking her eyes off Mrs. Keller, "it's as if she's lost her mind? I don't know. She's not aware of what's going on. It's scary. I'm worried about her, and I don't know what to do, Max."

"Does she have any emergency contacts?" he asked, and Remi wanted to praise his sound and logical mind in her moment of panic.

"Yes, I have her son's number, but he's not the best."

Mrs. Keller just sat there, watching TV, as if Remi weren't in her apartment at all.

"Okay, call him first, give him an opportunity to come get her. If he can't help, you're going to have to call an ambulance."

"Okay."

"Send me the address, so I can come be with you."

"Yeah, yeah," she said.

"And Rem?"

"Yeah?"

"If you're in danger at all, I want you to leave and go wait in your car. I'll be there as soon as I can."

"Okay," she said absentmindedly.

"Okay. I'll see you soon."

Max hung up first and she sent the address right away.

"Mrs. Keller," Remi said from the kitchen, receiving no response. "Mrs. Keller I'm going to call your son, okay?"

The older woman looked up at her this time, with complete peace on her oblivious face. "Yes, tell him dinner will be ready at five."

***

It was the first time Max had really felt the weight of his condition affect him negatively outside of hockey, past a minor inconvenience here or there. Driving slow at night wasn't bad, until you were trying to get somewhere fast. His head spun with worst-case scenarios. He hated the thought that Remi was alone in a scary situation, and he couldn't drive past 35 fucking miles-per-hour to get to her. Sweat gathered on his upper lip, and his heart hammered in his chest, anxiety flooding his body from head to toe. He kept driving, slowly, steadily, and blinking repeatedly. It was like a nightmare where the bad guy is chasing you and you can't run because your legs feel like they weigh a million pounds, only this was real life. This was his reality.

When he finally pulled into the small apartment complex, he spotted Remi's car immediately, but she wasn't inside, to his relief. He opened the text she sent with the apartment number and bolted up the stairs to the woman's apartment. The door was propped open, and the smell of hot trash hit his nose before he knocked on the door frame, not wanting to barge in.

Remi appeared from a room off the narrow hallway, her hair tied up on her head, wearing rubber gloves that came up to her elbows. Max hated the look on her face, it reminded him of the night she found him drunk. It reminded him of the way she looked when she returned from the beach. He hated that he had made her feel like this before.

"Tell me how I can help you?" he asked, taking a step into the trash-covered apartment, no sign of Mrs. Keller to be seen.

Remi stood before him, her hip popped out and her body obviously exhausted, with dark circles under her eyes as she looked around. And then, without a word, she pulled out a trash bag and a spare pair of rubber gloves from her cleaning cart and handed them to him. Max knew what she was asking without saying anything at all. He pulled on the gloves—a tight fit for his massive hands—and then he got to work. Anything that looked like trash, he added to the bag, as Remi wiped down countertops and scrubbed burnt food and a melted bowl from the metal coils of the stove.

Max moved on to sweep, and sweeping led to the mop, and then the vacuum. With each space freed of its litter, he felt hope swell in his chest and the anxiety of his drive melt away. He watched his girlfriend come back to life as the small apartment became livable again, breathable again, and safe.

Very few words were shared, and yet they both completely understood what needed to be done.

Max was never good with words, and Remi had already carried the conversation for them both so many times since he'd met her. But now, in their silence, he was grateful they felt safe enough to not say anything when the words were too heavy for them both to carry.

He loaded her cleaning cart into the back of her Subaru as she locked up Mrs. Keller's apartment behind her.

"Thank you for showing up to help," she said, leaning her body against the driver's side door.

"You're welcome."

"They took her away in an ambulance. She was so scared, Max."

"I'm sorry you had to see that. I'm sorry you had to be the one to find her in that state," he said, guilt from the other night flooding him, knowing she had also just found *him* in a scary situation.

"I just want to forget about it for a while, is that awful of me?" she asked.

"No. If you need to protect yourself right now, I say sweep it under the rug and come back to it later."

This made Remi smile. "Do I sense cleaning lady humor embedded in that last statement?" she asked.

"I've been known to have a pun or two up my sleeve," he said, offering her the most welcoming smile he had.

"I want to hug you so bad right meow," she said, a tired smile on her face and a speck of dirt above her eyebrow.

Max smiled and her cat joke, which had become a secret language of sorts between them. It was their own way of saying, *I'm yours*, and *I'm safe with you*. Max moved toward her without a second thought, pulling her into his arms. She tried to push away, but he just held her closer, his physical strength winning this round.

"Max, I'm so filthy," she protested.

"So am I," he said quietly.

She looked up at him and smiled. "This is the most disgusting hug of my life."

"The absolute worst," he teased.

"You stink," she said.

"So do you."

They both began to laugh and Max, despite the smudge across her forehead, leaned in and kissed her there.

"My place or yours?" he asked.

"Mine? I need to feed Bozo."

"Okay, your place it is. Let me grab my bag from the jeep."

Remi's eyebrows quirked up in question.

"I don't think I should drive at night anymore, Rem," he admitted, his smile faltering at the admission. It was the first thing he knew he officially had to give up.

She fell into his arms. "Oh, Max, I'm so sorry. Was the drive here bad?"

"Pretty bad. I don't want to risk it anymore. I kinda knew it was coming to this."

She pushed up on tiptoe and kissed his lips with affection and care. "I can bring you to get your Jeep tomorrow."

"Sounds like a plan."

"Now, let's get home so we can shower away this awful day."

And it had been an awful day. The Condors had lost in Colorado with Max in front of the net, and Remi had walked into a nightmare at work. While her shower was so small he wasn't sure how the two of them would fit, they would make it work because there was no way in hell he was going to let her wash away the sins of her day alone.

Chapter Twenty-Eight

R emi started the shower for her and Max, and piece by piece their clothing fell to the floor. The remnants of their day would be washed away down the drain.

She stepped into the shower first, holding out her hand to welcome Max to join her. It was a tight fit, but she didn't care. She wanted to be close to him. She *needed* to be close to him. The hot spray pushed his perfectly styled red hair back on his head, and she never knew someone could be so beautiful when wet.

Reaching for the bar of soap, she began to lather it in her hands. "Let me," he said, taking it from her, working it between his calloused palms.

Remi tilted her head back in the small space as he brought his soap-covered hands to her neck, lathering her skin while he pressed firm fingers against her sore muscles. Trailing his fingers down her breastbone, he stopped to lather soap over her sensitive nipples. As he ran the suds on his fingertips under her arms, she slowly began to lift them above her head, making room for him to wash everything away. His hands moved up her body, from the heaviness of her ass to the very tips of her fingers, and then back down, making her giggle as his knuckles slid across her more sensitive parts.

As the spray from the shower washed away the soap, Max lathered his hands again, this time bringing them to cover her back, stopping to admire the shape of her body, her ass, her thighs, and the soft smooth skin between her legs.

"Give it here," Remi said, taking the soap from him. "Let me get you now." She turned Max's body to face away from her and reached around him in a hug, washing him from behind. Her hands swept over his defined abs, brushing over the soft trail of red chest hair that led to his already hard length. Sliding her soap-covered hand over him, she gave him a long, slow stroke. His hand met hers there and encouraged her to keep going. Gripping her hand with his they began to stroke him with slow and sure movements.

She let her hand glide over his length with the help of his still wrapped around hers, the soap easing the movement while her head lay against his back. As she brought him closer to orgasm, she could feel his muscles begin to tighten against her face. Max, pulling his hand away from hers, turned back to face her, pressing his erection against her lower belly. She lathered her hands with soap again and brought them back to finish what she had started. Pushing her hands between their bodies, she stroked him with a firm touch. The thickness of his erection made her ache to feel him inside her.

"Rem," he moaned, the water dripping from his beard. His eyes closed as his head fell forward while she stroked him quicker, her hands gripping him tight.

"*Come*," she said, and it wasn't an offer, it was a demand. She wanted to watch as his beautiful pink cock spilled his release.

Max's body fell back against the cool shower tiles as he came in Remi's small hands. His eyes closed tight, and every muscle in his beautiful body was on display, the tally marks on his ribs contracting with each of his heavy sighs. *This*, she thought, was not a loss. This kind of comfort, this kind of intimacy. The act of cleaning one off, only to make a mess again. It felt like a win.

Right now, this tiny shower stall was *their* sanctuary. Together they had entered this porcelain alter dirty, and together they would leave cleansed of their day's iniquities naked and alive.

***

Max settled into Remi's full bed for the night, appreciating the way the size of it made their bodies instantly draw close together with no room to move away. Their warm, naked skin from the shower was cooled by the inviting pale green sheets and lightweight blanket.

"Do you want to talk about the game?" Remi asked, her head on his chest, her fingers tracing over the fine black lines on his ribs.

"We lost." It was all he said because it was hard to focus on anything else with her legs tangled around his and the idea that all he had to do was pull her body onto his to slip between her thighs.

"Well, *yeah*. I know that part. But do you want to *talk* about it?" she pressed.

Max let out a heavy sigh. He knew talking about the loss would help, but that didn't make it easy to do. He had promised her he would open up and stop taking the easy way out of these hard conversations, and he would keep his word.

"We lost, and it was equal parts *my*—" He still wasn't sure what he was calling it, so he landed on, "My *eye* issue, and equal parts anxiety. The lights came up, and I knew we needed the two points. In the back of my head, I knew Brown should have had the start, because my morning skate was bad, Remi, like, *really* fucking bad. The mix of my vision failing, and the fucking guilt I get when I take the start; I was fighting a battle against my vision and my nerves and the pressure to win. Not to mention the night before, I told Brown what was going on with me. So, I had that going on too. It was just a lot to carry."

Remi sat up on her elbow to look at him. "You told Brown?"

"Yeah, I told him about what's going on," he said again.

"Do you think he'll tell your coach?"

"No. But, Rem, I'm going to have to talk eventually. I can't keep playing like this, the weight of it is too heavy. I feel like my chest is caving in 99 percent of the time I'm on the ice."

"So, what's your game plan?"

"I want to play through January if I can. And then, I'll see the team doctor."

Remi leaned down and pressed a gentle kiss right over his heart.

"That's a good plan."

"Yeah?" he asked.

"Yeah, it's—" she said, pausing for effect, and smiling before finishing, "purrrrfect."

Max pulled her up to his mouth and kissed her, their lips starting slow with soft pulls and teasing caresses, their tongues delicately meeting. Her body pushed closer to his, causing the heat of their want for each other to warm their skin, both of them knowing exactly where this would lead.

Max broke the kiss and looked down at her, her eyes somehow managing to be a vibrant shade of blue, even in the darkness of her room. "Remi," he said, "I know I'm not great at saying what I'm feeling,"

"Then let me say it first," she offered, the smile on her face knowing, if not a little cocky.

"Okay, say it then," he challenged, opting for the easy way out, curiosity getting the better of him.

"Max Miller," she said.

"Yes?"

"*You* are in love with me."

They both burst out laughing. The kind of laugh that starts in your stomach and rolls its way up to your throat in a punishing burst of joy.

He brought his finger up to her nose. "Ding-ding-ding," he said with each pressing boop.

"And?" she asked.

"Well, I think you might love me too?" he asked.

"You think?" she said sitting up to straddle him, pushing his massive arms above his head. "You *think*?"

Max loved her power, her confidence, and her ability to lay him out below her and have her way.

"Ok, I don't *think*." He paused, before taking a deep breath and announcing with certainty, "Remi Davis, *you* are in love with me."

"You're damn right I am," she said, leaning in to kiss him the way two people kissed when they had just admitted their love for one another. The kind of kiss that left lips swollen, necks covered in purple marks of passion, and fingerprints on wrists, hips, and thighs in the act of being too rough, too excited, leaving no room for second guesses.

It was Remi lowering herself onto him.

It was Max letting her be in control.

It was Remi rolling her hips against his body as she held his arms in place.

It was Max submitting to the woman he loved, to show her that he would, while also needing her to know that he could be in charge too.

He flipped her over in one swift movement, using the weight of his body to thrust deep inside of her. Pulling her legs up with a punishing grip on her ankles, he spread her wide open as he pumped into her with no refrain. Remi braced her hands on the headboard as he fucked her good and hard.

The sounds in the room were raw. Skin slapping against skin. Uncontrolled breathing. Heavy moans. Mumbled words: *right there, oh fuck, Max, Max, Max.*

With one final push, Remi called out his name, her body trembling around him, her fists clenched tight as he came deep inside her.

Chapter Twenty-Nine

Max awoke to the distant sound of the ocean outside Remi's window and her voice carrying from another room. He found his sweat suit from yesterday cleaned and neatly folded at the end of the bed. Making his way to her kitchen, he caught the tail end of her phone conversation.

"Ok, thanks for keeping me up to date. I hope you find the right care for her. Okay, thanks, you too... Bye."

Remi was sitting at her small dining room table wearing nothing but an oversized t-shirt with a skull on the front; maybe a band logo of sorts, Max couldn't be sure. Her smile perked up at the sight of him, his bare chest, his joggers hugging his thighs, and his feet cold on the old beach house's wooden floors.

He leaned down to kiss the top of her head and her arms effortlessly wrapped around his waist. "Good morning," he said to the woman he loved.

She looked up at him, her arms still wrapped around his lower half. "Good morning. Do you want coffee? It's the worst coffee on the planet, but it's what I grew up drinking, and old habits die hard, ya know?"

She went to stand to get his coffee, but Max pressed her back down to her seat. "I can get it," he said, making himself at home and feeling proud of how naturally he took up space in someone else's kitchen. There had been billet homes he lived in for months and months where he never once felt safe enough, or welcomed enough, to serve himself there.

He took the seat across from her at the tiny two-person table that was pressed up against the open window, the chill of November adding an element of laziness to the day. "How's Mrs. Keller doing?" he asked, assuming the bit of the phone call he heard was about her.

"She has dementia. I don't know how I didn't see the signs before, but now that her son confirmed it, it all makes sense. I guess last night was a really bad episode. He feels like it's time to move her into a facility that can take care of her."

"How does that make you feel?" Max asked, sipping the bitter coffee.

"Sad. I just want to save them all, you know? All the lost souls, the people like me and my mom who society gave up on. I want to rescue them from their personal hell, their mental illness, their loneliness. I want to save them so badly, and I know I can't."

"Hey, you do save them—one house cleaning at a time. That might be the only safe place they have in their lifetime. That moment you give them, even if they're just going to mess it up again, and again, and again... you give them that peace. Even if it's short-lived."

She reached across the table and ran her fingers over his knuckles, a few of which were busted. "Thanks again, for helping me last night," she said softly.

"It felt good to help you. Lately, I wonder what my life will look like when I'm unable to do the thing I've built my entire identity around. And I worry I won't know how to fill that space, or how to be fulfilled.

But last night was a huge eye-opener for me—no pun intended." This made Remi laugh, and honestly, it was nice being able to joke about it all with her. If he couldn't laugh about it, he feared it might consume him completely, essentially breaking him.

"How so?" she asked.

"I guess I got to see how important you are to so many people. You come in and you clean people's homes. Some of us pay you to do it, but you do it for some of these people for free, like Mrs. Keller, out of the kindness of your heart. Some of your clients are just too lazy to clean their own homes, and some of them are entitled, like me, but some of these strangers that you help actually *need* you, and you show up for them, no questions asked. You help them because you have a good heart, Remi. Not a lot of people have that kind of purpose. Not many people are as quick as you are to give back. I guess it just helped me see that there is no task, no job, no deed too small. You give me hope that when I'm done with hockey, when my eyes won't allow it anymore, that I might be able to find my purpose in something much bigger than being a professional athlete. I might be able to find some way to really give back."

Remi got up, tears filling her eyes as she took her place in his lap. Straddling him in the small, rickety chair, he feared it might break under the weight of them, but it wouldn't stop him from wrapping his arms around her to keep her there.

"I think you'll find your purpose, Max. I think your story will be one they talk about for ages. You *know* you have this platform and this spotlight, and I can see you using it for good. I know that you will bring this unfortunate circumstance from darkness to light in the most beautiful way. And I, for one, cannot wait to see the way you change the world, Max Miller."

She eased her hand down the plane of his chest, over the black inked lines, her eyes heavy with contemplation.

"What is it?" he asked.

"It's just, I think it's time you stop counting your losses and started celebrating your wins."

"It seems silly now, all these immortalized reminders of each game I've lost. Had I known then, what I know now, I might have focused more on what really mattered, and less on forgetting what didn't."

"And what would that have looked like for you? If you hadn't done this?" she asked, her fingers trailing over the small black slashes covering his bare skin.

"I would have stopped watching the clock countdown to game over and tried harder to enjoy the seconds I had left in the moment. In my team's wins, and even their losses, the celebrations, the friendships, and just life in general. I've spent my whole life waiting for the final minute to be up, and now it's too late. I'm out of time."

"You're not out of time, Max. You just need to reset the clock."

Max pulled her body into his. Her sweet coffee-hinted lips pressed against his, and he kissed her. He kissed her like this moment was theirs because it really was. He was finally done counting down to his end and ready to start living in his now.

Chapter Thirty

Remi pulled her bleach-covered gloves from her hands and placed them in the bathroom sink to answer her phone, knowing Max would be finished with his early morning practice. She had been waiting for the call. Lately, she felt like she was always waiting for *this* call, it had become a part of her life over the past few weeks. The moment she picked up his call she would know the answer to the million-dollar question from the tone of his voice alone: Would Max Miller get the start in front of the net?

"Hey, how was practice?" she asked on pickup.

He sighed. "Not great."

"That's okay. Everyone has off days," she said, offering up optimism in a hopeless situation.

He laughed on the other line, and it sounded out of character for Max: cruel and annoyed.

"An off day is being overly tired despite going to bed early, struggling to focus, or something. I'm not having an off day, I'm going fucking blind, Remi, there's a big difference. No one else is having a few days off that will ultimately lead to an entire *life* off," he said, his tone snippy and harsh, catching her off guard.

"*Hey*, don't do that," she said gently, trying her best not to poke the bear. He was *her* bear, her big cuddly, redheaded bear, who was evidently not handling his situation well tonight—which was to be expected from time to time considering.

"Don't do what? Don't be mad that I'm going fucking blind at twenty-six? Don't be mad that my team is set to make the playoffs and I'm the number one thing that could stop them? Don't be mad that I gave up my entire adolescence training for this sport, only to have it ripped away from me by genetics passed down from a man who has never spent a day of his life trying to be my father? I'm mad, Remi. I'm mad as hell."

She could hear his heavy and erratic breathing on the line.

Remaining silent for a moment, she let him sit with his words. They were good words for a man who at times, didn't have any.

And then she spoke.

"You done?" she asked.

"No," he snapped.

"Okay then. Say whatever else it is you need to say. Yell, scream, cry, then start your Jeep, and drive home safely. I'll meet you there when I'm done cleaning for the day. We can eat good food and go down to the beach and do something fun. Will it still suck that you're not getting the start? Yes, it will absolutely suck. But we can, at the very least, try and take your mind off of it."

"It's just, I don't want—" he said, then paused.

"You don't want *what*, Max?" she asked, gently.

"I don't want to lose hockey," he said, his voice cracking.

She felt her heart breaking for him, and she wanted to save him, even if it meant lying and telling him he wasn't going to lose hockey. She wanted to lie, just to make him feel better in this moment. But she didn't, because Remi was a lot of things; she was brash, loud at times, and a little bit of a perfectionist, but she wasn't a liar. So, she stayed silent as the man she loved so much grieved the loss of his first love, his passion, his entire identity, and she silently accepted that some things he had to mourn on his own. Sadly, this was one of them.

"I don't know who I am without it, Rem," he said, and she could hear the defeat he was feeling through the phone.

She took a shaky breath and then offered the only thing she thought might help him understand this, process it, and maybe even find a place to lay blame for it all.

"Max, I think you need to meet your dad."

He was silent on the other line for just a beat.

"I know. I've been thinking the same thing," he finally admitted.

"Should we arrange it? I can go with you," she offered.

"You would do that?" he asked.

"Yes, I would go with you. I said yes to *everything*, Max Miller."

Chapter Thirty-One

They pulled up to Max's father's house in Remi's car. She offered to drive more often than not lately, and for that, he was grateful. Driving had become scary, even during the day over the last few weeks, his vision majorly declining seemingly overnight. Taking the time on the drive over to get his head in the right place, he focused on preparing himself for this unconventional family reunion. Nothing seemed to work, so he sat back in his seat and let the sounds of Remi singing along to her punk mix drown out the intense panic he felt in his chest.

He loved how easy she was. She was so free; she didn't hold back or edit her actions around him, or anyone else for that matter. One day he wanted to know the words to these songs too, and to sing along with the windows down, his hand flying outside the window of his Jeep as they drove along PCH together. He wanted to say the first words that came to his mind, even if they were harsh or offensive or passionate. Looking over at Remi, she smiled up at him, and his heart raced with affection for this woman, drowning out the nerves he had about meeting his father.

When they pulled into the driveway, they found that his father's house was a faded shade of brown. Not because it wasn't taken care of; it was just an old house that had been lived in. The harsh California summers had taken a toll on its exterior. Remi took Max's hand in hers, pulling him up the small pathway that led to the front porch, his feet hesitant and his body stiff with fear. When she rang the doorbell, several dogs began to bark, followed by the sound of a woman telling them to settle down. The woman, who Max assumed to be his father's wife, opened the door with a warm smile on her face and a small white chihuahua in her arms.

"You must be Max and Remi. I'm Nancy, Jim's wife," she said, opening the screen door to let them in.

Max was hit with an intense wave of panic. His face flushed hot and he felt his eyes glaze over. It was a lot. People were hard, but with the new people being his estranged father and his wife, it was even harder. Remi gave his hand a reassuring squeeze and he couldn't be more grateful that she was here with him. It was like she had come into his life at the exact moment he needed her and filled every void, helping him overcome his fears, calming the raging storm that was in his chest.

"Thank you for having us," Remi said, then added, "We could have met you somewhere, taken you out for lunch."

"No, it's fine. We don't go out as much these days since Jim started collecting stray dogs," she said with a laugh, the small dog in her arms shaking nervously as she led them through the house. "Your father has never met a dog he didn't want to rescue."

Anger towards the man swelled in Max's chest at those words.

Never met a dog he didn't want to rescue, but he was more than willing to abandon his son like a mangy stray.

"Just right through here," she said, leading them into the small kitchen where Max saw his father for the first time in his life.

The red hair was a dead giveaway. It was very obvious that the two of them were related, and Max hated that looks weren't the only thing the man had bestowed upon him. He hated that his father couldn't just pass down the thick red hair, freckled arms, and stocky build, he had to give Max this curse too, this life-altering disease.

The walking cane by his father's side was the other indication that this was indeed his dad. Max wondered if he would need a cane one day too and his heart raced at the sight of it. Of him, his cane, and the dogs, there were so many fucking dogs. It was too much. He gripped Remi's hand tightly, and she responded by whispering, "You got this."

The man stood at the sound of their entry, and Max knew this part all too well; the way your other senses seem to step up when your vision starts to fail.

"Max, this is your father, Jim. Jim, this is Max. He's the spitting image of you. He brought his girlfriend Remi as well," she said, introducing Max nonchalantly like he was a missionary off the street popping in to tell him about the second coming.

Max's father offered up a hand to shake and Remi encouraged him forward to take it. He hesitantly shook it, despite wanting to tell the man that he would like to pass on the formalities. It was surreal, meeting him and seeing him after only ever having wondered what he would be like.

Remi spoke up, breaking the silence between them all. "It's nice to finally meet you, Jim. Thank you for having us over on such short notice."

Max's father looked over to where Remi's voice had come from, following the sound of her.

"Well, you don't sound like I remember from the phone call. Your voice was a bit deeper last time we spoke," Jim joked, hinting at Max not saying anything, and Remi gave the man's joke a small laugh.

"Yeah, thank you for having us over," Max finally said.

"It was long overdue, kid. Have a seat. Nancy will get us all a beer and you can start your interrogation. How does that sound?" his father asked, and without agreeing verbally, he and Remi took a seat at the small dining room table.

"So, how's your mom these days?" Jim asked, and it felt like a strange introduction to the conversation, but Max was grateful he didn't have to get the ball rolling.

"I don't know what you remember about her," Max said.

"Not much to be honest. Me and her were never a love match. She was from money, and I was young, dumb, and drunk most nights. You weren't something we planned for."

"A mistake," Max said under his breath.

"That's one way of putting it," his father agreed.

Remi ran her hand over Max's thigh before pressing it firmly against his knee that had begun to bounce anxiously, trying to calm his nerves.

"So, when you met my mom, was your vision already going?" Max asked.

His father took a long drink from his can of beer with a chuckle. "We're diving right into the vision stuff then?" his dad teased.

"With all due respect, I am twenty-six years old and going blind. I think diving in this late in my life is the least you can do to help me understand what the fuck is about to happen to me."

"Well, son," the man started.

"I'm not your son," Max bit back.

The man let out a gruff laugh. "Well, technically you are, but if you'd rather I didn't call you that..."

"I'd rather you didn't call me that," Max said, cutting in. He wasn't usually this aggressive, but something about this man in front of him, with his brown lab at his side, another lab at his feet, and two small dogs on a dog bed under the table; it made Max angry.

"Well then, to answer your question, when I met your mom, I was already noticing signs, but I chalked it up to being drunk, hungover, or hungry. I was young, dumb, and in denial."

"When did you finally find out you had... it?" Max asked, avoiding calling a spade a spade.

"I found out I had *it*," his father said, also avoiding using the proper medical term, and Max couldn't tell if he did so to mock him or out of respect for him. He didn't know the man and didn't expect to understand his humor after five minutes with him. "I found out when I was twenty-three. I couldn't see at night by that point, and if it wasn't up against my nose, it would be blurry. I thought I just needed glasses, but instead, it landed me with a walking cane."

"How long?" Max asked.

"How long what? How long do you have left in the game? Until you can't drive? How long do you have left to watch a movie, a sunset or to see your own two feet?"

Max's hands curled into fists.

"How long until I'm blind?" Max said, because that was what this all came down to. He would lose everything, but the end game was losing his vision completely, and Max needed to know how long he had to enjoy what he had left.

"Mine went completely by thirty. You could be different. Not everyone loses it entirely, but genetics say you might."

"Why didn't you tell me?" Max asked.

"Sooner?" his father asked.

"At all. Why didn't you tell my mom? I spent my whole fucking life training for this sport, this fucking game. Chasing the Cup that one day I won't be able to see. If you had told me sooner, maybe I wouldn't be here. Maybe I wouldn't want it so bad or love it so much."

Max felt his eyes grow hot with tears. He didn't want to cry, not in front of Remi, not in front of his father and his wife and their nineteen fucking stray dogs.

"If you had known sooner you never would have made it this far with the NHL, because you would have given up before you made it. Wouldn't you rather have had a taste of it, than to never have experienced it at all?"

"No. Because no loss in this lifetime will ever be as great as this one. I'm going to suffer when I tell my team this is my final year. I'll have to announce my retirement. I'll eventually skate onto that ice knowing it will be my last time. Nothing will ever hurt worse than giving up that fucking net."

"I think you're wrong, Max."

"Well, you don't fucking know me, so you don't get to think anything about me."

His father cleared his throat and went on. "I think you're wrong in thinking the biggest loss of your life is losing this sport. The biggest loss of your life would have been to never have gotten to play it. You're a goalie for the NHL, you know how many young men dream of that? And *you* achieved it. It's not about how long you got to do it, but that you got to. I know I wasn't a father to you. Your mom didn't make it easy, and I'd be lying if I said I tried. The truth is, I passed on some shitty genetics, and for that, I'll always be sorry, but I'll never apologize for not telling you this sooner, because you would have started living in the future and forgot to live in the present."

Max felt his stomach drop.

He didn't have it in him to tell his father that he hadn't lived his life in the present anyway. He thought of his sterile, pictureless home, and the relationships he had denied himself, with teammates, friends, and women, and how he hid from them all until he met Remi. He thought about the ocean, mere feet away from his back door, and how he had taken it for granted, until now. He thought about each sunset he closed the curtains on, and each sunrise he slept through.

He thought about the Cup, and how if he held it now, before things got too bad, he might be able to see the flash of the lights against the crisp, clean silver and how he might still be able to make out the names of the men who came before him. He knew he had to be honest with his team, even if it broke his heart, even if it broke *theirs*. He knew the only way they would have a chance at the Cup was by him walking away from it.

Max looked at his father and noticed the gentle line on his brow, Max had that line too. He noticed the way he seemed okay, relaxed, happy even, surrounded by his wife and his rescue dogs in his comfortable home, with his mobility cane close by.

Was there a life after hockey?

Yes.

Was there a happy life after hockey?

He looked over at Remi and she gave him a simple smile, her single dimple a reminder of the first time he met her, stumbling over his own two feet, breaking the lamp; the writing was on the wall. It had been for a while now. The wheels were in motion long before he accepted it. And like his father, he had chalked up his condition to anything else: anxiety, low blood sugar, not enough sleep. But it was time to face the music. It was time to see it for what it was, no pun intended. He needed to talk to the right doctors, get the diagnosis on paper, and take his first step toward helping his team win the Cup without his skates, pads, or his custom mask and stick. Without him in front of the net.

"Thank you," Max finally said. "I know this hasn't been easy for either of us."

"It hasn't been, but maybe we can try our hand at this whole relationship thing over time. I know I won't ever be a father in your eyes, but maybe I can be a friend, and a sounding board as you navigate this new way of life."

"Yeah, I'll think about it," Max said, and he wasn't being cruel, he just wasn't sure he could commit to anything with this man just yet. Not now. Not when he had so much to unpack that didn't involve long-lost parents and emotional voids he carried since childhood.

"That's more than I can ask for," his father agreed.

Nancy appeared as if on cue. "Should I see them out?" she asked knowingly.

"Yeah, Nance, I think we're done here."

"Bye, Jim," Remi offered, "thanks again." He didn't say anything in return, he just gave her a nod before they turned to leave the cramped kitchen.

The sun was long gone when they got out to the car.

"Thanks for driving, Rem."

She leaned in and kissed his cheek

"I don't mind driving, you know that."

"I know. But while it's just me asking you to drive at night for now, there will be so much more that I'll have to ask of you later," he warned.

"I know."

"I don't want to hold you back," he said quietly.

She pulled him in to kiss her, a kiss fueled by reassurance, leaving no room for doubt in the way her lips praised his.

"The only way you're holding me back is by not getting in the car fast enough. I need a donut and the beach, and I need you, as you are, as you will be, no matter what, Max Miller."

"Yes... to everything," he said.

"Yes, yes, yes. A million times yes. Now get in the car right meow."

Chapter Thirty-Two

Max sat in the locker room with his head down. If he didn't look at them, they wouldn't be able to see that he was hiding something. If he didn't look at his teammates, he wouldn't have to accept the fact that they looked blurry from across the locker room.

It was getting worse.

Each day.

Each minute.

The clock was ticking down to the moment he was exposed. His truths laid out bare, one loss at a time, one tally mark at a time, one bad save, one last fumble.

Only, the season had taken off since November, prolonging his delusion.

He had every intention of coming clean after he saw his father. After he got the backup seat. After he handed over his keys to Remi each night as they drove along the Pacific Coast Highway with the windows down, her music blasting, his hand on her thigh, her hands on the wheel, his vision nonexistent; the ocean breeze single-handedly keeping air in his lungs.

He was two clicks away from a mental breakdown and two steps away from falling over something he didn't see. He was a few wins away from clinching a playoff spot, and the thought of losing that chance because of his condition made the weight of it all unbearable.

Without Remi he would be lost, she was his siren song. She was his anchor. She was every generic ocean metaphor he could think of that said she was his everything, his lifeline, his safety vest, *and* if he asked, he wondered if she would be his forever.

The second he kissed her goodbye and made his way to a new arena, a new city, a new hotel, and found himself on the ice, the weight of it all came crashing down. He would never feel free again, light again, or confident in front of the net again. Darkness was closing in on him.

He blinked once. It was just enough.

He blinked and blinked again. It was hardly anything.

Soon, he would blink, and blink, and blink, until lights out.

He took his spot in front of the net. Practice had become harder than games. All eyes were on him as if they knew. They had to know. If they all looked closely enough, they had to see that he was faking it. He was fumbling his way into the starting lineup and was putting on the show of a lifetime. He might never hoist the Cup, but he sure as hell might win an Emmy for this performance.

"*Miller*! Wake the fuck up, man," Carter yelled from across the ice as another puck made its way into the net.

He wished he could wake up, but this was the kind of nightmare that kept going even after your morning piss and cup of coffee. This was the kind that you didn't escape.

"Miller, get your ass over here," Coach shouted from the bench.

Max did the skate of shame.

He blinked, and it was no help.

It was an off day. His ass would be cozy on the bench tomorrow night for sure.

"What the ever-living fuck is wrong with you?" Coach asked.

"Can't focus."

It was a half-lie. Or was it a half-truth?

"You're telling me that you think a multimillion-dollar goalie thinks he gets to chase butterflies and sunshine on *my* fucking ice, on *my* fucking clock?"

"No, Coach," Max said.

"Then explain to me what the fuck is happening in front of the net?"

Max looked out at the ice, and the boys continued running the drills. But he knew they were all watching from the corners of their eyes. He felt shame heat his body, and he knew all he had to do was be honest and tell his coach everything. Break the news. Lighten his load while simultaneously ending his career.

"I've had this bad headache all day. I took something earlier." He lied for sure this time. "But it didn't put a dent in it. It's making it hard to focus."

"Sounds like a migraine."

"Yeah, I don't know, it might be." This was *not* a lie; this was evading the truth. This was Max spinning it any way he could to save face for a game longer.

"Why didn't you see the team doctor before practice?"

"I thought Tylenol would do the trick."

Coach looked up at the timer to make out how much time was left on the clock. Max did too, but it was a blur.

His stomach dropped. How was he supposed to count down the minutes left of a game if he couldn't see the clock?

"We got a good ten minutes left, I want you to go see the doctor, make sure you're good to play tomorrow night."

Fuck, Max thought, feeling disappointed about his start in front of the net for the first time in his career. "Right on, Coach."

"And Miller, so help me God, if you ever tell me you can't fucking focus again over a goddamn migraine when we have a team doctor, I'll pull Brody up from the minors to fill your spot so fast you'll get whiplash. I'm not missing the playoffs this year. Not with this team. Get your shit together and come back tomorrow ready. You get the start, don't make me regret it. We got one last game before the holiday break, and we're fucking winning it."

"Got it," Max said. Heading to the locker room, he heard Coach mumble, *"Says he took fucking Tylenol,"* under his breath, and Max knew his time was up. Whether he owned up to it, saw the doctor, and got the diagnosis on paper or not—he was done for.

Chapter Thirty-Three

Remi pulled up to Lighthouse Rehabilitation after she finished cleaning her last house of the day. It was only a half-hour drive from Max's house and forty minutes from her place, which was important to know now that Max had taken to staying with her more nights than not. It amazed her really, that he could have the best house in San Clemente, and yet he chose her little nugget of space to be at. He said he liked that it felt lived-in and safe; it felt like home. She loved that she felt like home to him because he felt like home to her too.

Today was his last practice, tomorrow would be his last game before the holiday break, and she couldn't wait to spend that time with him.

Looking back on it, Remi had seen Max's eyesight fade since they started seeing each other, since that first day; the boxers, the shattered lamp, the donuts, and the hummus. The night swim, Halloween, and cat jokes into the late hours of the night. Since making out in dark closets and making love in bright bedrooms, she had seen his vision slip. She had watched the struggle, the panic and the uncertainty wash over him. He was really good at faking it most days, but sometimes his fears showed in his panicked blinking, the way his hands braced for impact, and the way his breathing grew heavy. Some days he drank too much, and she drank with him. Some days he wouldn't leave the house with her, so they snuggled up and asked all the questions that came to mind.

"Have you ever been in love?" he had asked.

"No. You?" she said.

"With a girl, Allison, in a billet home. Her brother found out and beat me up. That sort of ended it," he had said.

"Beat you up?" she asked.

"Well, I didn't fight back."

Even the more difficult questions had come up.

"Do you sleep with hockey fans?" she asked.

"No... yes... sometimes... not much," he stuttered.

"So, you do, or you don't?"

"I have, but I didn't like it. I never knew how to initiate it. I'm not great with..."

"Words, yeah, so you've told me."

He went on, *"I want you to know I don't have any STDs or anything. I get checked, I get physicals and stuff."*

"I don't either. I don't sleep around much. I have, in the past. But not since my business took off," she assured him, and it was a good thing to establish since they had taken up the bad habit of not using protection in the heat of the moment, as dummies in love often do.

"I kind of want to fuck you right meow," he said, with a straight face, cat joke and all.

"Max Miller," she had purred. *"Bad kitty,"* she said, pouncing on him playfully.

Some days, he simply handed over the keys and let her drive until they both grew too tired to drive anymore.

That was why she was here, at Lighthouse, one of the best rehabilitation programs in all of Southern California. She wanted to educate herself, so that when Max was ready, she would already know each step he needed to take. She would have the answers to his questions, the guidebooks on her shelves, the technology at her fingertips, and the apps on her phone. She wanted to be ready, so when he said go, she could take his hand and walk him through the biggest life change anyone could ever experience. A lifetime of vision, replaced by a future without it—it wouldn't be easy, but she wouldn't let him fail.

When she entered the facility, the door chimed, and she was greeted by a young woman who found her way to Remi with the help of a guide dog. Remi hadn't even considered a guide dog as an option, but now that she saw the woman with the beautiful golden retriever at her side, she couldn't help but feel an inkling of hope surrounding all of this.

"Hello, I'm Nicole, and this is Shepard," the young woman said, holding out a hand to shake.

"Hi, I'm Remi. Thanks for squeezing me in today."

"No problem. I'm happy you reached out."

The dog, Shepard, looked up at Remi, his eyes oddly human. "Can I pet him?"

"Absolutely. Shep loves a good head scratch from new friends."

Remi leaned down to pet the beautiful, well-mannered guide dog. "How long does it take to train them to behave like this?"

"Why don't we let him guide us around the facility as I answer all of your questions; he loves to give tours."

Remi smiled, hope filling her heart as Shepard led them through the building with confidence. This looked like a life that had promise—a future that had meaning. She saw a life where everything was going to be okay.

"So," Nicole started, "Shepard was selected to be a guide dog as a puppy. He went through assessments and once he passed all of them, he began to train. He is my second guide dog since I lost my vision at fourteen to a condition called Stargardt disease. It was something we saw coming on, no pun intended, so my mother started preparing me for a life with vision loss right away, including getting me my first guide dog, Wendy, when I was seventeen, and now I have Shep. He's the best boy." She leaned down to pet the dog, whose tail began to wag excitedly. "Aren't you the best boy?" she asked, and the dog knew he was, in fact, the best boy.

Shepard led Remi and Nicole with ease and confidence through the facility while Nicole explained what the facility offered: training, classes, technology, community, and counseling. All things both she and Max would need to navigate their future together.

The tour ended with the two of them in Nicole's office, where Remi found a folder with all the information she could possibly need about Lighthouse sitting on Nicole's desk.

"Can I ask you something a little more personal?" Remi said, taking a seat across from Nicole.

"Ask away. Part of my job is being an open book."

"How hard was it for you? Losing your vision after having experienced life with it?"

Nicole took a treat from the glass jar on her desk and handed it to Shepard who happily took it to his dog bed nearby.

"That's a good question, and I'll answer it as honestly as I can, but take into consideration that everyone's experience is different. I lost my vision at an early age, so there were many different emotions involved. I was mad as hell, because why me, ya know? I was depressed. I was also motivated to not let it ruin my life or stop me from living. I was scared, as anyone would be, and all of these emotions hit me at separate times. Some days were good, and some days I wouldn't leave my room. But I had a good support system; I had loving parents who would stop at nothing to accommodate my disability. The second we knew what my future looked like having Stargardt, I started therapy, which I strongly recommend for your friend. I attended a facility similar to this and started to just prepare myself as best I could."

"My boyfriend," Remi started, "he's got a pretty specific job."

"Okay, there might be a way to navigate his career with his vision loss. Being blind isn't always a career-ending disability."

Remi wished Nicole was right, but she knew there was no saving Max's spot on the team roster, not even with all the rehabilitation and preparation for what came next in the world.

"It will though," Remi stated. "This will absolutely end his career."

"Okay, do you want to share? I would love to talk through some options, and if there are none, and you think losing his career to vision loss will be hard on him, I can send you home with resources, and numbers for therapists that can be on call, for when he's ready."

Remi looked over at Shepard, happily gnawing on his treat. She looked around the facility and saw happy faces, kids smiling; people learning how to live happily while being blind. But they weren't NHL goalies. She almost wished Max never knew what it felt like to be in his position, just to save him from the hurt he was going to experience, no doubt, once it was gone.

"Do you want to share? Or would you rather he shares when he comes to visit?"

"It's just, no one knows yet," she said, not wanting to blow his cover before he got the chance to tell his team.

"Ah, yes. He might need some time to wrap his head around it before he can admit it to others, let alone himself."

Remi couldn't agree more, only, she didn't know how much longer he would have before he was forced to tell his team, essentially ending his spot in front of the net with the Condors. Two major losses in one year would be hard, and she realized she was terrified of what this looked like for Max, the man she loved.

Chapter Thirty-Four

Max had somehow made it into December without hurting himself or his teammates while on the ice. Each game felt harder than the last, and now it was his last game before the holiday break, before quality time with Remi, the woman he loved, who he had somehow convinced to love him back. He had never been so excited for a break from hockey.

It all felt *too* heavy, each game, each puck drop, each save.

But something about tonight felt different.

He took his spot in front of the net knowing he didn't deserve it. Not with Brown on the bench, healthy, and fully aware of what Max was up against. The lights went down as the Canadian anthem was sung, and then the national anthem came next.

Max kept his eyes on the ice below him. It was dark in the arena, darker than normal. Shifting on his skates, his knees felt weak, and his heart began to race.

Don't panic, the lights will be up soon, he told himself.

Don't panic, you've been playing like this all season.

Don't panic, you still have a few more games in you.

The lights came up and the crowd cheered. The puck was dropped, but his vision did not recover.

Max blinked. That was the trick, right? He blinked again, no improvement.

"*No*," he said under his breath as the game took off in front of him through a cloudy haze.

Sweat covered his body in a panicked cold chill. He blinked. And blinked. His heart hammered in his chest. The lights were up, he should be fine. He blinked again. His body felt heavy, and the ice moved below his skates. The cheers from the stands echoed in the distance.

He blinked.

"No," he said again. His chest grew tight—could you die from panic? Could you die from sheer shock and fear?

No amount of blinking was helping, his peripheral vision was nonexistent.

The game raged on, the Vancouver team had the puck, and he could make out the shift of the battle. He could make out his team's colors—white away jerseys with teal blue condors on the chest—chasing the dark blue blur of the Vancouver team. He felt all sense of balance and equilibrium shift.

He blinked.

He readied himself for the puck and looked out at the game around him, only to see the end of his career in front of him in a blur of bodies, and movement without any real defining features.

Max dropped his stick and pulled his gloves off in a panic, he couldn't breathe like this. He couldn't stop his heart from pounding. Could you die from this, from the weight of it all? Would he die? He ripped his helmet from his head and the quick movement was enough to send him to his knees, his body sliding along the smooth ice.

The whistle blew.

The game paused.

The crowd grew silent.

His team raced to his side, and he heard someone shout, *"We need a medic."*

He rubbed his eyes, gouging at them, if he could just get them to focus, he would be okay. If he could just get his heart to slow down, he would be okay. If he could just get a few more minutes, a few more seconds, he would be okay.

"Max, *Max*, look at me," the trainer shouted at him.

Max kept rubbing his eyes. "I just need to... focus... I just, it's my eyes. It's my heart, I think I'm having a heart attack," he managed.

"Max, we have to get you off the ice, we need to have you checked out. Can you skate for me? Can you make it off the ice?"

"I can skate, I just—" Before he could vocalize what he needed, his captain was by his side, with the team's trainer on his other side.

"We got you, Miller, let us help you," the familiar voice said.

They couldn't help him. No one could. This was it. Game over. Lights out.

Time's up.

They helped him skate off the ice, the deafening cheer of the crowd, their encouraging clapping, and his team patting him as he passed by felt like the final nail in the coffin.

Max knew this was it. This was the last time he would skate off the ice in this uniform, and he didn't know what hurt worse—the way he was leaving or the fact that it wasn't on his terms.

***

Remi watched it all happen from the comfort of her home. She watched as Max completely lost his shit on the ice, on national television, and she had no way to find out what the hell was going on. She realized Max had never introduced her to his team or given her emergency contact numbers, so she called the next best thing, the only person who might have some kind of advice—his dad.

"Hi, it's Remi Davis, Max's girlfriend."

"He'll be okay, hon," Max's dad responded immediately.

"Did you see? Were you watching?" she asked as she paced her small living room. The game resumed now that Max was off the ice, but the team was worried. She could see it on their faces as the camera zoomed in to the bench while Brown took his place in front of the net, replacing Max.

"I watch all of his games," Max's father went on.

"What does it mean? What do you think happened?" she asked.

He cleared his throat on the other line. "There comes a point in this disease when it hits you."

"It's *been* hitting him," she shouted.

"Yeah, it comes on slowly... until it doesn't. We call them dips. You see gradual change, but then you blink, and—BAM—you experience a dip, a drastic change in your vision. It's this moment where you realize it's gotten worse, and there's no going back. Maybe you realize you can't drive anymore, or you can't watch a movie on the TV anymore, or in Max's case, it was when those lights came up and he couldn't gain focus on his surroundings. When that happens, your entire body responds, because it's the moment you really comprehend the severity of this disability. It's the moment you realize you will never see more clearly than you did a split second ago, ever again."

"But he fell, he looked scared," she said more to herself, replaying the events she had just witnessed on the TV screen.

"Wouldn't you be scared too? If everything you ever worked for was nothing more than a blur in the blink of an eye?"

"I would be fucking terrified. I should have been there. I should be there," she said, her voice slightly hysterical.

He went on, "Now picture yourself in Max's shoes, or skates if we're being detailed here. He went out there to play that game with the weight of his team on his shoulders, and just like *that*," she heard him clap his hands together on the other line, "he knew he couldn't. He knew his time in front of that net was over for good and the panic set in. What you saw tonight was his 'oh shit' moment, darlin'. He'll be okay, might take some time, but he'll get through this."

Remi took a seat on the couch as tears began to stream down her face, because no, he wouldn't be okay. Not now anyway. Her heart broke for him as she watched the TV with her own blurred vision as tears filled her eyes—seeing things the way Max might see them. And the game went on, but he was nowhere to be found.

Chapter Thirty-Five

The flight back to Anaheim was quiet. The team was nervous, and Max knew the unknown was killing them, but he stayed silent. He let them wonder, he let them hurt for him because he was hurting too. Max sat with his head down replaying the night. Taking the start. Blinking. Panic setting in. Skating off the ice. Seeing the team doctor. Telling him the truth.

The boys knew something was wrong, they just didn't know *what* was wrong. He had hidden it from them, and he hid it well. He had always been good at being invisible, not taking up any space, not bringing unwanted attention to himself, and all his years of practice, of being invisible around his mother, and invisible in his billet homes, had paid off. He had managed to skate by, unnoticed until tonight.

Coach made his way down the aisle of the plane, using the other seats to keep himself from falling over as it bounced around with turbulence while they flew over a storm in Oregon.

"This seat open?" he asked.

Max removed his iPad from the empty spot to make room for his coach.

"What did the doctor say? When I asked, they said you should be the one to tell me."

Max ran his hands through his hair. He didn't know how to say it. Words were always his worst enemy, and right now, they were hard to find, like a game of hide and seek in the dark.

"Max, whatever it is we can fix it," Coach encouraged.

"No," Max said, his voice low. "We can't fix it, Coach."

"And why's that, son?"

"Because what I have isn't treatable."

"And what *do* you have?"

Max looked over at his coach and it hurt to see such worry in his eyes, a man who was known for having thick skin—an unshakable man. Seeing him this distressed unnerved Max.

"What happened on the icc was just the start of something that only gets worse. I have something wrong with my vision, something that is essentially making me go blind. It's called retinitis pigmentosa. My father has it and he is completely blind too. It's hereditary, and there's no stopping it."

"Max, I—" His coach tried to articulate any kind of appropriate response, but Max wasn't sure there was one, so he spared his coach the trouble of trying to find the right words. For the first time, Max said what came next.

"When the lights came up, I couldn't focus. It's happened before. I've been selfishly playing knowing I wasn't capable of getting the job done anymore. But with Brody injured in the minors, and the Condors so close to clinching a spot, I just let my heart's deepest desire take over to maybe, possibly, play long enough to win the Cup, before I... before I have to hang up my skates for good."

"I wish you would have told me sooner," Coach said, and Max couldn't be sure if it was disappointment or pity that lined his face. He didn't want pity, anything but pity.

"I should have. I should have been honest with you and the team. I could have cost you the playoffs, but I couldn't give it up. I just didn't know how to walk away."

"What's next, Max? Where do we go from here?"

"I don't know. I need to be seen by a specialist. I need to take the steps to prepare myself for being vision impaired for the rest of my life, and I need to announce..." He didn't know how to say it, they would be the hardest words to leave his mouth in his lifetime.

His coach cut him off before he finished the damning statement. "We can put you on leave. Injured reserved. That way you can still be on the roster until the season is over and then—" Coach paused, and Max worked up the courage to finish the sentence they were both trying like hell not to say.

"And then I can formally retire."

"Max," Coach said, his voice cracking.

"I'm sorry I didn't tell you. I'm sorry I kept playing. Are you disappointed in me?" Max asked, realizing that the only validation he had ever gotten in his life was from his coaches, trainers, and other players, and he needed it again, this one last time, to be told that he was okay.

"Son, I could never be disappointed in you. Not when I know I would have done the same damn thing. We have hockey in our blood, and we will fight or die trying to win that Cup."

Chapter Thirty-Six

Remi watched in silence as Max got into the car to head home from the airport. His body language showed his defeat, and while she knew she had said no more passes, tonight she would give this man anything he needed.

Before he buckled in, he leaned in and kissed her cheek. "Thank you for picking me up."

"Of course. Your place or mine?" she asked.

"Mine," he said, thinking about it before adding, "but first, donuts."

Remi smiled over at her big, red teddy bear of a man. He was beautiful on a good day, but the sadness in his eyes only made them that much more green, more real, more relatable. She loved him. That she was certain of, and if he wanted donuts, then donuts he would get.

They drove in silence down PCH towards Seal Beach. Having no words with Max was normal for them, she accepted his silence but was grateful for his touch. His hand rested on her thigh, a reminder that while he didn't always have the words to articulate his need for her, his physical connection was always strong.

"You're so beautiful, Rem," he said breaking the silence.

She looked over at him, his gaze on her didn't waver. "You okay?" she asked, knowing damn well he wasn't but giving him every opportunity to speak about what happened at the game.

"It wasn't low blood sugar the day we met," he said quietly.

"No, I guess it wasn't."

He looked out the window, and then back at her. "I wish it would have been low blood sugar, Rem."

"Me too, Max," she said, placing her free hand on top of his.

"I'm scared," he said, voice cracking.

She brought the car to a stop; they had made it to Donut Palace. "What can I do to make you feel safe?" she asked.

He brought his rough hand to her cheek, running his thumb across her bottom lip, then down the bridge of her nose, then over her jawline. His eyes were intent on her. Taking her in. Memorizing her.

"Don't let me forget what this looks like," he said.

"I won't. I promise."

"I don't want to forget the details, Remi."

She leaned over the center console, bringing the tip of her nose to trace across his. "You won't. We will spend every waking moment memorizing each other. Loving each other. Learning how to navigate this together."

"I love you, you know?" he said.

"I know you do," she said, because she did.

"It's going to be hard... *I* might be hard."

She brought her lips to his in a delicate kiss, her breath heavy against his lips. "I'm not afraid of hard things."

"I'll need a lot of help," he said between soft kisses.

"I know, and I'm ready for it."

"After the break, I'm telling the team. Coach told me to take the time off to prepare for it, but I almost wish I had told them after the game. I wish they already knew so I didn't have to face them again."

Remi shook her head at his words, taking his hand in hers, gripping it tight. "Don't say that. Just because you won't be able to play again doesn't mean you're not a part of that team. They love you, and they're going to rally behind you, Max. Your name, your number, and your jersey will be woven into the history of that team for eternity. You're Max Miller. You have your face on banners leading to the Condors arena."

"I'll never win a Cup."

"Neither did Henrik Lundqvist, but he's still one of the greatest goaltenders of all time."

"How do you know that?" Max asked, cocking an eyebrow at her random hockey trivia.

"I've been doing my research. And what I found is that not all of the greats win a Cup, but it doesn't diminish the careers they had. Nothing will steal the legacy you've already left with the Condors."

"You overestimate me."

"No, you underestimate yourself. You've been doing it since I met you and I think it's high time you stop tattooing your losses on your side and start enjoying your wins."

Chapter Thirty-Seven

Max was sitting on the beach, with a box of donuts, half glazed twists, half maple bars, with Remi at his side. It was going to be okay. He was going to be okay... with time. He knew speaking his truth out loud to his teammates would be hard, maybe the hardest words he would ever say in his lifetime, but he could do it with this woman by his side. Playing the words over and over in his head, he thought about how he would tell the team, wondering how they, the media, and the fans would respond.

"So, the night is young and I'm in the market to distract you from hockey shit," Remi said, playfully bumping her leg against his. "Blow job perhaps?" she joked.

"I won't say no to a blow job." Max blushed. "But that wasn't exactly what I had in mind if I'm being honest."

"Okay, so what did you have in mind, and I *swear* my ego isn't bruised that you're not constantly thinking about me blowing you," she said playfully with a wink.

"I didn't say I wasn't constantly thinking about you blowing me, my brain is 98 percent you blowing me, 1 percent hockey, and the other 1 percent 'oh shit I'm going blind,'" he teased.

"At least I know I can keep your brain distracted."

"You're the *best* distraction, Rem. I feel like you came into my life right when I needed you," he admitted.

"I don't think I knew just how lonely *I* was before *you*. As a kid, I never made friends because I was so afraid they would find out about my mom, and that just kind of carried on into adulthood. I've just been filling my time with work and caring for others. I didn't know I needed a Max Miller in my life."

"Black briefs and punk music," he said.

"The perfect start to any relationship," she agreed.

"Speaking of punk music, that's kind of what I was thinking we could do tonight."

Remi threw the last bite of her second donut back into the box. "You want me to start a punk band with you?" she asked.

"No." He laughed, and he couldn't push back the image of him on stage, all redheaded and sweaty, playing a bass guitar. "I was thinking more along the lines of you showing me new things to fall in love with. All I've ever known is hockey. Train, eat, sleep, play, repeat. But if I don't have a backup plan, I'm afraid I might get depressed. I'm going from living a very structured life to retirement. I think it might be a big adjustment, and I have no idea what else is out there that I might like. I remember that day, when you woke me with your music, being a little annoyed, and a lot embarrassed, but I also remember feeling excited, and I haven't been able to stop thinking about it, about the music you played that day. I think it might be something I could get into."

Remi's body language perked up at the mention of this, of exploring new things together.

"Max, the world is so big and so full of wonderful things to discover, not only will I single-handedly introduce you to all the best bands, but I will also take you to see them. There's so much good music here in Southern California. So many amazing small venues to see shows. This is going to be so fun," she said, doing a bit of a happy dance.

"What else can you introduce me to?" Max asked.

"Blow jobs?" Remi teased.

"Yes, that too. But what else is out there, Rem? What am I missing? What do I need to see and do before this gets bad?"

He watched as she thought this through, her eyes out on the ocean, her brain ticking away, making a list, he could see it all on her beautiful face.

"I think we should just live freely and do as you asked me to do; I think we should say yes to everything. That's the only way we won't miss out on something you might love."

"Sounds like a plan."

"So, what's the first thing we should say yes to, Max Miller?" she asked with an all-knowing raised eyebrow and a sexy grin revealing not one, but two dimples.

He took her hand in his and brought it up to his lips to place a gentle kiss, his eyes laced with something devious.

"There's only one right answer and you know it," he said, his voice low and gravelly.

"Blow job?" she asked, yet again, but this time it wasn't a joke.

"Yes, please."

Remi shot up from the sand, gripping his hands in hers as she helped him to his feet before she took off running towards his house.

"Wait, the donuts," he called after her. She swung around and ran back to grab them without missing a beat, the smile on her face wild and playful.

"Let's go," she said with the pink box tucked under her arm, the poor donuts didn't stand a chance, "We have *yes* shit to do."

They ran all the way to his house, a trail of heavy footprints in the sand leading them there.

The second they entered through the back door Remi was on him in the most beautiful way. Her hands slipped under the hem of his t-shirt, pushing it up his body, her mouth following the happy trail of red hair that led to his chest as she lifted his shirt over his head. Her mouth was wild on his. Heavy, hot kisses pressed against the muscles of his chest before she moved to his ribs, kissing the tattooed tally marks.

She looked up at him through hooded eyes. "No more losses. Just wins," she said.

Yes, this was definitely a win; this woman here with him, her mouth on him, hands fumbling to unbutton his jeans.

His dick begged to be free, and his brain was far too scrambled with anticipation to do anything but watch as his pants came undone. She pushed them down with rushed hands before they got caught on his thick thighs, a goalie blessing and curse. While he took over undressing himself, Remi wasted no time getting to work on her own clothes. In one swift movement, her shirt came off, leaving only a thin lacy bralette underneath cupping her small, beautiful breasts, the deep pink of her nipple showing through the delicate pale blue fabric. She pulled the bralette off next, exposing her breasts, her body gloriously on display in front of him.

Before she could remove any more clothing, Max pulled her into his naked body, and in one swift movement, picked her up and threw her over his shoulder. A scream of laughter escaped her as he began to carry her to his room; her ass only covered by a matching pair of lacy blue panties sat gloriously close to his face. He couldn't help but press his mouth to it and playfully bite her, panties and all.

"Max Miller put me down," she cried out, laughter still carrying through her every word.

"No way. My brain said *carry this woman to your bed*, and my heart said, *yes, absolutely do that*. And we're doing yes shit, are we not?" he asked.

"We are," she agreed through fits of laughter.

"Then I think this is a *fuck* yes."

They made it to his room, Remi still squirming in his arms as he flung her onto his bed gently before falling to his knees before her, gripping her ankles and yanking her down to the edge of the mattress.

"Ummm, this is not what a blow job looks like, Mr. Miller," she said as he pulled the pale blue lace from her body in one swift motion before bringing a finger to her nose, tapping it three times.

"Ding-ding-ding," he said, making Remi laugh at him stealing her signature move. "This is a taste test," he said nonchalantly.

Remi laughed and watched as he trailed kisses down her body, pausing to pull her nipple into his mouth. "A taste test?" she asked incredulously.

"Yeah, trying to figure out what I like more, maple bars, or your come all over my face."

This made her chest blush and her smile fade into something sexy and needy. "Max Miller," she moaned as he sucked on her sensitive nipple, "and you said you weren't good with words."

"I'm not good with words, but I'm great with my mouth."

He fell between her legs, pushing them wide open as he knelt before her. The bright red of his hair glowed against the warm tones of her tanned skin as he pressed his nose along the entrance of her sex, causing a giggle to escape her.

"Your beard," she said.

"Tickle?" he asked.

"Mmmmhmmm," she moaned as he nuzzled his face against her inner thigh before bringing his mouth down to kiss her there. "This was not what I had in mind," she said.

"I can stop," he offered, looking up from between her legs.

Remi sat up on her elbows and looked down at him, a wild smile on her face. "No, no, finish what you started, by all means. No one likes a quitter," she teased, and immediately after she said it—*quitter*—she felt her stomach drop as he recoiled away from her.

It all happened so fast, the mood shifting all around them in the blink of an eye. She sat up and wrapped her arms around his shoulders, giving him a moment of vulnerability, allowing him to hide his face away from her gaze.

"Max, I'm sorry. I need to choose my words more wisely. I know that. I was just being snarky, and you were so sexy, and it was just so playful. I didn't stop to think." She paused, going silent, and she hated that she had ruined this moment.

He looked up at her after a moment of silence, trying to convince her with his half-smile that he was okay. Maybe he wasn't fully okay in this moment, but he would be, eventually. He wouldn't be this hard to handle, this sensitive, this fragile forever.

It wouldn't be this hard forever.

"I don't want you to have to choose your words wisely around me," he said, pressing up to kiss her neck, "I just want you to say whatever you say, and if it triggers something in me, I just need you to do *this*. I just need you to do exactly what you're doing right now."

"Holding you?" she asked reluctantly.

"Helping me feel safe enough to be vulnerable. Helping me to live through this unashamed. Because I can't push these heavy emotions away. If I do, they'll just fester inside me until I explode."

"I'll always be safe, I promise," she said, pulling him up to sit next to her on his bed, both completely comfortable in their nudity.

"I killed the mood," he said sadly.

"*I* killed the mood," she argued.

He took her hand in his and brought it up to kiss it. "Can we try for a different mood? Just for a little while. Just until I can get my head in a better place. Can this be a *to-be-continued* kind of thing?"

"What do you have in mind?" she asked.

"I was thinking you could show me some of your favorite music."

Remi's smile grew wide, the awkward moment fading with ease. "Should we stay naked?" she joked.

"Do cat ears count as clothing?"

Chapter Thirty-Eight

Remi pressed play on the next song she chose to share with Max. So far, they discovered he liked the faster songs, and he was a huge fan of heavy bass lines. She wore one of his Condors tees and he wore a pair of athletic shorts and his black cat ears, which made Remi smile. She thought she had ruined the night with just a few simple words. She didn't think Max was a quitter by any means, and she didn't think *he* thought he was a quitter, but she knew right now, he might react differently as he processed what he was up against. Tonight, she knew that donuts and blowjobs aside, in the back of Max's head, he was preparing himself for the moment he walked back into the locker room to tell his team that he would never return to the ice.

While that didn't qualify as quitting, Remi understood why Max might feel that way.

His emotions were too big right now, and Remi was fine helping him navigate those big emotions. She was a cleaner, a fixer, and ultimately, she was a lover. And she loved this man. She couldn't fix him, but she could stick around, even when things got hard.

The music had stepped in like a crutch to save the night after their intimate fumble. Remi was grateful they were able to go from the exposure of their naked bodies to the exposure of the deepest hurt so gracefully.

With the music blasting, Max gave her a nod of approval as one of her favorite bands filled the space around them.

"I like this one," he said.

"Yeah?" she asked.

"Yeah. This might be my favorite so far."

Remi did a little happy dance before climbing up onto his lap to straddle him on the massive couch. "So, this is just an idea, but this band is actually playing a show tomorrow night at a little venue in Huntington."

"What does that even mean? I don't speak this music language."

Remi leaned in and kissed his nose. "Okay, so a show is like a concert, but smaller. It's usually in a dive bar or a small venue with standing room only. People crowd in, get really sweaty, and sometimes a little rowdy. You drink shit beer, and the music is so loud your ears hurt afterwards. There's usually a hot dog vendor outside when the show is over, and it's just... it's the best," she said with a huff.

Max looked at her, his face a little unsure before he said, "And they're playing a concert on Christmas Eve?" he asked.

Remi laughed. "A *show*," she corrected. "And yes, not everyone has a family to cozy up with by a Christmas tree, some of us have always spent the holidays wherever we could find company."

"Do you go to a concert or a *show* every Christmas Eve?" he asked.

"No," she said, "I don't have any holiday traditions."

"Me either," he admitted.

"To be honest, you're the first person I've spent the holidays with since my mom passed away."

"You're the first person I've spent the holidays with since I was a boy."

"Do you want to start our own tradition this year?" she asked.

"You mean like going to see this band tomorrow?"

Remi knew going to a punk show was completely out of Max's comfort zone, but what if he loved it? What if they went, and it was everything he didn't know he needed?

"Yeah, what else do we have to do? I don't go back to work until the 27th and you, well—" She stopped to look at him.

"I don't really go back to work ever," he said, and Remi was worried he was about to spiral, but then he smiled instead, catching her by surprise. "So, I guess I better find out if I like going to punk shows."

She leaned in and kissed him. She was so proud of him. He was so brave, kind, funny, and wearing cat ears. He surprised her more often than not, and she loved that.

"We didn't even get a tree, or hang lights, or do anything festive," he said, looking around his bland living room.

"That's okay, I'm more of a Halloween girl myself," she said, running her finger over the headband of the cat ears.

"I think we should finish what we started meow," Max said, bringing his hands to grip her hips, pulling her up against his already very turned-on body.

"I think that's a purrrfect idea," she said, her head falling back, making room for his mouth to kiss her neck, his beard making her skin tingle.

"Lay down," he said, easing her body onto the couch, a new song booming through the house; one of her favorites.

She laid back on the couch and watched as Max made his way down her body in a trail of kisses, pushing the Condors tee up just enough to nuzzle his face against the soft skin above her panties.

His fingers hooked on the elastic band and slowly tugged them down, past her hips, his hands gripping her legs, trailing his fingertips against her bare skin as he pulled them all the way to her feet before tossing them to the floor.

"Purple," he said, noticing her toenails were painted a new color from the last time he had seen her.

"So observant."

He brought her foot up to his mouth, kissing the deep arch.

"Max Miller, I think you might have a foot fetish." She giggled as the scruff of his beard started to tickle up along her leg.

"I think you might be right," he said, breaking his kisses to look up at her. "I still can't believe I get to do this to you."

Remi laughed. "I still can't believe you're wearing cat ears *as* you do this to me," she teased.

This made Max laugh, his eyes were wild and carefree—he looked so young like this, smiling and confident between her naked legs—she hoped they always kept each other wild.

"Is this considered roleplay?" he asked.

She laughed and thought before responding, "No, I think it might be cannibalism."

Max's smile dropped as he pondered what she had said, and then it hit him. He was a cat, eating her *pussy?*

They both started cracking up, his face pressed against her thigh. Her hands came up to cover her face at the crude joke she had just made.

"I love laughing with you, Max Miller," she said through giggles.

"I love laughing in general," he said, and she wondered when the last time was that he felt safe enough to be this carefree.

She reached down and ran her fingers through his thick red hair. "The distractions are strong tonight." She sighed.

"Yeah, but I can't be deterred," he said, picking up where he left off, "I always finish what I start."

"I know you do," she said, her voice a hint lower, more serious.

They had come full circle.

And he was ready to finish this.

His mouth pressed against her center, kissing her there gently, a slow build-up to an already drawn-out moment—she would cherish these memorable times. She would always try and remember to make laughing and joking a priority, and never forget to postpone sex for a good cat pun, or a well-thought-out punk mix.

Max pushed her legs up, giving himself better access to her, running his tongue along her core and stopping to focus on what mattered the most. He pushed a finger inside her and her body instantly tensed around him. She didn't realize how badly she wanted this, *needed* this.

His mouth worked her clit while he expertly moved his finger inside her, the perfect pressure and perfect curve that hit all the right spots.

Her orgasm came on faster than she expected. Maybe it was the cat ears between her legs, or maybe it was the slow-burn of the night, laced with heavy emotions. This was the release she needed, and she couldn't wait for it to come so she could return the favor.

Her knees began to shake, her body instinctually trying to pull her legs together around his head, but he firmly held her legs in place, making her entire body come alive as he continued to lick her clit. The sensations of it all flooded through her, the tickle of his beard, the pressure of his finger deep inside her, the soft fur of the cat ears against her thighs.

It was purrrfect.

He was purrrfect.

Max kept his pace, never trying to switch things up when he felt her getting close. So perceptive. So aware. He was already so masterful of his senses.

Her body trembled as her breathing went shallow. A soft hum of moans grew to an encouraging string of words for him to *keep going*, that she was *so close*, her entire body jerking below him. Her hips pressed up off the couch as her fingers latched onto his strong freckled covered shoulders as she came hard—the release like no other. It was more than an orgasm, it was an emotional release, too.

Max climbed up next to her, the couch deep enough for the both of them, his cat ears a little off-center on his head from her legs clenching against him.

"Me-owwww," she said in a deep release of breath as she tried to slow her heart rate.

"Good?" he asked.

"Great," she affirmed.

They were talking about the *sex*.

"And how are *you*?" he asked.

"Also, very good." She smiled.

They were talking about the *heart*.

He pulled her into his body in a hug that engulfed her, his heart racing against her cheek as she pressed her warm face against his bare chest.

"You feel like home, Max."

"I do?" he asked, "Is *this* what home feels like?"

She looked up at him, a lazy post-orgasm smile on her face, and pressed her finger to his nose to boop it three times. "Ding-ding-ding. I think it is. I really do."

"Then stay here forever," he whispered against her head, his lips kissing her there.

"I like the idea of that."

"Of staying here?" he asked.

"Of forever, with you. Of home. I think it's high time we both know what that feels like."

"You bring this place to life, Remi."

"One potted plant at a time," she said, kissing him right above his heart.

"One single-dimple smile at a time."

"How about two?" she asked, looking up at him, her smile spread across her face, both dimples present.

"Two is better than one, they say."

She pressed up and kissed his jawline, sliding her tongue down the salty skin of his neck, sucking and nipping. Her hand pushed below the elastic band of his shorts, his erection hard, his tip wet with anticipation. She wiped her finger over it firmly and then gave him a slow stroke.

"I remember a conversation about a blow job," she said nonchalantly.

"Yeah, I think there was mention of that," he said through gritted teeth.

"Well then," she said, sliding off the couch, encouraging him to sit back, his legs spread wide, making room for her in front of him on her knees.

"Well then," he repeated, bringing his hands to push away the unruly blonde hair that fell across her forehead.

She leaned forward, pressing a single kiss to his tip, just to greet his beautiful cock in a friendly manner. She looked up at him, his eyes heavy on her, his hands gripping his thighs in anticipation, the cat ears still atop his head.

Remi burst out laughing.

"Max." She laughed.

"What?" he asked, slightly confused.

"I can't do this with the cat ears on. I just can't."

Max began to laugh along, and without another thought, he yanked the ears from his head and tossed them across the room. Remi pushed up on her knees, Max meeting her there halfway as she kissed him in a soul-crushing kiss, the sound of laughter still finding its way from the corners of their mouths.

Her lips fell away from his, landing on his neck, nipping at his ear and his freckle-spattered shoulder—she couldn't get enough of him. She kissed him everywhere she could, every inch of this man was perfect and worthy of love.

The lower she got, the more her frantic kisses slowed, a trail of red leading her to his perfectly thick length. Without hesitation, she took the whole of him deep, with no reservation. She sucked him hard, a moan escaping her as she felt his hands assertively grip her hair to guide her. She slid up his length, the flat of her tongue pressing against his tip before sliding back down, sucking him down to the hilt.

Max groaned, deep and restrained.

She didn't want him to hold back.

His grip grew firmer in her hair and the sting of it made the ache between her legs worsen. Bringing her hands up between his thick thighs, she cupped his balls, massaging them as she took him as deep as she could, staying there and sucking, using the vibrations of her own moans to let him know she wanted this as much as he did.

His body shifted under her, his hips bucking, causing her to take him even deeper, his tip hitting the back of her throat. She kept sucking, waiting for his release, but his hands tugged at her hair, willing her to pull away.

"I'm going to come," he hummed, trying again to pull her from his body.

Slowly, she lifted up, her lips sliding to the tip of his cock and sucking his sensitive head. His body completely tensed up at the sensation of her mouth there. She took him deeply once again, despite his warning that he was about to climax, her jaw stretching to fit his girth. Max jerked under her, letting out a rough, deep moan as he began to come. She gripped his thighs tight and swallowed down every drop of his release.

"Oh, my... oh, fuck," he said as he came, realizing that she wasn't pulling away. "Oh, fuuuuuu..." he said again, and she couldn't help but smile, her lips swollen and her jaw aching in the best way.

"Remi, Remi, Remi," he said, pulling her up into his lap.

"Good?" she asked.

"Better than a maple bar, that's for damn sure."

Chapter Thirty-Nine

The little band venue—The Pig Pen—was packed, considering it was Christmas Eve. Max stood at the back of the crowd, his size and red hair made him stick out like a sore thumb amongst the others: a girl with green hair, a guy with a mullet, lots of piercings, and angry-looking tattoos. Max took in all the black clothing and Dr. Martens boots, and for a crowd that liked music that sounded a bit angry at times, everyone was so extremely kind.

"This your first time seeing them?" the pocket-sized girl next to him with dark hair and perfectly straight bangs asked, as he waited alone while Remi went to get them a beer.

"Yes," he said... because words.

"You're in for a treat. I've seen them six times. They're the only thing I would ditch my murder documentaries for on the Eve of Christmas," she said in a monotone voice, slightly bouncing on her toes in anticipation.

"This is my first show," he managed.

"First show at The Pig Pen?" she asked, needing more information.

"Yeah, and just, like, in general," Max said.

Remi reappeared, handing him a can of Pabst Blue Ribbon. She looked over at the girl Max had been talking to. "Making friends?" she asked, bumping his shoulder.

Max opened the beer and took a long drink. "I was telling her it's my first time."

Remi laughed and elaborated for him. "Yeah, it's his first time at a show. He's new to the music world."

The girl, without hesitation, pulled him in for a very sweaty, mildly musky hug. "Welcome to The Pig Pen family, and the music world, and all that jazz." She looked over and motioned to Remi. "Looks like you found a good one," she said, and Remi smiled back at her. "Anyone who shares their music with you is a keeper."

"I was in my boxer briefs, and she was blasting a punk mix..." he said, realizing that too was a story that needed more words—words he didn't have.

Remi laughed, and elaborated again, "He started as my client. I clean houses—*his* house—and I barged in on him half-naked one day." Max turned to show their new friend the back of his shirt, with a Busy-Bee logo on it. "Yeah, that's my cleaning service, and well, I kinda, sorta fell for him after that."

Max shrugged, a hint of a smile hid behind his beer can as he took a drink.

The girl smiled back, looking up between the two of them. "Wait, you met him because you were his house cleaner?" she asked.

"Yeah, I don't usually mix business with pleasure, but there was no going back after seeing him in the little black briefs."

"I fucking love that story!" their new friend said. "Good thing he didn't end up being a serial killer, right?" she asked, and Remi agreed. The dark-haired girl stuck out a sweaty hand to introduce herself properly, and Max couldn't believe how unbelievably hot the small space had gotten as the bodies continued to pack in.

"I'm Mia, and this," she said, introducing a bigger guy as he came up behind Max and Remi with two beers in hand, "is Chris, the only friend I could convince to come with me tonight." Chris rolled his eyes and took a long drink of his beer, his face wincing at the taste.

"Well," he said, pulling the tiny girl to his side in a friendly hug, "it's not really my scene or drink of choice, but anything for my Mia. And be forewarned, she's obsessed with murder. I blame Netflix."

They all began to carry on like old friends as they waited for the band to take the stage. Max watched as Remi took up space so effortlessly, she was easy and cool, and he realized he had never done anything like this. He had never randomly met strangers and made a toast with cheap room-temperature beer to celebrate a holiday he often forgot existed. Hockey crept into the back of his mind and panic threatened to ruin this moment for him, but before it got too bad, Remi's hand found his and gripped it tight, willing his entire body to loosen up.

He didn't want to think of hockey.

Not now.

Tonight was about music.

"You okay?" she asked, leaning into him.

"I'm more than okay."

"Yes to everything?" she asked.

"Yes to everything," he said.

The band took the stage, and the crowd shifted; a surge of warm bodies moving forward to get closer to the front. The temperature grew hotter still, and Max loved the sweat on his brow and the heat of Remi pressed against him.

The lights dropped.

The stage lit up.

Max blinked.

He blinked again.

His heart raced, and then before he could panic, Remi was wrapping reassuring arms around his massive body, holding him close—she knew. She knew and she responded without him needing to ask for help.

The band's frontman yelled, "Merry fucking ho-ho-ho, or some bullshit like that!" And the crowd went wild. A beat later the band began to play, and it was the song Remi said was her favorite.

Their bodies swayed as the crowd surged forward. He let all of his senses come alive as he closed his eyes and took in the way the heavy bass line made his bones rattle. Every element of the punk show was crashing into him.

He loved this.

This life with Remi, and music, and the beach, and hummus, and new plants, and cat ears, and closets, and sex, and Remi... full circle. *Remi.*

The next song began to play and the room around him was a blur, but the vibration of the music brought every inch of his skin alive. Remi bounced on her toes as she shot her hand into the air while the band played a sort of anthem; the whole crowd knew the words. It was like an unspoken understanding that you shouted these lyrics and pumped your fist.

Max wanted more.

He wanted to be a part of this.

He had never been a part of anything outside of hockey.

Hope filled his chest.

He was going to be okay.

This was going to be okay.

"I love this," he shouted into Remi's ear right as the music stopped. A few people around them laughed, and the lead singer looked out into the crowd and responded.

"Good. I'm happy you don't hate it." The crowd all laughed again, and Max felt his face grow red at the newfound attention he got as the next song started.

Remi turned to face him. "This is my favorite new tradition," she shouted.

"It's our only tradition," he said, leaning in to kiss her mouth that tasted like beer and the mint gum she had gotten from their new friend, Chris.

"For now." She smiled.

"I want you," he shouted, only realizing it for himself as the words escaped his mouth.

"You have me," she said, not grasping what he was asking.

He took her hand and placed it on the crotch of his pants, his want for her very obvious, the music doing something to the entire makeup of his DNA.

"Oh," she said, her smile turning mischievous. "You *want* me, want me."

"Yeah. I *want* you. *Now.*"

She scanned the crowd; the band's set was just taking off. "I have an idea."

"Yes," he agreed.

"I didn't even tell you what I was thinking yet."

He pulled her in to kiss her. "I said yes."

She gripped his hand, beginning to move away from the mass of people. "Follow me."

And he did.

They pushed through the crowd, his hand in Remi's as the outline of bodies in the dark blurred around him.

She pushed on the bathroom stall door; it was locked.

"A bathroom?" he asked skeptically.

"You said yes," she said, biting her bottom lip teasingly between her teeth.

Max pushed her up against the wall of the dark hallway, the music and the sound of the crowd singing along carried through the space around them, loud and heavy. He pressed his body against her, his mouth taking hers like he owned it, like it was his to keep. Her hand gripped him through his pants, and he didn't care that they were only hidden away by the dark hallway, no one here would notice, and if they did, he was certain they wouldn't care.

"This is becoming a bad habit of ours, ya know?" she said as his mouth sucked at the skin below her ear.

"You mean fucking in public?" he asked.

"Yeah. I hate how much I like it."

"Let's call it a tradition then, it sounds worse when you call it a bad habit."

His leg pushed between hers and she let her body roll against the dark denim of his jeans, her black faux leather skirt hiked up around the fishnets she wore under it.

The bathroom door swung open and a drunk man stumbled out, looked at them, and slurred, "Niiiiiice," giving them an enthusiastic thumbs up.

Max pulled her away from the wall and tugged her into the graffiti-covered bathroom stall. Band stickers, political posters, and things like *"Natalie Jane Rudolph is a dick biter"* written on the walls only made the small restroom look even more grungy than Max had anticipated.

"This is not up to my cleanliness standards," Remi joked.

"It could be worse?" Max asked.

"It could," she said, pulling him into her, her ass up against the chipped porcelain sink that was hanging on to the wall for dear life.

A small puddle of water under the sink made for dirty footprints that seemed to be etched into the existence of this bathroom—it probably hadn't been mopped since The Pig Pen opened in the '80s.

Max brought his hand between her legs and began to massage her over the fish nets and panties she wore. His mouth crashed against hers in a punishing kiss as her hands tugged at his zipper. The band started a new song on the other side of the wall and the deep bass line rattled the janky mirror that seemed to only be held up with double-sided tape and grime.

Remi worked Max's jeans down to his knees, pulling his briefs with them, his dick springing free, hard and ready.

Max spun her around and her hands braced the sink in anticipation. The moment arose, and their frantic need to see it through had them both pushing aside all rationale. Remi raised her ass for him in a teasing wiggle as he hiked her skirt up around her waist. Tangling his fingers in the holes of her fishnets Max ripped them open. Pulling her thong to the side he lined up his erection with her entrance, his thick head pressing and teasing against her.

With both hands on her ass, he pulled her cheeks apart, and with one quick motion, he pushed himself deep inside her. Remi gasped at the sudden fullness of him, bottoming out against her.

"This is so fucking hot," she moaned, locking eyes with him in the battered mirror.

"Hold on," he warned, preparing her for what came next.

She moved her hands to press against the graffiti-covered wall in front of her, and right as she braced herself, he pulled out to the tip and slammed back into her, gripping her hips as his body crashed against hers, the timeworn sink rattling against the wall.

"Oh fuck," she said. "So good, so deep."

He did it again, and again. Finding his footing and holding her tight, Max used her body to hold on to as he began to pound into her from behind. The sound of their bodies smacking together was almost loud enough to drown out the music on the other side of the wall.

Remi moaned, and it was deeper than she had sounded in the past. "Faster," she encouraged. "I want to feel it tomorrow. Make me remember this in the morning, Max."

Max lost it. He had never felt so out of control and yet completely in control at the same time. Remi's head fell back. She was saying his name, over and over, every time he slammed into her again.

"Too much?" he managed, a little worried he was being too rough.

"No, please don't—" she faltered, a whimper escaping her before she finished. "Don't stop, just, ohhh, oh shit," she moaned, and he knew he had her, he knew she was coming.

"I'm going to—" he said, and before he could finish his sentence, she cut him off.

"Do it. Go ahead. I want it."

Max pulled her body against his with one last smack of skin against skin, as he came, buried deep inside her.

"That was kind of wild," Remi said, looking back up into the mirror as Max slowly pulled out.

"Kind of wild? We just fucked in a bathroom at a punk show on Christmas Eve."

"A story for the grandkids," she teased as Max pulled the last of the paper towels from the dispenser and handed them to her, suddenly feeling guilty that she had to deal with the mess—*his* mess.

"I ripped your tights," he said.

She pushed them down and maneuvered them off carefully, slipping one foot out of her checkered Vans at a time so she wouldn't step on the disgusting floor. "Yeah, you did. You know, you could have just pulled them down."

Max took the fishnets from her, turning to throw them in the trash as she ran the paper towels under water to clean up the mess between her legs.

"I know. I thought about pulling them down, but the truth is, I had been thinking about ripping them off you since you showed up at my house wearing them today."

"Did we just unlock a Max Miller fantasy?" she asked, tossing the paper towels in the overflowing trash can.

"I don't think it actually was one until tonight, but yeah, that was pretty fucking hot," he said, pulling her in for a kiss.

A loud knock on the bathroom door startled them apart and the person on the other side shouted, "Are you done fucking yet? I gotta piss. I broke the seal."

Max looked at Remi like a deer in headlights. "He knows," Max said, a little worried he might get found out. He *was* still an NHL player, and he did have a certain reputation to uphold, he didn't need a Roman Graves situation right before he announced his retirement.

"It's fine. We're not the first, and we won't be the last to fuck in the bathroom of The Pig Pen," she said, taking his hand and pulling the door open to find the same guy as before, standing in front of them doing the pee-pee dance.

They walked by him, and again, he gave Max a thumbs up and said, "Niiiice."

Max gave him a smile, because it *was* nice, doing whatever he wanted, knowing that his life was his, *all* his. Even if he lost hockey, and in the end, his vision too, he could see it being a pretty good life with Remi.

"Should we finish the show?" she asked, as the lead singer announced, "*We have a few more songs and then you can get the fuck out of this shithole to go do whatever it is people do on Merry Ho-ho-ho night.*"

"Yes, let's stay for the last few songs," he agreed.

"For tradition's sake?" she asked.

"Yes. And because I think I really like this."

Chapter Fourty

The holiday break went by in the blink of an eye. It was crazy how fast time went when you were having fun, and Max *had* been having fun. He and Remi ate terrible food and made love as much as his body would allow him—twice in his closet—just because they could, for nostalgic purposes. She showed him old bands that he wished he had known about when they were still together. They laid in bed—*his* bed—and ordered random things off Pottery Barn for his house: decorative pillows, a gigantic painting of the ocean for above his couch, picture frames for pictures he hadn't taken yet, and different jewel tone glass cups, because Remi said they would be *aesthetically pleasing* to drink fancy drinks from in the fall.

The fun helped.

It pushed away the reality of what he was up against.

The NHL Network had replayed his mishap on the ice several times over the holiday break while giving little insight into *"What was really going on with Max Miller?"* He hadn't watched it, he couldn't. The sight of him stumbling around on his skates, his helmet being frantically ripped from his head in panic—it was too much to watch happen over and over again when it already lived rent-free in his head.

Max made his way down the cool, long corridor that led to the Condors locker room, where he would find his team getting ready for practice.

This was it.

This was the moment he had been dreading.

His heart hammered in his chest and the words he had to say out loud played over and over in his head. Words he knew well by now. Words he thought he wouldn't have to speak for years and years to come.

But that didn't hold true for him anymore.

And now, his exit music would play.

When he entered the locker room, the sound of his team's chatter went instantly silent, and he looked down at his feet, avoiding their gaze. When he finally found the courage to look up, he found comfort in the gentle smile of his fellow goalie, Brown. He gave Max an encouraging nod, and the simple, silent gesture set the wheels in motion for what came next.

Max made his way to his locker and took a seat. He could feel the pause of motion throughout the locker room in anticipation. The familiarity of this moment was stolen from him by his lack of equipment present, he didn't have a bag to hang, or pads to put on, not even a protein shake that would carry him through the practice. The blades of his skates were haunting, still dull from his last game, his last skate, his final start. His practice jersey was nowhere to be found, and it was so solidifying, how real this had all become.

The foreshadowing was an awful reminder of why he showed up today.

The team watched on in anticipation as he sat there, his head hung low, his silence a deafening scream.

Brown made his way across the locker room to Max and the team made room for him, like the parting of the Red Sea. Out of respect for Max's old superstitions, Brown took the seat to the left of him, because the right was off-limits. Even if Max didn't believe in superstitions anymore, even if he didn't need them, he was grateful for this simple nod to his legacy.

Brown placed a sure hand on Max's shoulder, and that simple act of kindness poured an overwhelming amount of comfort and reassurance into Max.

"You got this," Brown said.

Max looked up; all the boys were looking at him. Waiting. Watching.

He had left them in the dark long enough.

Max stood, running anxious hands through his thick red hair, the words sitting on the tip of his tongue.

Brown patted his back, and repeated his words, "You got this."

Max looked around, these men, these teammates, these Condors—they were his family, his constant, his *home*. He somehow hadn't realized it until it was too late, and for that, he would never take them or this opportunity to have known them, sharing this locker room and this arena with them, and the wins and the losses with them, for granted ever again.

He loved hockey.

He loved this team.

He... *would* be okay.

"So, as you all know, I'm not a man of many words," he started, happy a few of the smart-asses on the team made jokes of agreement at his statement—it was a much-needed ice breaker. "But sometimes all we have left to give is our words. I guess that's what I'm here to do, I'm here to tell you the truth. A secret I have selfishly kept from you, hell, a secret I tried to keep from myself. Denial is an ugly thing, but oblivion was where I chose to hide for the majority of this season. Over the past few years, I have noticed small signs that my vision was not as strong as it had been in the past. These were things I think many people face in their lifetime, things that can be fixed with glasses or a procedure." He paused, and Brown gave his back another reassuring pat.

"But as time went on, I started to notice my performance struggle on the ice because of my vision, which led to severe anxiety. I started to notice that this was something more. It was more than struggling to see at night, or floaters when the lighting suddenly changed." Max took a deep breath, steadied his voice, and went on. "I went to see an eye doctor under the radar, and he saw something in my eyes. Something bad. He told me I needed to see a specialist, which instantly freaked me the fuck out. But what scared me more was the look on his face. I knew from his look that whatever he saw wasn't good. I knew at that moment that this wasn't going to end well for me. Before I left his office, he told me to try and contact my biological father, and that he might have answers for me."

Several men in the room gasped, they knew his story, they knew enough about his past to know that Max had never met his real father.

"I tracked him down and the doctor's suspicions were confirmed—my father is legally blind."

The whole room grew eerily quiet, their breaths held, even their hearts seemed to pause beating to allow Max to go on.

"My father has a condition called retinitis pigmentosa, and along with his red hair, he passed this on to me as well. I *will* go blind. This outcome is unchangeable, unfathomable, and heartbreaking. I will spend the rest of the season on injured reserve, and I think we all know, without me having to say it, what comes after that."

The team's captain, Patrick Carter, made his way to Max, bringing him in for an embrace. Brown stood next, and hugged Max as well. Slowly, one by one, his team packed in around Max until the ever-growing hug he was at the center of was completed, every player in the room wrapping their arms around the next in solidarity for Max. The locker room remained silent, and Max knew this was their way of saying goodbye, in true Max fashion, with words being too hard to speak.

Because words were hard when you were losing a game, but words were impossible when you were losing a teammate.

Coach was the last to join the hug. Max looked up from the sea of heads lowered around him in the embrace and found his coach looking back, a single tear running down his cheek accompanied by the proud smile of a father.

Chapter Fourty-One

Max found himself sitting in his garage at home while the rest of his team were across town taking the ice at the Condors arena for a practice he wasn't a part of. The paperwork for his medical leave sat on the seat next to him, his years of dedication and training summed up in a neat manila folder; it felt like a smack in the face because that folder made it official. He was counting down the days until he was no longer an Anaheim Condor, or an NHL goalie. The only two things he had ever known himself to be.

He was supposed to be signing his big bridge contract this year, not announcing his retirement.

This was *not* okay.

He was *not* okay.

And this time, Max knew it was okay to not be okay.

The team had taken it harder than he expected. The questions they asked were all ones he'd readied himself for, all questions he had asked himself a million times already: Is it treatable? Is there a medicine that could cure it or slow it down? Can you play a few more games? Can you finish the season?

The answer was no.

Then there was the hardest question: Will this be your final year with the Condors?

The answer was yes.

The hardest yes he had said since he had decided to live a life of yeses.

His phone buzzed, and he knew it was Remi. She both worried about him and reminded *him* not to worry. She was the only thing keeping him grounded at this point, and he couldn't help but think back to the day they met and wonder if some higher power had it all planned out for them, for her to come into his life just when he needed her. He remembered sitting on his bed after he had broken the lamp, and the way his body came alive at the simple brush of her finger against his—his connection to her was instant.

He opened his home screen and found that the text was not from Remi at all, but from Jack Brown, inviting him to meet up after practice to talk, and maybe grab some food if Max was up for it.

He wasn't up for it but agreed to it anyway.

For too long he had said no, and where had that gotten him? A big house that had never seen guests. Great accomplishments with no one to celebrate them with. A whole hockey team of great men who felt like family, yet they knew almost nothing about him. Max was done hiding, with his words guarded, tucked away in the back of his mind.

So, he said yes.

And then he called Remi.

"Hey, you," she said cheerfully. She knew that today was the big day, so he wasn't surprised she was using her extra welcoming voice.

"Hey. I'm sitting in the garage," he said.

"Did you just get home?" she asked.

"No, I just can't seem to pull myself out of it."

It being the moment, the spiral, the reality—the manila folder on the seat next to him, mocking him.

"That's okay. If sitting in your Jeep is where you need to be, then stay put. There's no rules about this, Max. No books written on how to properly handle what you're going through."

"I told them," he said.

He could hear her breath falter on the other line. "How'd it go?"

"It went as to be expected. Big emotions. Lots of support. Lots of tough questions."

"How do you feel about it now?"

"At first, I felt numb. And then angry. Now I'm a little relieved. I keep having this weird sense of freedom knowing I don't have to be the last line of defense for my team anymore. Which also feels kind of shitty."

"Do you think that might be a sort of defense mechanism? Almost like your brain protecting you from the reality of what's going on?"

"Maybe? But I try and buy into it, ya know? I don't want to play into the opposite of those thoughts, the ones that tell me I'm nothing if I'm not a goalie."

Remi took a second, and for a moment he thought the call had failed.

"You there?" he asked.

"I am. I'm just trying to comprehend how you're taking this so well. I'm just really fucking proud of you, Max."

"I'm not taking it as well as I'm letting on, Rem. But I think I might need to fake it for a while, just to help me through the rest of this season."

"Sometimes that's all we can do."

The line went silent again. Remi made silence safe.

"Jack Brown," he started, "the other goalie. He wants to get dinner tonight to talk."

"And how do you feel about that?"

"I think I want to go."

"Good. I think you need to rely on your team now more than ever."

He ran his hands over the steering wheel, they were clammy with anxiety. "I rely on *you*," he said.

"You do, and you always can, but they have something I can't offer."

"What's that?" he asked.

"They know what it's like to be an NHL player, I don't. I can't even imagine how hard you worked to get there, but they can, Jack Brown can—especially with him being a goalie. They're going to know how to console you in ways I can't even fathom, Max."

"How do you always know what to say?" he asked.

Remi let out a long sigh on the other end, and then playfully said, "Because I'm fucking awesome."

Max laughed. "This is true."

"So, should I just head back to my place and call it a night?" she asked.

"I was actually thinking you might come with me?"

"You don't think it'll be weird? He might want you all to himself."

Max took a deep breath, and then gently reminded her, "I can't drive myself, Rem, it'll be dark. I'm sorry to ask. I can just call an Uber."

"No," she nearly shouted, "no Uber. I'm sorry. I just—it just slipped my mind."

"It's okay, I don't expect you to be my personal driver. It's more than that really. I think I want you with me, I want to introduce you to someone I know. I want my team to know you."

"Okay. I would love to come meet him. And Max?"

"Yeah?"

"Driving with you has become one of my favorite things to do, please don't ever feel like it's a burden."

"That's going to take some work," he admitted.

"I know, but I'll keep reminding you."

"See you soon?" he asked.

"I have to go home and get ready first; I cleaned four houses today. I smell like pine sol, bleach, and sweat."

"Mmmm," he said, "my favorite smells."

***

Max held Remi's hand as they walked into the restaurant, letting her take the lead. On the drive over she shared with him that she was nervous about meeting his teammate, and ultimately the man that would take Max's place in front of the net. She said she couldn't be sure if she resented him or not, and while Max didn't admit it to her, he shared the same feelings. He didn't want her to resent Brown just as much as he didn't want to resent his teammate, but Remi was allowed to have big emotions in all of this too. Even if she was new to all of this, she was allowed to mourn the end of his career. She had fallen in love with him, claiming that part had come easy to her, and with loving him, came loving hockey. She told him she would miss watching him play and that she hadn't realized that until now—now that it was all so final.

The host showed them to their table and Max was shocked to find his team captain, Patrick Carter, there as well. Both men stood and brought Max in for a hug, their faces inviting, but he didn't miss the underlying hints of sadness.

"Guys, this is Remi, my girlfriend and personal driver," he said, only half joking.

Remi shook both of their hands and handled their introductions with ease.

"I'm Patrick Carter, sorry for inviting myself," he said with a warm smile that showed a missing front tooth.

"That's okay," Remi said. "It's a double date now," she teased with a wink.

"And I'm Jack Brown. Thanks for joining us."

Remi gave both of them a single-dimple smile and thanked them for having her.

"We're happy you came," Carter said to Remi, "Max is kind of a closed book. It's nice to finally see into his world. To know that he has someone caring for him."

They all took their seats and placed drink orders with the server.

"So, this is weird," Carter said jokingly.

"If you invited me for good conversation, you should have known better," Max teased back.

They all laughed.

"Today was a lot," Brown spoke up. "I guess me and Carter just wanted to see you and make sure you're okay. It all happened pretty fast. It was like one second you were telling the team you're retiring and then we had practice, business as usual. It felt unfinished I guess, like there wasn't any real closure. Not for the team anyway, and I'm guessing not for you either."

Max looked over at Remi, she gave his thigh a reassuring squeeze, a reminder that she was with him, and that he was safe.

"I felt the same way. I just sat in my garage when I got home," Max said, and they all laughed again.

"Is that what you've been doing for all these years when we've invited you out with the team after a win?" Carter joked.

Max took a second, sipped his drink, and then answered honestly. "Yeah. Pretty much. I mean, I didn't sit in my garage, but I definitely hid away. I wish I had done things differently," he said, his voice trailing off at the end.

"We all have those thoughts," Brown said. "But what's important is that we realize that sort of thing before we live our whole lives without making any necessary changes."

"When did you get so wise?" Carter asked the young goalie.

"I've had a great mentor," he said, looking over at Max.

Max, surprised, brought his hand to point at himself. "Me?" he asked, shocked.

"Yeah, you," Brown said. "You may not say much, but when you do talk, it's exactly what people need to hear. I became the goalie I am today because you *didn't* say a lot. When you gave me feedback, I knew it was genuine, I knew it was important, because you didn't give it often. I hung on to every word you ever told me. And more often than not, it was exactly what I needed."

Max wasn't expecting this. He didn't come prepared for admissions of the heart. He hadn't even known anyone felt this way about him, but he was grateful it was being said.

"You know, when I first met Max," Remi started, "he told me he wasn't great with conversation, but I think I agree with Jack. I think he's just cautious with his words, and I think that makes being someone he chooses to share them with feel extra special."

Max took a drink of the cocktail the server had brought and ran a nervous thumb over the condensation dripping down the side of his glass. "There is one thing though, that I wish I had said more," Max admitted.

They all waited in a safe, but still a little awkward, silence for him to go on.

"I wish I had said yes to the celebrations, the dinners, and the friendships. I wish I had gotten to know the team on a more intimate level. I was always so afraid of not knowing what to say that I missed opportunities to listen. I missed opportunities to get to know amazing people—" He paused and looked over at Remi. "But I'm working on that, thanks to this girl," he said, bringing her hand to his lips to kiss her there.

He smiled over at her, and she leaned in to kiss his cheek. "One yes at a time," she said.

"One yes at a time," he agreed.

Carter took a piece of the complementary bread, dipping it into the accompanying oil mixture. "How did you get him to open up to you? I have to know. I've been trying to lure him into my web of bullshit for years," he said with a mouth full of bread.

Remi smiled, this time a double-dimple smile, and Max couldn't believe, in this moment, that she was his.

"Hummus," she said simply.

"Hummus?" Brown asked with a chuckle.

"Yup." She beamed. "That was the first time I got a yes out of him. I asked him to have a picnic with me on the beach. And then there were the donuts, cat ears, and even a punk show," she said, then paused and added, "Oh, and one hard rule: No more passes."

Max shook his head and lowered it, a small grin on his face.

"No more passes?" Carter asked.

"Yeah," Max said, "it turns out if you tell me I'm not allowed to pull away and chicken out, I actually stick around and do scary things."

"Do scary things," Carter repeated quietly, and Max knew he was thinking back on the moment in the hotel room when Max had lost his shit over those simple words.

"Yeah, she helps me do scary things," Max said.

Brown looked between the two of them, his eyebrows raised. "Yeah, doing scary things is cool and all, but are we really going to act like she didn't mention Max in cat ears?"

They all began to laugh, and Max began to talk with his teammates more freely than he had in all the years leading up to his last. He wondered if it was too late to create the memories that should have lined the halls of his home in picture frames long before now.

Time didn't stop for anyone, but Max was certain that he wanted to spend the rest of his saying yes.

Chapter Fourty-Two

The hockey season for the Condors continued on without Max, as he knew it would. He watched the games with Remi, and sometimes he resented his team for winning so effortlessly without him in front of the net, and some games he cheered them on with nothing but respect and admiration for a team he loved so dearly.

Max found himself doubling down on his time off the ice. He could sit back and let his disability become his entire identity, or he could ready himself for the future with it. He had his moments where he still freaked out, and nights where he laid awake angry and bitter, his heart questioning his misfortune. There were also days where nothing filled the void of hockey, not Remi, not the beach, not sex, food or even his newfound love of music.

This was to be expected.

He tried to show himself grace when he wasn't the best version of himself.

Sometimes he failed.

And sometimes he slept too long.

Sometimes he just needed to get out of the house, so he found himself in a stranger's home, his Busy Bee Cleaners shirt on as he mopped the floors while Remi scrubbed a toilet in the next room over. Max was grateful that she shared her outlets with him, invited him to get his hands dirty with her, to be a part of *her* day-to-day.

He was happy she wasn't sick of him yet.

"Hey," she said, as they loaded her cleaning cart into the back of her Subaru after they finished cleaning the last house of the day. "I was thinking that tomorrow, if you're up for it, I can take you to check out Lighthouse, that rehabilitation facility I told you about."

"I'm nervous," he admitted, slamming the trunk shut and circling around to get in the passenger side.

"Tell me what about it makes you nervous."

He had a long list of reasons why he was apprehensive about visiting the facility. This wasn't the first time he had thought about taking the recommended steps for preparing for the future with his disability, but something about acting on it felt so final. He still technically had his vision; he could drive during the day, he could watch TV—even if blurry—and he could still do the simple acts of life with just his peripheral vision being affected, though he knew it didn't stop there. He knew what came next, and he knew the best thing he could do was prepare himself for it.

But getting there was hard.

"I'm afraid I'm not emotionally ready to learn what this looks like in depth. Right now, I have a general idea, you know, the common misconceptions of what life looks like with a vision impairment. I know enough, but I'm choosing not to be informed, because the more I know, the more real it will become and I'm struggling with that."

"That's a very valid thought process, Max. But don't you think the unknown might be scarier than just ripping the Band-Aid off and speaking to people who are not just living, but thriving with a vision impairment? Maybe what you're really afraid of is thinking there is no silver lining, and because of that, I think you might want to go take a look for yourself and see that there is so much technology and support out there for you. I know it's out there, because after we met with your dad I started to dig. I wanted to be informed, so I did some research. I wanted to understand this, I wanted to know for myself what *we* are up against, because I'm in Max, I'm all in, and we have a lot of fucking life to live together."

Max took her hand in his, bringing her knuckles up to his lips to kiss. "Okay. Let's go."

"Yeah?" she asked.

"Yeah. I think I'm ready."

***

Hand in hand, they entered the Lighthouse Rehabilitation Agency. Remi could feel Max's nerves in the stiff way he held her hand, his palms clammy against hers. The facility was welcoming, the lights were bright, and the room was free of any unnecessary clutter. Along the far wall was a line of desks with computers, and in the far-right corner there was another desk where a young man sat as an older woman explained contrast and labeling to him. At the far back of the facility there were two closed-off rooms, one for counseling, and one that Remi had visited last time, which was the office that belonged to the facility manager, Nicole, and her sweet dog, Shepard.

"Right back here," Remi assured Max as she led him through the facility slowly, giving him time to take in the surroundings.

"It's nice," Max said.

"It's very nice. It's one of the top-rated facilities in California."

"Everyone seems... happy."

Remi gave his hand a squeeze. "Of course they are. Look at all this amazing technology and support. This is going to be really good for us."

"Us," he said under his breath, giving her hand a squeeze back.

Remi knocked on the doorframe of Nicole's office and announced that it was her and Max. She had been researching ways to be respectful of the vision-impaired community, and one of the things she read was announcing yourself, and making your presence known.

"It's Remi and Max," she said.

Nicole's face lit up with a huge welcoming smile, and the beautiful golden retriever next to her sat up, ready for action, his tail wagging at the sight of new visitors.

"Come in," she welcomed. "Make yourself comfortable."

They entered the small office; Max took a seat across from Nicole as Remi went to properly say hello to Shepard.

"Hi, buddy. Remember me?" she asked the happy dog.

"He remembers everyone. He's a people person." Nicole beamed.

Remi went to take a seat next to Max.

"Welcome, Max. It's nice to meet you. I'm Nicole, the facility manager, and Shepard here is the mascot. He is also my seeing-eye dog," Nicole said, formally introducing herself.

"Hi," Max said awkwardly, and Nicole giggled. Remi had warned her he was a man of few words.

"Let's start with some basic 'getting to know you' formalities. Break the ice. I know the first visit to a place like this can be overwhelming and a little unsettling even."

Max nodded his head to agree, and Remi noticed the realization on his face that he needed to use his words more now than ever. "Yes. I'm feeling a little anxious, that's for sure," he agreed.

"That's completely normal. It's kind of weird when you think about it; knowing you're going through a drastic life change and having all these tools to help you transition into that life change, but actually doing them and learning them can be challenging. There's always this want to hold out a little longer. To try and avoid the inevitable."

"Yeah, I'm definitely in that phase, the denial phase," Max agreed.

Nicole gave Max an affirming head nod. "Well, I'm happy you came, and that you have Remi here to give you that little push. It's nice to have that support right out the gate."

Remi leaned over and squeezed his shoulder, mouthing *I love you* to him for encouragement.

"So, Max, tell me a little bit about you. What are some things I should know that might help me understand you better, help you transition into this lifestyle better, and help me understand what tools we have here at the facility that might be the most helpful for you," Nicole asked.

Max looked over at Remi, seeking strength through her. If she could, she would give him all of her confidence in this moment, all of the words that came so easily for her, she would give them to him—she would give him everything, but this was something Max had to do. These were emotions Max had to portray for himself, because only *he* could get it right.

"So, the biggest thing I think you should know is that I'm a professional goalie for the Anaheim Condors," Max said, and Remi watched as the smile on Nicole's face faltered for a split second.

"Wow. That's incredible. I've never worked with a professional athlete before," she said.

Max cleared his throat and went on. "It's already affected my career. I played my last game before the holidays. It ended badly. I'm officially on injured reserve for the rest of the season."

"That's got to be hard," she said, her voice dropping an octave from its usual chipper tone.

"It was the lighting in the arena. The contrast. I struggled to keep focus on the puck, and then at the last game the lights came up and it was like my vision had gotten significantly worse in the blink of an eye."

"Sounds like you experienced a dip. It happens with RP. Your vision can be slowly deteriorating and then you just blink once and experience a major change—a dip. Those moments are hard. I'm sorry that had to happen to you at a game."

"I freaked out," Max added.

"I'm sure you did. It's terrifying. Even if you had known it was coming, nothing could have prepared you for it."

"I think I may have been able to finish the game if I didn't freak out over the 'dip,' but I couldn't keep playing, not well or safely, at least. I knew I was becoming a liability to my team, and myself. So, I finally told them."

"That must have been a hard conversation to have. I'm so sorry. I'm not a huge sports girl myself, but I can only imagine how important your career is to you."

Max let out a sigh. "It's *everything* to me."

Remi's heart ached for him.

As if on cue, Shepard got up from his bed next to Nicole's desk and made his way over to Max's side. Looking up at him with puppy dog eyes, he laid his head against Max's thigh.

"Can I pet him?" Max asked.

"I think he might not let you leave if you *don't* pet him," Nicole said, her sympathetic smile returning.

Max looked down at the dog and brought both of his big hands up to scratch under Shepard's ears. "Are you a good boy?" he asked, Shepard's tail instantly started wagging. "Did you come over here to cheer me up buddy?" Max asked, the dog nuzzled his head against Max's hand.

Remi looked between Max and the dog. It was the best smile she had seen on his face in a while, it was childlike and gentle. With each tail wag and nuzzle of his face against Max's hand, Remi watched the anxiety in Max's body melt away.

Max looked up at her, catching her smiling at him and Shepard. "I like the dog," he said simply.

"Shepard is an amazing boy. Sometimes I feel like he can read emotions," Nicole added.

Max looked back down at the dog. "Then you must know that you are making me very happy right now, Shepard," Max said.

The dog's tail wagged some more.

This was never going to be an easy visit, but Remi was grateful for Shepard lightening the mood.

"Have you ever had a dog, Max?" Nicole asked.

He shook his head and looked over at Remi and smiled. "No, but I have an adopted betta fish named Bozo."

Remi's heart warmed with love for this amazing man, pushing back tears from her eyes.

"Well, you can't have a seeing-eye fish, but dogs are incredible resources for the vision-impaired community," Nicole teased, and Remi found it refreshing that there was humor to be had here.

Nicole went on for the next hour of their meeting detailing the levels of technology and resources that were out there for Max. Remi took notes and opened tabs in her search browser of things she wanted to have a little more in-depth look into when she got home. And while Remi knew all the technology in the world wasn't going to make this any easier on Max, she was grateful it was available. Even more so, she was thankful that he was willing to be here at Lighthouse when she knew what he really wanted to do was avoid it altogether, to live in denial until what vision he had left was gone.

Chapter Fourty-Three

It was game one of the playoffs.

His team had made the playoffs.

He wouldn't be playing, not tonight in Anaheim, and not at the next game in San Jose against the Threshers. While it pained Max to be back in this arena in a suit instead of his jersey, he knew he had to be there. For his team, for his own mental health, and because he wanted to share this with Remi while it still felt like it was his.

She sat next to him, holding his hand, and he couldn't help but love the way she looked in the fresh Condors hoodie he got for her to wear to the game. The other players and Condor's affiliates in the box welcomed Remi with open arms, like a family member, while they expressed their condolences to Max. Some of them handled it better than others; they asked good questions and didn't shy away from his situation. Some treated him like he was given a death sentence—those were the harder people to deal with. At the end of the day, he just wanted everyone to treat him normally and look him in the eyes when they spoke to him. He didn't want his vision loss to be the main character in his life, not when only a month ago he was Max Miller, the goalie.

They all stood as the National Anthem was sung. Max closed his eyes to steady his breathing, to try and calm his heart rate, to prepare for what was to come. Puck drop. Brown in net. The timer showing fifteen minutes. Game one out of a possible seven-game series.

The Stanley Cup playoffs—it was the hardest trophy to win—and he would never know what it felt like.

This would be okay.

He would be okay.

The anthem ended, and everyone in the box clapped and cheered as the lights came up. Max blinked. He blinked again. If he was in the net at this very moment, he wouldn't be able to see his own feet, let alone a tiny black puck. His stomach ached with longing to turn back time to when he still thought he just needed glasses for night driving, a time when he thought everyone struggled to make out sharp images in the dark, a time when he was unaware and naïve enough to hide away in his denial.

The puck dropped and the game was officially underway, but Max couldn't make out anything past the box.

"You, okay?" Remi asked, leaning into his ear, "You look pale."

"Low blood sugar," he joked, but both he and Remi knew that wasn't the case.

"Blood sugar aside, how's your heart? How's your head?" she asked.

He wiped anxious hands on his deep blue suit pants. "Heart is very happy that you're next to me. Head…" he said and stopped to think, "My head is a mess, Rem."

"You know, we don't have to stay," she assured him. "Your team will understand."

He looked around the box, some of the people affiliated with his team were standing and watching with plates of food in their hands, others sat in their seats, their focus intent on the game. He didn't miss the way their eyes found his before darting back to the ice. *Pity.* He hated it.

"I want to stay," he said.

"Okay. Is there anything I can do to make this easier?" she asked.

"Yeah, let me know if the other team scores," he said, his voice a fine line between sarcasm and defeat.

The crowd was loud. Their cheers seemed to rattle the arena, and Max could feel the pulse of the building under his feet. A good save: they cheered. A goal: they jumped to their feet to sing out the Condor's anthem. A bad call: boos, and chants that the refs sucked filled the air. And the win—the *first* win—of this round of the playoffs against a West Coast rival team, and Max could feel the excitement all around him. He could feel the victory. Even from the stands, even in his suit, even without being able to make out *his* teammates on the ice celebrating, he could feel it all.

Winning *still* felt good.

It still felt like this victory was his to celebrate.

His heart raced with joy for his team, and it felt really fucking good to win, even if he wasn't the one in the net.

They drove down the Pacific Coast Highway back to his house in silence after the game. Max could feel Remi's need for conversation, he knew her mind must be flooded with questions, and concerns.

"I need you to do something for me when we get home," he finally said.

"Anything," she agreed, she always did.

He pulled her hand up to his lips and kissed her knuckles. "Okay," he said.

"Okay? What does that even mean? What did I just agree to?"

"You'll see," he said.

Remi laughed. "Max Miller, tell me right meow."

Nope. Even with a cat joke, she would have to wait.

***

They got back to his house and as part of their new routine, their new lifestyle that had somehow fallen together so effortlessly, Remi led the way, flipping on each light switch as she walked through the house.

"Sit at the bar," he said, disappearing into his room.

"If you don't come out naked wearing only your hockey helmet, I'm leaving," she teased, draping the floral print farmers market tote he had gotten her months ago over the back of one of the barstools.

"I don't even have a helmet here, but it's good to know I still have a reason to own one," he shouted from his room.

When he returned, he held a little leather box with a zipper keeping it closed. He set it on the counter, then circled around the bar to grab the plastic wrap from the pantry. Piece by piece he lined a small portion of the bar top.

"Well?" she asked as he unzipped the black box.

"I need you to tattoo me," he said, at the same exact moment that Remi saw the tattoo gun.

"My name?" she joked.

He looked up at her, his cheeks blushing, his eyes so green. "One day."

"Ha," she said. "Okay, for real, what am I tattooing on you, because I can't even draw stick figures. Art is not in my wheelhouse."

Max poured black ink into a small cap and then turned on the gun, testing to make sure it worked. It buzzed in his hand, then he turned it off and set it down. Button by button his dress shirt came off. Remi instantly knew what this was about the second she laid eyes on his naked ribs.

A tally mark.

"But you didn't lose tonight, Max," she said under her breath.

He lifted his right arm and exposed the bare skin there, not a single tally mark to be seen.

"I'm done keeping track of my losses Remi. I thought I would do one last tally mark, but this time, to signify my wins. I have you, I have this beautiful house, the beach, and my whole life ahead of me. I'm ready to lay my losses to rest."

Remi climbed into his lap, straddling him, kissing him like this was the only way she knew how to celebrate him. His arms wrapped around her, holding her close as he kissed her back. At first, the kiss was rushed and messy, but realizing they had all the time in the world, it slowed to something sweet and reassuring.

A kiss can say so many things.

Tonight, it said, I'm proud of you.

As their lips slowed and his grip on her loosened, Remi pulled away just enough to take in the sight of him up close and personal. His beard and mustache were so perfectly trimmed. His hair thick and well-kept. His eyes were green and heavy. His cheeks flushed by just their kissing alone—the beauty of dating a ginger. He was handsome and wonderful, and she didn't know how this man of few words had transformed into the one giving her the best conversations of her life, but she wouldn't question it. No one questions the way the waves tease, threatening to move forward onto the shore only to pull back just when you thought it might touch your bare feet in the sand. So, she wouldn't question how she got so lucky with Max.

Once her client, now her lover.

Life was weird and wonderful, and for the first time in a long time, Remi wished her mother were here to see this, to see her in love, successful, and thriving.

"So, how does this work?" she asked, eying the tattoo gun and fresh cap of ink.

"Just press the needle to my skin like a pencil."

"What if I press too hard?"

"You won't. It's easy to grasp how deep you are the second you touch the needle to my skin."

"Why can't you just do it? You did all your other tattoos," she asked.

"I'm not left-handed," he teased.

"It's a simple line."

He leaned in and kissed her, pushing her hair behind her ears. "Exactly."

Remi shook her head with a playful grin and leaned across the bar to get the tattoo gun. She turned it on, the buzz tickling her hand, then dipped the needle into the black cap of ink. Max sat back in the chair and lifted his arm above his head, his strong body elongated, his ribs exposed, the muscles in his arms stretched. She felt something stir deep in her stomach. Something about this exchange was so intimate, so sexy. His trust in her—it made her want him more than ever.

"Okay," she said. "Here it goes."

His eyes locked on hers. "To celebrating the wins," he said.

She leaned in and kissed his cheek before bringing the needle to the soft skin of his ribs. Drawing the gun down, she felt the buzz and pull as she watched a single line appear there.

A tally mark.

A forever of wins.

Chapter Fourty-Four

It was a Wednesday and Remi woke up to her phone buzzing on her bedside table at 4 a.m. She reached over, trying to grab the phone without waking Max. They slept at her house last night after watching the game at the local bar. Max had been incognito in a hat and sunglasses as they watched the Condors advance to the second round of the playoffs after absolutely destroying the San Jose Threshers in the first round.

"Hello?" Remi answered.

On the other line one of her cleaners, Miriam, responded, "Hey, Remi, I can't come in today. Sebastian is running a fever, and my mom is out of town. I don't have anyone to watch him and there's no way I can send him to school like this."

"Yeah, yeah. Family first," Remi said. This was her golden rule as a small business owner.

"I know it's your light day. I'm so sorry to do this," Miriam said on the other line.

"No, it's fine. The house I clean on Wednesdays is flexible," Remi said with a smile, looking over at Max, whose house *was* her Wednesday morning house. He looked up at her through sleepy, hooded eyes and mouthed, *Everything okay?* She patted his shoulder, gave him a reassuring smile, and went on. "Keep me posted. If you need tomorrow off as well, I can cover it between me and Maria."

"Okay, thank you, Remi," Miriam said.

"No worries, girl. Go take care of your baby."

She reached over and put her phone down on the bedside table right before Max pulled her into his body, nuzzling his face into her neck.

"I have to cover a few houses today," Remi said as Max began to trail slow kisses across her collarbone.

"Okay," he said. "I'll come with you."

She leaned her head back, making room for his lips. "You going to help me clean, or just cheer me on?"

"Both?" he asked, the heat of his mouth warming her skin.

"Deal. But we need to leave right meow," she said.

Max grumbled. "You kitten me? It's too early, and I'm a little hungover."

"Nope, I'm not kitten. We have to be at this house by five."

Max pulled her on top of him. "Who gets their house cleaned that early?"

"A doctor who works graveyard shifts," she said, rolling her hips against his morning wood despite knowing they didn't have time for this.

"Makes sense," he said, reaching down to push his hand below her panties, slipping a finger against her clit, rubbing it gently.

"Max Miller," she said in a low purr.

"Real quick?" he asked, but his hips were already lifting below her, making room to pull his boxer briefs down his thighs.

Who was she to say no to a morning quickie?

"Fine," she agreed, rolling her eyes, but really, she wanted him too. Their sex was electric, needy, and silly, and most times, it was really passionate. A million unsaid words seemed to play out between them when he was inside her.

Remi slipped off her panties and climbed on top of Max, his chest heaving with deep breaths as he watched her pull her shirt over her head before taking his erection in her hand, lining him up to enter her, and taking him with one drop of her body.

They both moaned at the same time, their voices deep and raspy with sleep.

Remi circled her hips, grinding her body flush against his, her sex shaved with a small beauty mark resting on the skin above the sharp point of her hip bone. She had tan lines, dark and distinct, from long days at the beach. Max was pale in contrast, with trails of red freckles spattered across his naked skin, his body hair well-kept for a hairy man. She loved it.

His hands found her hips and gripped them tight as she began to move her body up and down his length with the roll of her body. She always came so fast when she was on top, with Max's girth stretching her in the best way possible.

She wanted to take her time and draw this out; ride him fast and hard, then slow and steady. Make him beg. But they had houses to clean. Using his chest to brace herself as she quickened her pace, his hands gripped her tight, forcing her to take him deep with each thrust.

Remi felt her body contracting around him, the muscles in her legs tightening, her toes beginning to curl as her orgasm came on strong.

Max, without hesitation, moved her off his body, repositioning her onto her stomach, lifting her ass up in one swift motion before pushing back into her with a punishing thrust.

"Oh. Fuck," she cried out. Another orgasm was already building as he fucked her like they were on a time limit—and they were.

He pulled her body against his with each thrust. The slapping of their skin, groans, and deep breaths filled the room. Remi felt herself about to come again. Twice before work, not a bad way to start your day.

"Keep going," she managed. "So good."

Max's athletic strength proved to be a complete game changer in the bedroom, his stamina never wavering as he thrust against her from behind, good and hard.

Remi's head fell and she gripped the sheets tight, coming for a second time.

"Are you?" he asked, his words short.

"Yes," she moaned.

"Again?" he asked, never missing a thrust.

"Yes," she said, this time laughing a hint.

"Damn, Remi," he said, somehow managing to fuck her harder, the sound of his body against hers echoing through her small bedroom. "So. Good," he said, slamming his body flush against hers one last time as he came; the heat of his orgasm spreading deep inside her.

She wouldn't be able to walk, let alone clean after that.

Max slowly pulled out, leaning down to kiss the center of her back.

"You sure we have to clean these houses today?" he asked, and she knew why.

She knew he asked because that was the kind of sex that needed a follow-up, and after the follow-up, a shower. And then after the shower some heavy petting. That was the kind of sex that could have very easily led to an entire day of making love on every surface of her tiny house.

"We *have* to clean these houses," she said, rolling over onto her back, her legs still shaking and her body aching in the best way. With the throb between her legs, she could feel phantom thrusts against her entrance even with him gone.

"I guess we should get ready," Max said, looking over at her, his smile still managing to be a little groggy and his beard lopsided from sleeping on his stomach.

"I have a Busy Bee shirt for you here," she said, and his face lit up.

"I like wearing your company shirt. It makes me feel official."

Remi leaned over and kissed his smiling mouth, then his nose, then his eyes that fluttered shut under her lips, then his forehead.

"I like seeing you in it," she said.

"I want to see you in my jersey... before the season is over."

"I would love that."

His hands trailed across her bare skin, down her breast, over her nipple, then outlined her tan lines in a non-sexual nature, in a "just because I can" kind of way.

"It's going to be hard," he said.

"Seeing me in your jersey?" she asked.

His hands stopped moving. "Seeing you in my jersey knowing it's the last year that number is mine."

She leaned over, draping her body across his in a blanketing hug. "Thirty-one will always be Max Miller's number to me."

"What if they win the Cup?" he asked, his question lined with some kind of heavy meaning.

"Then you celebrate with them. You're still a part of the team."

Max went silent, it still wasn't an uncommon thing for him to do, to go completely quiet, but this was a different kind of silence.

"If I don't play a game in the playoffs, or at least get dressed as a backup goalie, I don't get my name on the Cup."

Remi sat up, her face twisted with irritation. "Why? That's so stupid and entirely unfair."

Max brought his hands up to rub his eyes. "It's just the rules."

"Well fuck the rules," she said, standing aggressively to head to the bathroom.

Chapter Fourty-Five

The playoffs went by in a blaze as Max sat back and watched his team push forward win after win. Brown was mesmerizing in front of the net, making the hard saves look easy; Max found himself toeing the line between jealousy and pride. If he couldn't be the one making the save, he would be happy it was Brown. Even the few games Brody, the backup goalie, played had left Max feeling like his team was in good hands. He could let them go knowing they would thrive in the future without him.

Free time between playoff games and cleaning houses was filled with visits to the Lighthouse facility. Max was learning how to prepare his home for the future with things like bump dots and playing with lighting options, as well as hiring a painter to paint all the door frames in the house to create a contrast of colors while that would still help. They had also done some simple fixes, removed area rugs that weren't necessary, got special bump coded cutting boards, and even added floor and table lights to help with his night vision.

He found himself letting go of his denial towards his diagnosis little by little with each trip to Lighthouse. Being around other people with vision impairments helped him accept that he needed to start learning things now, because they would be even harder to grasp later when his vision was gone entirely. He signed up to learn how to use a cane, and how to navigate different apps and technology that would help along the way with things he didn't even consider, things like telling time, and reading a dinner menu.

Since he found out about his retinitis pigmentosa, he had only focused on the loss of his career. He hadn't even considered the day-to-day things he would eventually have to relearn to do without his vision.

The community of people he met through Lighthouse were slowly becoming his second family, Shepard the guide dog included. They offered encouragement and reminded him it's okay to laugh and make jokes, because if you didn't, someone else would, and why not laugh at your own expense.

Max had even let Remi and Nicole, the facility manager, convince him to sign up for counseling. At first, he was hesitant to accept the idea. The last thing he wanted to do was talk about going blind in a stuffy room with someone he didn't know, when words were not his strong suit to begin with. But, after his first session with Dr. Hill, he realized this was bigger than going blind. He was going to have to rethink his entire lifestyle, so, why not get a head start on the overwhelming anxiety and deep bouts of depression before it got out of control?

He and Dr. Hill didn't only talk about RP. Some days they talked about hockey. Those days Max left wondering what was harder, losing his vision or losing his spot in front of the net.

He couldn't be sure.

The hockey season was almost over. Even from the box, with the cool arena air on his warm, anxious face, Max felt it coming to an end. If the Condors won tonight's game against the Carolina Storms, they would secure the most coveted trophy in hockey, the Stanley Cup, ending Max's career for good on the highest note possible.

He helped Remi pull the teal blue jersey over her head, his number thirty-one on the back along with his last name, Miller; it looked so good on her it hurt. He almost wished he had never seen her wear it, and he almost wished she had never known him in this season of life at all, never experiencing these two parts of his world overlapping: Max before RP and Max after.

Even with those thoughts swirling in his mind, he noticed how Remi handled it all so effortlessly, with simple jokes and greeting his fellow Condors with ease, like they were family. A few other players on injured reserve were in the box with him and Remi, and the overall mood was intense. This could be the night; the Condors could win their first Cup in sixteen years. As the arena filled with fans wearing jerseys, some with painted faces, some with his number on their back, Max could feel it, he could feel the win deep in his bones. He knew it was their night, he could feel it in the way the tips of his fingers tingled like they used to when he was in the net.

His goalie intuition had returned one last time.

They went to take their seats; the Cup was in the building and the game was about to start. Remi went to sit on the right side of him, and on instinct Max stopped her. "Not here. You have to sit to the left of me, if you sit to the right, its bad luck."

Remi took the seat to his left, a small smile on her face, an understanding that only a goalie girlfriend got, even if she had only been introduced to this crazy world months ago. "We're going to win tonight," Max said.

"Yeah?" Remi asked.

"Yeah. I can feel it." He looked out at the ice and it was nothing more than a blur. His stomach dropped. He blinked. He blinked again, and if he did it quickly, he might be able to wipe away the tears without anyone noticing.

Remi took his hand and in the palm of hers was a tissue. She gave him a comforting squeeze, then placed her head on his shoulder.

"You okay?" she asked quietly.

"No," he said, glad he didn't have to lie to her.

"That's okay," she said, and he could tell by the way the voices in the box grew hushed that the puck had dropped.

***

The first period ended with the Condors up 1–0. Brown was standing on his head, and their captain, Patrick Carter, had the first goal of the night. Max felt his anxiety growing with every cheer and boo of the crowd on a play he couldn't see, with every kiss-cam on the jumbotron—he would never know if it was him and Remi on the screen.

But the Condors were winning.

This was going to be okay.

"Max." Clay Adams, a marketing director for the Condors, greeted him during intermission. "Any word when we'll see you back on the ice?"

"Well," Max said, "if they win tonight, it won't be this season," he joked, to avoid admitting the truth. Some of the team's affiliates knew, some didn't, and in those cases, he found himself bullshitting his way out of admitting his secret.

"Big bridge contract year for you," he said, and Max could tell it was more a question than a statement, but Clay would have to wait like the rest of the Condors community to find out what the future held. Max wasn't giving anything away, not here, not now. Not in the box at the Stanley Cup finals.

"I can't talk about it yet." Max lied again, remembering the time Remi gave him the green light to tell a lie, or hide the truth if he had to, and right now, Max had to. For his own mental health.

"Ah, right. Big hush-hush until the ink dries," Clay said, playfully punching Max's shoulder. It didn't hurt, but Max instinctually brought his hand up to rub there.

"Something like that," Max said, but he knew the only ink that would be drying was his signature on his resignation letter.

The lights in the arena went down, and before Max could panic at the sudden shift in lighting, Remi had his hand in hers.

"You're anxious," she said.

"I am."

"Do you want to leave?"

He looked over at her and simply said, "I can't."

She leaned her head onto his shoulder. "I know. I don't know why I offered that."

"Could you maybe try and tell me what's going on in the game?" he asked, his voice cracking as it came out.

Remi looked over at him, a single-dimple smile on her face, her eyes sympathetic and kind. "I can try."

"I'd really like that."

"I don't know the proper terminology," she said.

He leaned in and kissed her forehead. "That's okay. I don't think anything could make me happier right now than you trying to explain hockey play-by-play to me, in my jersey, at the Stanley Cup finals."

Remi laughed, but not her happy-go-lucky laugh that he had gotten used to. This laugh was love, understanding, and the emotional depth that he never realized a single laugh could hold.

"Okay," she said, steadying herself next to him. Her chest puffed up as she prepared to take on the role of his personal announcer for the remainder of the game.

He looked over at her, her eyes were wild and so blue, but then the lights came up in the arena.

He blinked.

He blinked again.

She was still there.

Nothing else mattered.

"Okay, so they are going at it behind the net, and the Storms player is like, pinning the Condor up against the wall-thingy," she said, then laughed, "I'm going to butcher your sport, and you are going to dump me."

"No way." He smiled over at her. "Keep going."

"Okay. So, the big dude finally eased up. Your guy has the puck and he's going with it..."

He corrected her. "Is he *skating it up the ice?*" he asked, giving her some proper terminology.

She looked over at him and pressed her finger to his nose. "Ding-ding-ding," she said, booping him. "Those are exactly the words I was looking for."

He laughed, the box around them was noisy, the drinks were flowing, and no one was focused on them, and even if they were he didn't care. His secret would come out after the playoffs were over anyway, he might as well enjoy this last game on his own terms.

"Ohhhhh," Remi shouted, "Brown just made a super good save."

Max felt his body recoil. Remi leaned in and kissed his neck, and his skin heated instantly. "He's good, but he's no Max Miller," she whispered.

The crowd was loud, a drumbeat played out on the speakers and the fans knew to clap and cheer, *"Go, go, Condors. Go, go, go!"*

Remi joined in, clapping and chanting. She looked over at him, her brows lifted, challenging him.

He rose to the occasion. "Go, go, Condors," he shouted, clapping along. "Go-go-GO!"

They laughed, and Remi gave him her best play-by-play into the end of the second period. The Condors were up 2–1.

***

Remi leaned into Max, her hand in his, gripping it tight. The emotions in the box, hell, the emotions in the entire arena were high, and the excitement in the air was so thick you could cut it.

"Three minutes," Remi said. Her play-by-play of the game had turned into a countdown. A loss of words swept over her as she experienced the best hockey there was for the first time in her life—playoff hockey—Stanley Cup hockey.

"Two minutes..." She paused, bringing her hands to her chest in panic. "Fuck, I thought they had that one." She released a deep breath, and went on, "Two minutes, or less than two now."

Max didn't even try to watch the ice at this point. He didn't even care what the blurry figures below looked like, not when he could watch the final moments through Remi's facial expressions. Her deep inhale of breath, followed by a sharp exhale. She gripped his thigh and then dug her nails into his arm, then slapped his leg in excitement.

"Oh my god. Oh my god. Max. Max. Max," she said, bouncing up and down in her seat.

He knew exactly what she meant.

"Oh, my fucking... Max. Max," she kept on saying.

He knew exactly what was happening.

She pulled him to his feet. His heart raced. His eyes blurred. He blinked.

"Five seconds."

He blinked.

She began to jump up and down.

The whole arena counted down.

"Four-three-two..."

Remi jumped into his arms. She was screaming, "We did it, Max! We won the fucking Stanley Cup."

He blinked.

And then he celebrated as tears fell from his eyes, down to his thick red beard.

They did it.

The Cup was theirs.

Only he wouldn't be hoisting it, and he wouldn't be getting his name on it. He wouldn't be drinking lemonade from the farmers market from it with Remi, or eating hummus and pretzels from it. And he wouldn't be skating on the ice with it held over his head, nervous he might drop it, too excited to care.

He blinked and pulled Remi into his arms.

"We sure did, Remi. We won it," he said, because he was celebrating the wins, and despite all the things he couldn't and wouldn't do with the Cup, he still felt like he won.

Chapter Fourty-Six

The press room was packed with reporters. Max peeked in to see what he was up against, and despite having practiced his speech with Remi a million times, words were still hard, and press releases were harder, but announcing a retirement was the hardest of all.

His coach took a seat at the desk, a black tablecloth draped over it, a microphone and two bottles of water all lined up on the table. Max wondered if anyone ever drank the water they provided. The reporters' phones, cameras, and recorders all shot into the air as a loud hush settled around them in the press room when his Coach leaned forward to speak.

"Thank you for being here today. After a big win this past week, the Stanley Cup is back home in the beautiful city of Anaheim for the first time in sixteen years. With spirits high surrounding this franchise, this is not the news I was hoping to bring into the press room today, but full transparency is the only way to go about what I have to share with you. It might be the hardest thing I've had to say at a press conference, so I'll keep it brief so you can get more information from the source.

"Today, I am here in support of one of the greatest goalies to protect the net for the Anaheim Condors, Max Miller. I have been lucky enough to watch him grow as a player, and a person, and become a man I respect wholeheartedly as a friend, teammate, and son. Max Miller came to Anaheim a shy redheaded teen with a killer glove save and a lot of weird superstitions, and he will leave here today a Stanley Cup winner, even if he wasn't on the ice that day. The work he put into this team in the years leading up to this big win played a vital role in why we were able to hoist the Cup last week. The extra hours he put into practicing and mentoring with our up-and-coming goalies was the foundation and future of men like Brown and Brody, and many goalies to come as Max Miller's infinite wisdom, passion, and composure will trickle down to the next generation even after he is gone.

"There will never be another number thirty-one for the Anaheim Condors, and if I'm being honest, I doubt any player would feel worthy to wear that number again after today, as we say goodbye to the legacy of Max Miller and wish him a happy retirement."

The press room went wild. Cameras flashed. Hands raised into the air. Reporters shouted out questions.

"Please allow me in welcoming Max Miller."

Max blinked, wiped his nervous hands on his suit pants, and made his way to the press table.

Looking out, he scanned the sea of reporters, all of their faces distorted, the flash of the lights making his focus struggle. He knew Remi was out there, in the sea of strangers. He knew she was there giving him the go-ahead. She was there, with a double-dimple smile, encouraging him.

He blinked again, and then he began to talk.

"This wasn't the press release I thought I would be giving this year. I think it's safe to say this isn't the press release any of you were expecting today. This was supposed to be my big contract, my gap year, locking in my time with the Condors, the only team I played for in the NHL and the only team I'd want to. But last summer, during training, I noticed a shift in my reality that would forever change the course of my life and ultimately my career.

"As you all know, after the events that took place on December 23rd in Vancouver, I was put on medical leave, and not much information has been shared since. So, with full transparency, I'm here today to not only announce my retirement from the NHL, but to take this opportunity to use this platform, this moment, with all eyes on me, to bring awareness to my condition.

"I have an inherited eye disorder called retinitis pigmentosa. This disorder will eventually leave me legally blind, and there is nothing I can do to stop it or slow my vision loss. It's out of my control, and I'm still working on accepting that fate. Some days I find optimism in the programs, technology, and support that I have been lucky enough to find in the vision-impaired community. And some days, I couldn't buy a positive thought, even if I drained my entire life savings.

"This is one of the hardest moments of my life. Right now. Sharing this with all of you, with my fans, with my Condors community... my Condors *family*. But if I can, in this moment that feels so heavy and bleak, bring awareness and share the deep-rooted hope that I have found with others in the vision-impaired community, then that's the only way I want to spend this press conference.

"I started to see signs of vision loss far earlier in life than I realized. Looking back now, I remember being a young boy and already struggling to see at night. Things that other kids did with ease, I struggled with, but my naïve mindset told me this was normal, no one could see clearly in the dark. As time went on my night vision progressively got worse, but denial set in, and I continued to do things that could have jeopardized my safety along with the safety of others. I continued to drive, despite knowing how dangerous it had become, and continued to tell myself I just needed glasses to fix it.

"But still, I put off seeing an eye doctor. I think that was because deep down, in my gut, I knew there was something bigger that needed to be addressed. Over my years in the NHL, I continued to play and found ways to work around the symptoms that were slowly creeping in. My struggle with different lighting, floaters, contrast, and eventually the loss of my peripheral vision beat out my denial, forcing me to see a doctor. From that day forward, my journey with RP began.

"I know you are probably wondering how knowing you have RP can help if there is no way to stop it, and I want to say I sadly don't have some magical cure. If I did, I wouldn't be announcing my retirement today, but I can say there are steps you can take to prepare yourself for the future. There are tools, technology, and support groups that can ease you into your future with vision impairments. I'm here to encourage my community, both hockey and vision impaired, to get your eyes checked regularly. I want to encourage you not to hide your diagnosis from friends and family. I want to encourage you to see a counselor. It's important to protect your mental health, because I will be the first to admit that while right now, I look composed and unbothered, I'm actually terrified. I am heartbroken, and I too, did not want to talk about it. But even as a man who has not always been great at words, I want my final thought today to be this:

"Vision impairment is not my entire identity now. I am still Max. I still want to sign your jerseys and talk hockey. I still want you to treat me like a person, look me in the eyes, make jokes, and most importantly, ask me the hard questions about the things you don't understand, because the only thing that sucks worse than going blind, is being treated like you're invisible.

"So, as I enter my retirement, I want to start it off with a donation to The Lighthouse Organization for the Blind. If you, or anyone you know, might be experiencing the symptoms I described today, there is a link at the bottom of the screen, as well as a link in the Anaheim Condors Instagram bio that will bring up eye clinics near you for exams and a resource link.

"If you want to help me celebrate my retirement, please donate to a vision-impaired charity of your choice, remember to be kind to one another, and go easy on Brown, he's a good man, and he's going to take good care of this team. Go Condors."

***

When Max entered the family waiting room, he found Remi having what seemed to be a deep conversation with his captain, Patrick Carter. He was happy she had found her footing around his team. His captain pulled him into his arms in a brotherly embrace when he approached.

"I'm proud of you, Millsy. I know that wasn't easy," Carter said.

"Hardest thing I've ever done," Max admitted.

They broke the hug as a few more players surrounded him. "I donated to that foundation," Brown said, patting Max's back.

Max was surprised when several other players agreed that they had made donations as well.

"That's great. Thank you all and thank you for being here to support me."

"It's what teammates do, Max. We show up for each other," Carter said, and Max was almost certain his eyes were tearing up.

"I wish I could have been on the ice with you when…" Max trailed off, it was too hard to say.

"We all wish you could have been out there, man. It's still your Cup, you know that right?" Brown asked.

"Yeah. It just would have been nice to actually be able to *see* this season through," Max said with a laugh.

"*See* this season through?" Carter asked, bumping Max's shoulder, "Was that a vision joke?"

"It's all I got these days," Max said. "Vision jokes and a super cool cane," he said, smacking Carter on the ass with it.

"You should put a skull on top of it," Levi Holland said.

"A golden skull," chimed in Brody.

Max laughed. "I'm going blind, not becoming a pimp."

"So, what now?" Carter asked.

Max thought about it. He thought about his future, and a life full of new things to say yes to.

"I was thinking you all could come to my place. We could enjoy the beach and eat some food. Remi and I can stop and get some donuts from our favorite place," Max offered.

The guys looked at each other in amazement at the invitation—this was new—and Remi looked over at Max, her expression both puzzled and excited.

"I guess we're going to the grocery store?" she asked.

"Yeah," he said, "I was thinking hummus and pretzels, and maybe some donuts. A proper beach picnic," he said with a wink.

Remi smiled up at him, it was a good fucking smile, two dimples, wild blue eyes, long sandy blonde hair tucked behind her ears, the soft glow of the sun on her cheeks, and his name on her back.

This was going to be okay.

He was going to be okay.

Epilogue

Max unloaded the last box of full-sized candy bars into the massive black plastic cauldron in his entryway. He and Remi had gone all-out with decorations this Halloween. Spooky music, fog machine, spider webs and, orange lights. Remi was dressed up as a dog, she had floppy ears, and a brown body suit of sorts that she had glued spots onto—she looked equally sexy and cute. Max decided to return to his roots and wear his cat ears, this time allowing Remi to tack a fluffy black cat tail onto his dark Levi jeans. It was, he decided, his new tradition. He was slowly replacing his superstitions with them, one by one.

"Do you think we'll get many trick-or-treaters?" Max shouted from the hall.

Remi met him there, her phone in her hand buzzing three times before she clicked the home screen dark and pressed up on tiptoe to kiss him. "Are you kitten me?" she said. "We have full-sized candy bars. We'll be a hit."

"Purrrrrfect," he said back, doing his best cat paw hand motion.

Max clicked the switch that turned on the fog machine, the cackling pumpkins, the ghost that played eerie music, and the orange lights Remi had wrapped around the mini palm trees.

"And now we wait," he said with a huff. Remi leaned up to kiss him again before pushing him away quickly towards the living room.

"Go turn on the movie, and I'll get the junk food," she said, looking back down at her phone.

"Okay, but if we get a trick-or-treater, I want to be there to hand out the first candy bar," he said, looking over at her only to catch her on her phone, again.

"Mmmhmm," she said, still looking down at her phone, seemingly distracted as she loaded up the wooden snack board with all of their favorite things.

"You know," Max said, "you look super good dressed like a *cactus*."

She sent another text. "Mmmhmm, it turned out cute," she agreed absently.

"We should watch a Christmas movie instead," he said, just to see what she would say.

"*Scream* right? We decided on *Scream*?" she looked up momentarily only to be pulled back to her phone ringing. "Be right back, I have to take this call."

Max didn't know what could have made her so distracted tonight of all nights. It's not like anyone was cleaning houses at this hour, so it couldn't be work-related.

He shouted out to no one, "Do you mind if I put hockey on for now?"

Remi didn't respond.

He clicked on the TV; the Sports Center pre-game was on. The announcers stated there was news of big trade deals happening. Max flopped down on the couch, his tail creating a weird bump under his butt, so he lifted his hips and pulled it out from under him when he heard the doorbell chime. He jumped up so fast his vision blurred, but not wanting to miss the first kids of the night, he grabbed his cane and headed for the door.

"Rem, we got trick-or-treaters," he called out excitedly.

He looked for her in his bedroom quickly, then knocked on the bathroom door. She was nowhere to be found.

"Rem, you're going to miss the first trick-or-treaters of the night," he shouted, and the doorbell rang again.

He couldn't put it off any longer, he pulled the door open, and to his surprise, standing in front of him was Remi, and at her feet sat the tiniest golden retriever puppy he had ever seen.

"Happy Halloween," she said, letting go of the black leash. The puppy bolted straight for Max, covering his face in puppy kisses.

"Remi, what is this?" he asked stupidly. He couldn't even comprehend what was happening.

"Well, it's a puppy, Max," she said sarcastically.

He picked up the pup and felt his shirt go warm and wet along his chest. He pulled the puppy back to notice the dog was pissing.

"And," Remi said laughing, "he seems to be so excited to meet you that he did a little happy pee on you."

"Is it... Is it mine?" he asked, sincerely shocked and completely unbothered by the puppy piss on his shirt.

She leaned forward, pressed her finger to his nose, and said, "Ding-ding-ding."

He pulled her into a hug, the small puppy wriggling between their bodies, excitedly licking them both wherever its little mouth could reach.

"It's a boy. He's going to train with the same person who trained Shepard. He's going to be your guide dog one day," Remi said.

Max's hand came to rest on her lower back, pulling her against his body, his forehead pressed to hers. "I love you, Remi," he whispered, and just as he went to kiss her the doorbell rang again.

"Trick-or-treaters," he said, the tiny dog letting out the cutest little bark he had ever heard. His heart raced, but he was okay. This was okay.

Remi rushed forward. "I'll get it, you hold on to the pup," she said, and before she opened the door, she pulled out her phone and before Max could process what came next time seemed to speed up in a blur of emotions.

The door swung open, and again, what he found in front of him wasn't trick-or-treaters at all. What he saw in front of him was better than anything he could have imagined.

Sitting on his doorstep, surrounded by fake fog and the sounds of Halloween, was the Stanley Cup.

Max felt all the blood drain from his face as his jaw hit practically the floor. He looked at the puppy, and then at Remi who was very obviously recording him, then back at the shiny silver trophy.

He started to walk towards it, then paused. "Rem, is it real?" he asked.

"It's real. And if you look closely, it's got your name on it."

He handed her the puppy, and right as he moved forward to touch it, to hoist it, his teammates jumped out from the sides of the house.

"Surprise!" they shouted.

Carter smiled at Max and gave him a nod of approval. "Well, what are you waiting for, Millsy, hoist that mutha-fuckin' Cup!"

Everyone cheered and Max, without hesitation, took the Stanley Cup into his hands and lifted it over his head. The puppy barked excitedly as Remi began to cry. The boys cheered all around him, as a group of kids asked if they could still get some candy; Brody handed them all king size Snickers bars before shooing them away.

Max blinked.

He blinked again.

It was real. It was his.

This was going to be okay.

His teammates poured into the house, and one by one Remi handed them cat ears to wear. Somehow this had gone from handing out Halloween candy to a Stanley Cup celebration.

"How did you do it?" Max asked his captain once he had finally broke free from pictures with the Cup, and the puppy, *and* the puppy in the cup.

"It was all her idea," Carter said, hinting at Remi. "She hit me up at your press conference," and Max remembered seeing the two of them huddled in the corner of the waiting room that night.

"She asked you to do this?" Max asked.

"No. She did her research. She came to us and told us about the appeal process to have your name added. We all signed a petition and started the appeal the next day. It had to go through all the board members, and we almost got denied, but in the end we won. *You* won. You're a Stanley Cup winner, Millsy."

Max brought Carter in for a hug, then shouted, "Alexa, play a punk mix." The music blasted through the house, and it was officially a party.

Trick-or-treaters came and went, and each of his teammates took turns handing out candy, with Brody getting caught giving out more than one candy bar to anyone dressed in a Star Wars costume.

Remi called Max over, the Stanley Cup sitting on the countertop, next to it was a bag of pretzels and hummus. He knew right away what she was getting at.

"Should we?" he asked.

"You know it," she said.

"Thank you for this," he said, leaning in to kiss her with his eyes closed tight and his heart full and alive.

Carter came over with the puppy in one hand, a beer in the other, his cat ears lopsided. "So, what are you naming this guy?" he asked.

Max took the dog and sat him in the Stanley Cup. The little guy slid down inside, and just as Max went to grab him, his little floppy ears reappeared as his tiny paws held on to the lip of the cup.

"Stanley. I'm going to call him Stanley Pup," Max said.

They all cheered again. The music blasted, and people laughed and celebrated. Max ate a donut out of the cup, then the hummus and pretzels with Remi, and then the guys suggested some puppy kibble for Stanley. The TV played in the background, but no one heard it. And no one recognized the picture of the player in the corner of the TV screen as the subtitles read: Liam Harvey of the LA Knights is officially headed to the San Jose Threshers as both teams have come to an agreement with his trade.

THE END

Acknowledgements

First and foremost, I have to thank my husband. You supported me through book one, pushed me to finish book two, and you continue to be my biggest fan. I could not do this without you.

My daughter, this year you have also accomplished so many goals of your own. Side by side we tackled hard things. I couldn't be prouder of you.

Sara, my sister, and best friend. Your wisdom from years in ophthalmology helped keep this book accurate and medically sound. Thank you for answering all my calls/texts to answer questions about Max's condition. Because of you I published this book confidently.

Lindsay, my alpha reader extraordinaire. You came into my life by chance, and you are here to stay without an option because I'm never letting you go! Thank you for reading this book through the eyes of a mother with a child who is vision-impaired. You and Gemma are so dear to me.

My street team, I will never stop thanking you. My reach is small, but all of our arms stretched out together is what keeps my books in the hands of new readers. I love you all dearly. Keep dry humping!

My artist, Sam, at InkandLaurel, you are my favorite ever. I continue to be blown away by the covers you provide me with.

Katie, thank you for going in and finding the little mistakes that slipped through the cracks. I can't thank you enough. Fuck meals, eat snacks.

My editor, Kirsten, thank you for making this such a safe process.

And Bella, my sweet yorkie girl. Thank you for giving me the best 15 years any dog mama has known. I will love you forever and now you will live on forever in the pages of this book.

If you would like to support the vision-impaired community listed below are a few organizations that are doing amazing things.

GuideDog.org

HelenKellerIntl.org

About The Author

Lucille James is a Southern California native who recently relocated with her family to a small Southern town. While she will always love and miss the West Coast vibes; food, beaches, Disney days, Ducks Hockey and the sunny weather, she has come to love the sounds of the South, sweet tea, rural highways, and a slower life that allows her to write more freely.

Throughout her life, Lucille has found stories in her own experiences; from skateparks to cheer squads; hockey games to punk shows; fast food burger joints to Hollywood sound studios; and most importantly, always asking the people around her: What's *your* love story?

Lucille enjoys spending time with her husband, daughter, pup, and kitty. In her free time Lucille loves writing, watching Rom Coms, reading, cooking, concerts, coffee shops, and going to the roller skating rink.

Follow For More

If you wish to follow Lucille James for updates on her upcoming books, follow her social media platforms:

Click or scan.

www.lucillejames.com